ALPENA COUNTY LIBRARY
8604 9100 017 901 1
D0808006
ALPENA COUNTY LIBRARY
211 N. First St.
Alpena, Mich. 49707
DEMCO

The Arbor House Library of Contemporary Americana is devoted to works, both fiction and nonfiction, many of which have long been out of print. Included are a number of novels, highly praised and warmly received at the time of publication, that have secured a permanent place in the literature of twentieth-century America.

ALSO BY VANCE BOURJAILY

A Game Men Play
Now Playing at Canterbury
Country Matters
Brill Among the Ruins
The Man Who Knew Kennedy
The Unnatural Enemy
Confessions of a Spent Youth
The Violated
The Hound of Earth
The End of My Life

THE END OF MY LIFE

By Vance Bourjaily

Introduction by John W. Aldridge

ARBOR HOUSE
NEW YORK

First Published by Arbor House in 1984

 Published in the United States of America by Arbor House Publishing Company and in Canada by Fitzhenry & Whiteside, Ltd.

Library of Congress Catalog Card Number: 84-70363
ISBN: 0-87795-603-0

Manufactured in the United States of America

10 9 8 7 6 5 4 3 2 1

This book is printed on acid free paper. The paper in this book meets the guidelines for permanence and durability of the committee on Production Guidelines for Book Longevity of the Council on Library Resources.

This book was written for Tina,
and is still hers.

V.B., September 1983

ACKNOWLEDGMENTS
"I Got It Bad and That Ain't Good," words by Paul Webster, music by Duke Ellington, © copyright 1941 Robbins Music Corporation, New York, N.Y. Used by special permission of copyright proprietor.

"Shot? So Quick, So Clean and Ending," from *The Collected Poems of A. E. Housman.* Copyright 1924, © 1959 by Holt, Rinehart and Winston, Inc. Reprinted by permission of Holt, Rinehart and Winston, Inc.

Introduction
by
John W. Aldridge

The End of My Life was first published in 1947, the year Vance Bourjaily and I and thousands of other young men finally managed, after a long interruption for war service, to graduate from college, he from Bowdoin and I from Berkeley. After that event I moved from California to Vermont with a new wife, a little money, and an ambition to understand and write about the postwar fiction that was then beginning to emerge, particularly about the ways in which it resembled or differed from the literature of World War I.

If I had not been more interested in the work of my contemporaries, I might at that moment have decided to join the crowd and write a war novel myself, the obligatory true book that would expose to a stunned world the monstrous iniquities of the military establishment. But my impulse then as now was to be critical and analytical, although it must be said that Gore Vidal—back in the days when he could be whimsical rather than splenetic in his responses to what I wrote about him—used to find amusement in describing my first book of criticism, *After the Lost Generation,* as in fact my first novel containing characters with improbable names like Norman Mailer, Vance Bourjaily and Gore Vidal.

In any case, my own experience in the European theater had convinced me that even though so many of us had gone into the war with preconceptions about what it would be like derived from Hemingway, Dos Passos, Cummings and others, we had actually fought a very different war and would accordingly come to write about it in a significantly different way. It was already possible, even as early as 1946, to sense the beginnings of new directions. Alfred Hayes's *All Thy Conquests* had been published that year and so had Gore Vidal's *Williwaw* and Robert Lowry's *Casualty*—all rather terse and hard-bitten novels that must have disturbed older readers whose views of the war had been formed by the hygienic productions of Marion Hargrove and Ernie Pyle. Then, in 1947, John Horne Burns appeared with *The Gallery,* a very fine book it seemed almost everybody read, and Bourjaily published *The End of My Life,* a fine and quite different book that for some reason I did not discover until 1948.

These early war novels confirmed my impression—and the appearance of Norman Mailer's *The Naked and the Dead* in 1948 confirmed it again—that these writers differed from their predecessors of World War I in at least one vital respect: they were not producing, and in the nature of things could not produce, a fiction in which the central theme was the classic passage of the young soldier from naive innocence to bitter knowledge as a result of the war experience. As I saw it then my contemporaries lacked the important advantage their predecessors had shared, the opportunity—ghastly though it may have been—to confront the horrors of modern warfare for the first time. Hence, the writers of the second war were denied access to the experience that formed the subject of some of the best fiction as well as poetry produced by the earlier generation—the violent collapse of their romantic illusions about war after they encountered the unbelievably wasteful slaughter of troops in the largely stalemated fighting along the Western Front.

I went on to speculate that perhaps because Hemingway, Dos Passos and Cummings, along with Erich Maria Remarque in Germany and Wilfred Owen, Siegfried Sassoon and Robert Graves in England, had in effect completed the process for them, my contemporaries had no romantic illusions about the glories of war to lose, and so entered the various services with their minds already made up that what lay ahead of them was an ugly, undoubtedly stupid, but nevertheless necessary business that needed to be concluded as quickly as possible.

As I wrote in 1947: "In comparison with the innocent boys who set out, more than twenty years earlier, to save the world for democracy, the young men who went into the second war seemed terribly aware. The illusions they might have had about war—the patriotic illusions of courage and noble sacrifice—had all been lost for them that first time and long since replaced by cynicism and a conviction of the international doublecross which was sending them out to be killed. Unlike their predecessors, they had no need for adventure or relief from boredom. Their lives, as far back as they could remember, had been spent in a world continually at war with itself, in an economic order that fluctuated from dizzy prosperity to the most abject depression. They could remember nothing but domestic unrest, fumblings at peace conferences, Asiatic invasions, and South American revolutions. They came to consciousness in the midst of breadlines, strikes, and milk riots. . . . The generation of the Twenties had found themselves lost in a world they had never made. The generation of the Forties could never be lost because the safe and ordered world had never been theirs."

This attitude of cynical disaffection made it impossible for the second war writers to produce novels and poems with the kind of tragic power generated by the betrayal of idealistic expectations and by the disparity between patriotic oratory and the realities which, as Hemingway discovered, rendered the language of such rhetoric obscene. They therefore wrote nothing comparable in force to *All Quiet on the Western Front* or in poignancy to *A Farewell to Arms,* or that conveyed the brutal disillusion of the trench poems of Wilfred Owen and Siegfried Sassoon.

Yet the writers of the second war seem to have come

through their less traumatic experiences with an understanding that the evils that had sabotaged the idealism of their predecessors were merely symptoms of disorders endemic to modern society as a whole, and that the moral issues raised by war were far subtler and more complex than the earlier generation had been able to comprehend.

As a result, the novels they wrote were preoccupied not merely with the sufferings of the individual soldier in wartime but with problems of much wider scope such as the injustices inflicted by the mindless authoritarianism of the military system and the degradations of the civilian population in countries controlled by a corrupt Allied occupation force. Norman Mailer in *The Naked and the Dead* and Irwin Shaw in *The Young Lions* explored the dilemma of the combat soldier as Dos Passos and Remarque attempted to explore it before them. But what the earlier writers saw in terms of the wartime experiences of small groups of men, Mailer and Shaw saw in terms of entire armies and Western culture as a whole. Hayes, Lowry, Burns and Bourjaily emphasized in their novels the ugly contrast between our professed liberating intentions in fighting the war and the immoral practices that cost us the loyalty of those we had helped to liberate.

For all these writers, the enemy was no longer anything so simple as an opposing army, but had become a generalized malevolence of spirit, a sickness that was somehow implicit in all organizations and governments possessing absolute power. As Bourjaily's protagonist, Skinner Galt, says to his friend Jeff: "I want a nice small war . . . with clear-cut issues. There should be more than just a villain you can hate. There should be a side you can love, too." But Skinner is well aware that the nice, small wars belong to the past, the issues that were once simple are now extremely complex, and this time there are villains to hate on both sides. With this perception Bourjaily and his contemporaries anticipated, even as they contributed to, one of the most important developments in the fiction of the next decades, particularly in the novels of Joseph Heller,

Thomas Pynchon and Jerzy Kosinski: a growing obsessiveness with the idea that there exists some vast but unlocatable, conspiratorial system that is diabolically engaged in manipulating the lives of all of us—an idea most often expressed through a vision of contemporary society as a warscape of seemingly arbitrary violence and purposeless devastation.

In rereading *The End of My Life* after more than thirty years I have been impressed by the subtle presence in it of this developing awareness of an evil that cannot be precisely placed or condemned, but that will eventually corrupt or destroy all who are touched by it. The threat is not posed just by the existence of the war, although the war gives it clarity in the form of violence. It is not traceable to the fear of being wounded or killed. Rather, it is a curiously indefinable intuition that one's destiny is in the process of being determined by forces somehow implicit in the human condition as a whole; that, therefore, one is finally powerless to resist, and that the ultimate result of their pernicious influence will be a meaningless and arbitrary death of soul, the condition at which, in the closing pages of the novel, Skinner Galt arrives and for which, as he realizes, there is no one to blame. "You can only mourn."

It is this intuition of inescapable doom gathering like a thunderhead more and more ominously as the novel proceeds that gives it its quality of elegiac sadness. It is also what accounts for the hysteria of some of the early scenes of collegiate partying and horseplay, scenes that are insane in their frenzy just because they represent a temporary escape from feelings of the blackest dread. These feelings are given concrete justification by the cruel and ugly events Skinner is forced to witness during his war service—the horrors of the "Glass House" military prison, the injustice of his friend Rod's desertion, the brutal treatment of African soldiers by their British officers, the death of Johnny, the American nurse, for which Skinner is blamed and imprisoned. Such occurrences serve to particularize the causes of his disintegration of spirit and his final retreat into a protective listlessness that presages—and, indeed, may well represent—the end of his life.

Back in 1951 I wrote in *After the Lost Generation* that the story of Skinner Galt is the story of the "war-born," the generation that grew up without a childhood, without firm values, and with only a disbelief inherited from their literary predecessors standing between themselves and ruin. Today I would not put the matter quite so simply. Today the novel seems to me to have another and more complicated meaning, if only because the intervening years have provided some perspective. I now see that it represents an early and tentative effort to confront the condition of malevolent nihilism, which in recent decades has become a central subject of such novelists as Pynchon, Vonnegut and Heller. *The End of My Life* should properly be read as belonging to the contemporary apocalyptic tradition those writers have developed. For like them Bourjaily saw, back in a time when the insight was prophetic, that working against his sense of conspiratorial design of evil operating in the world is the possibility that there may, in fact, be nothing and no one in charge; that Kafka's castle may actually be empty; that there is no crime for which anybody stands eternally condemned, no order behind organization, no system behind bureaucratic structure, no governing principle behind government; that what is happening is happening for no reason, and that there is absolutely nothing to be done about it because the causes responsible cannot be located and the very idea of responsibility has lost all meaning.

The suspicion that this may indeed be the case is a central element of the modernist legacy in all the arts. For well over a century, especially in literature, the question as to whether there exists a design beneath the appearance of randomness in human affairs has preoccupied the modern artistic imagination. But the question has been inflated to the dimensions of paranoia, by the massive dislocation of reality from sanity, the increasing unreality of events that are at once real and too terrible to seem real, caused in part by the two world wars, the Nazi holocaust, the nuclear devastations that brought the second war to an end and the threat of wholesale annihilation that has tormented us ever since.

Most of the serious fiction produced in this country since 1945 has been divided in its approach to the question and has reminded us that there may be a convincing argument for both possibilities. Our best writers, therefore, have often expressed in their work emotions of the most extreme paranoia at the same time that they have tried to make sense of a reality that just may make no sense whatever except in their imaginative possession of it.

Vance Bourjaily, as a very young but very serious writer at the time, gave compelling expression in this first novel of his to some of the central elements of this ambiguity. The book is a poignant and lasting record of the ways so many of us felt before and during the war years and how we tried then—and are still trying today—to make sense of a reality that seemed complex enough in 1945 but that has grown increasingly baffling and ominous as the years have passed.

CONTENTS

It was thought to preface this book with a fragment from the hitherto and henceforward uncollected writings of Skinner Galt; but the piece under consideration seems remote on rereading, and, in a way, almost naive, now that the war is over and its complex states of mind all but forgotten.

PART ONE

A Note on Saying Goodbye

CHAPTER

1

LATER, thinking back, Skinner would remember it as a time when neither of them had spoken. He kept saying things, to be saying them, and she answered him, but it was as if the conversation made no sound in the room.

He moved around the apartment, doing the final things, putting razor and toothbrush into the musette bag, along with a couple of books for the first days, before the luggage would be brought up from the hold. He packed the little bag very carefully, frowning over the folding and arrangement, trying to look at Cindy no more often than he would if packing a musette bag were a part of every morning's routine.

She sat on one of the day-beds, watching him, not trying to pretend to do anything else, and when he let their eyes meet, they smiled at one another. During the night they had said all there was to say, and if they had started to say any of it over, they would have had to say it all.

Finally, he put the strap of the musette over his head, so that it stretched across his chest and rode on his left hip, put on his cap, checking in the mirror to see that it tilted correctly, walked over to the day-bed and held out his hands for her. She took them, pulled herself up standing, and smiled.

"Right," he said, and kissed her.

They walked to the door, went out without turning around to look, and Skinner caught the knob and pulled the door shut after them, still without turning around. They went down the stairs side by side, arms around one another, Skinner shortening his stride to hit each step on the way down, as she did.

"We'll get breakfast at the corner," he said.

They walked to the corner, past a little restaurant not yet opened for the day, at which they had often eaten, and on into the drugstore.

"Coffee's all I want," Skinner said, as they sat at the counter, and waited for the girl to come and take their order.

"Me too."

"You should have orange juice, and toast, too."

"So should you, darling."

"We both will."

Skinner ordered.

"How will you get down?" She asked him.

"Subway. There's no sense taking a cab."

"West Side?"

"Yes. At Fourteenth Street. Downtown Express. One red light and one white one. You're going to Jane's?"

"Yes. She's leaving the key for me. I guess I'll move back in with her."

"You can take the subway at Fourteenth Street, too."

"Right," said Cindy. "Uptown Express. But I don't know what color the lights will be."

"Be sure to watch for them, darling," Skinner said. "The color of lights is awfully important."

"Awfully," she agreed.

She picked up the last half-slice of toast, held it out,

and sat looking at it. He watched her for a moment, then reached over, took the toast from her, and put it back on the plate. They eased around on the counter-stools to look at one another, and smiled wry smiles; he took her hand and squeezed it.

"Triangular toast," he said. "Damned foolishness."

"I know," she replied. "But Euclid would have loved it."

They swung back facing the counter to drink their coffee. After a moment, she said, quite seriously,

"Skinner?"

"Yes, darling?"

"Didn't they let women into this in the last war?"

"I don't know. There were some women driving ambulances, but it may have been a different outfit. They did very well."

"The women did well?"

"Sure. Everybody did well. Everybody was magnificent in the last war."

"Why can't we go this time?"

"I don't know. There are other ways you could get across. The Red Cross sends people; and they send entertainers. Actresses."

"I don't care anything about just getting across. Would they promise to send me where you were?"

"I doubt it, darling. They send people to the Americans. I'll be with the British."

"There are no Americans where you're going?"

"I'm not sure. Some Service troops maybe. Observers. The Americans are all in England." He picked up the checks. "We'd better go, darling."

They slid down from the stools and walked to the cashiers' counter. Waiting for the man to come and take the money, Cindy said: "I'm glad we're not going to write every day."

"Right."

"Some days I'll write two or three times."

"Some days you won't feel like writing at all."

"Skinner?"

"Yes?"

"I'm glad Benny will be with you."

"Because he's a good guy?" The man came and took the money.

"Yes. And because he'll keep you from being reckless."

They went out of the store. "I won't be reckless, darling," Skinner said.

They walked across Sixth Avenue to the uptown side of Twelfth Street, and towards the subway station, very close together. Skinner kept wanting to put his arm around her, but it seemed better not to. They didn't hold hands, but walked slowly, deliberately keeping out of step, so that his right leg and her left leg moved forward at the same time, and hips and shoulders kept touching, all the way down the long block.

They went into the station, down the stairs, and Skinner put nickels into the turnstile, standing aside for her to go through. At Fourteenth Street, the Uptown and Downtown Express tracks are side by side, with no platform between. They stood one flight above the tracks, watching through the grillwork for the train to come.

Cindy said, "I wish we weren't so cool and modern. I wish I were standing on a dock, waving a handkerchief and weeping."

"I'll think of you that way, if you like."

Skinner's train came first. He waited until it was slowing down. Then he kissed her quickly, and pressed her tightly against him.

"We'll be okay, darling," he said, doubting that she could hear it over the roar of the train that filled the station. And whatever it was she said was lost in the noise, too.

He ran down the stairs to the platform, timing it so that he would make it just as the doors were ready to close, so that she could not follow him down, so that there would be no looking back and waving.

PART TWO

A Portrait of Jack, Nimble

CHAPTER

2

SKINNER and Freak got the window seats.

Rod sat beside Freak, where he would ride backwards when the train started, and Benny sat beside Skinner. The compartment was designed to seat six, but, with luck, no others would join them.

It was a second-class coach, stemming, Skinner suggested, from the Early Renaissance.

Rod said reflectively, "It looks something like a train."

"I don't think it's a booby trap," Freak offered, "or they would have made it comfortable."

Benny frowned. "It's enemy propaganda. It symbolizes decadent democracy."

Skinner shook his head at them. "You malign beauty; my train is beautiful," he said. "My train is lustrous with beauty. Look at the chandelier." He pointed to a tiny ten watt bulb, screwed into a crooked white porcelain socket in the ceiling.

"The grand manner," Benny agreed, reverently.

There was, consecutively, a jerk, a shudder, and a series of metalic groans as the pull of the engine communicated itself from car to car.

The train moved through the outskirts of Cairo, and Skinner noticed that Freak was the only one of them who looked out of the window. Arabs in ankle-length robes, dark-brown Egyptian business-men in European suits and red tarbushes, women in black, cheesecloth veils—these things seemed inexhaustibly interesting to Freak.

To Skinner they had been interesting until seen once; then they had joined the category of things known. He supposed that Benny had found them interesting until he had analysed them. For Benny, the color and the strangeness would not be so much to be seen as to be seen through, as though there were a general conspiracy in the Middle East to unfamiliarize itself to Western eyes, so as to disguise its poverty. As though an ankle-length robe and a cheesecloth veil pretended to have no equivalents in patched denim and faded gingham.

Skinner looked at Rod, darkly absorbed in his corner, staring at the floor. Neither the interest nor the significance of his surroundings would ever have any importance to Rod. He would simply accept them as he accepted all the other terms of his existence, as not worth either noticing or fighting. When they had gotten off the boat at Port Tewfik ten days before, Rod had seemed uneasy, but only briefly. Waiting on the docks for trucks to come to take them to Cairo, they had heard an Arab street musician playing reedy pipes, and later, in the trucks, driving by a bar with an open front, there had been a quick glimpse of a piano; and seeing these things, Rod had relaxed and said to Skinner, "It's going to be all right."

Half an hour out of Cairo, Skinner closed his book, laid it on the seat, and considered his window.

"This is not going to work," he said, and, pressing the catches at the bottom of the frame, heaved up on it. Surprisingly, it opened. Benny looked up from the pamphlet he was reading, and smiled.

"You've done well, Comrade," he said.

"Do I get the Order of Lenin?" Skinner asked.

"I'll recommend you for it. He on the other hand," pointing to Freak, who was pushing the window on his side up, "gets purged for not thinking of it before you did."

Freak got his window latched into position, and turned back to them. "You've got to purge Rod, too," he said. "For going to sleep."

"Is he really sleeping?" Skinner asked.

"I think so." They were all quiet for a moment, listening to Rod's breathing.

"I'll bet you can't get his necktie off without waking him up," Skinner whispered.

"What'll you bet?" Freak asked.

"Ten piastres."

"That's two beers. Its a bet."

Putting a finger to his lips to shush Skinner and Benny, Freak shifted in his seat so that he half-faced Rod. He leaned across him and put one hand gently on Rod's neck. He slipped his other hand under the necktie. Rod didn't stir. Freak loosened the tie a little, paused, loosened it a little more. When he had the knot about three inches away from the collar, he untied it, working the big end out. Then he began to tug stealthily at it, so that the small end slid slowly up towards the neck. Still Rod didn't stir.

Making sure that Freak was too absorbed to notice him, Skinner reached across the aisle between the seats and pinched Rod sharply on the leg. There was no sign that Rod had felt it.

Skinner looked at Benny, raising an eyebrow; Benny shrugged; and Freak turned back to them, triumphantly waving the necktie. "I win," he said, settling back in the seat, and arranging the tie around the crown of his head like a wreath. "Lacey, the conqueror."

"Hail," said Benny, and, to Skinner, "Render unto Caesar ten piastres."

"Right," said Freak, "Caesar wants his ten piastres." He held out his hand, and Skinner put the note into it, saying,

"Observe that I do this with good grace."

"And," said Rod, dreamily, without opening his eyes, "I do this with excellent grace." He opened his eyes, reached out, and took the ten piastre note away from the astonished Freak. "Half for me, half for you, Caesar, baby," he said, and, getting a smaller note out of his pocket, he handed it to Freak.

"Wonderful," said Benny, exultantly, "a double cross, a triple cross."

"A quadruple cross," said Skinner, jumping up and snatching the tie from Freak's head, "I've got the necktie." He sat down, and let the tie trail out of the window. "Sell you a fine necktie for five piastres, Rodney."

"A quintuple cross," said Rod, sleepily. "It's your necktie."

Just before the train got to Ismalia, another member of the ambulance group stuck his head into the doorway of their compartment.

"You guys can get your rations up in the first compartment if you want," he told them.

"Thanks," Skinner said. "What do we get?"

"Bully beef, bread, cheese, and you can get tea and sugar and canned milk, if you want them."

"But there's no hot water to make the tea with," Benny said. "Right?"

"Right," said the messenger, and withdrew his head from the doorway.

"Maybe we can get some wine at the next station," Freak said.

Benny looked at him disapprovingly. "Wait until such suggestions are made by the older members of the party," he said sternly.

"I'll bet I wouldn't have to wait long," Freak said.

"Hmmmm," said Skinner.

"Hmmmm," said Rod. "Pretty independent youngster, isn't he?"

All three looked at Freak severely.

"We'll have to punish him," Benny said.

"Make him go for rations," Rod suggested.

Freak stood up. He was within a year of being twenty-two, which was Skinner's age, but he had the features and complexion of a half-grown boy. When he grinned, he looked to be about fifteen.

"I don't know what you guys would do without me," he said.

"Get a little rest, maybe," Skinner told him.

"See these lines?" asked Benny, wrinkling his forehead and pointing to it. "All from worrying about you."

"But it's all right," Rod put in. "We'll care for you as if you were our own dear son, dead these many years."

"Nuts," said Freak, starting for the door, "I'm the Papa around this household. Look who's going to bring back the rations." He went out into the aisle.

"A little discipline needed there," Benny said ominously.

"We'll send him to military school next fall," Skinner suggested.

"Sure," said Rod, "there might be a war someday, and he'd have to do his bit."

Freak returned with four cans of bully beef, a small can of cheese, and two long, irregular loaves of British-army-baked white bread. "It doesn't look like much, does it?" He asked, putting the rations beside Benny on the seat.

"We get to Syria tomorrow afternoon," said Skinner. "That makes supper tonight, breakfast and lunch tomorrow."

"We'll be all right," Rod said, "we can buy more stuff at the stations."

"Right," said Benny, "Freak says he's Papa, so we'll let him pay for it."

"Some guys don't care if they never eat," said Freak.

Ismalia is the last town this side of the Suez canal, and, therefore, the last town before the Sinai desert. When they got there it was late afternoon.

Skinner and Rod got out and went into a shop near the station to try to buy wine. Wine was unobtainable. Yes, there was Arak, but he was not permitted to sell it to soldiers. They tried to explain that they were not soldiers at all, but American civilian volunteers who drove ambulances for the British. The distinction was not grasped. After all, they were in uniform, were they not?

Rod claimed an inspiration. He got out his phrase book, and looked up the words for Red Cross.

He pointed to Skinner's arm-band. "Salib Achmar," he said persuasively.

The Egyptian behind the counter shook his head. "No Salib Achmar," he said. "You Englissi soldier both."

Skinner decided the situation was hopeless. He leaned towards the clerk and said, confidentially, "Excuse me, sir, but you stink. Also your country stinks. However, you are quite right. We are not Salib Achmar. We are not Americani or Englissi either." He looked over his shoulder, as if to make sure that no one was listening, and then, stringing together two Arabic phrases he had memorized, he whispered dramatically, "Ana ibn Khalifa Baghdad. Huwwa sharmuta faransawi."

The man burst out laughing. "Kuwayis, kuwayis. (Good, good.)", and sold them a bottle of Arak.

"I'll be damned," said Skinner.

They left the store with the bottle concealed in Skinner's shirt, and started back to the train.

"What on earth did you tell him?" Rod wanted to know.

"Nothing," said Skinner, airily. "I just explained that I was the son of the Caliph of Baghdad, and you were a French whore."

They got back to the compartment without the bottle being detected, and were greeted with admiration by Freak and Benny. The bottle was carefully stowed beneath the seat.

The train started again, pulled out of the station, rumbled along for a moment without gathering speed, and stopped, just outside of town.

"For water," Benny guessed.

"Or to give us a ringside seat, maybe," Skinner said, and pointed out the window to a pair of camels about fifty yards away, quite absorbed in one another. It was quite clear that one was male and the other female.

The male was nibbling clumsily at his partner's neck; then, moving around to the other side, nuzzling her shoulders. She stood docilely, but her spindly legs were trembling, and after a moment she sank onto the sand, frothing slightly at the mouth.

Camels, thought Skinner, watching them, look like something that ought to be extinct, like some strain of puny dinosaur, dwindling and disarmed. Their necks are absurdly long, their bodies absurdly round, their legs absurdly thin. They are covered with ugly patches of shaggy hair; their faces are expressive of a sort of stupid surprise. And their love-making, like the love-making of all other mammals, is essentially comic to the beholder.

The comments in the compartment would not have been considered humorous by the camels.

Suddenly Benny had a thought. "Hey, guys," he cried. "The Freak. We can't let him watch."

"You're right, Benny," Rod said, and crooking his arm around Freak's chest, he pulled him away from the window onto his back on the seat. Benny sprang across the aisle and sat on Freak's chest. Skinner worked his way in beside Benny, pinning the legs, while Rod secured the arms.

"No corrupting of youth around here," Skinner said.

Freak struggled briefly, then relaxed. "He's saving up energy to catch us off guard," said Benny.

"He doesn't seem to realize it's for his own good," said Rod.

"And now," said Skinner, thoughtfully untying Freak's shoes and taking the left one off, "we can resume our natural history lesson with clear consciences." Then, to Benny, simulating great wonder, "Will you look at that? I wouldn't have thought it possible."

"Amazing," said Benny, "simply amazing."

"Incredible," Rod agreed, absent-mindedly flicking Freak's nose with his free hand. "You'd have to see it to believe it."

"Yeah, and look at the way . . ." Freak gave a great heave, broke one of his arms loose, dumped Benny off his chest, and pushed Skinner to the floor. He scrambled over to the window seat that Skinner had vacated, arranged his legs defensively, and said,

"Freak is going to be corrupted."

"Oh, well," said Benny. "He had to learn sometime."

"We can explain it to him later," Skinner said, returning the shoe. Rod moved to where he would have a better view.

They watched. Prehistoric flanks gathered, thrust, and regathered in the immemorial motion.

The train gave its familiar shudder, and moved out towards the desert.

By the time they were well into the Sinai desert, it was almost too dark to read. Skinner put his book down, and looked out at the sand. It was, they had agreed, more like being on a ship than like being on a train; every part of the desert was like every other part, and there was no way by which the eye could appraise speed and motion.

The Sinai looked like the deserts Skinner had imagined: white sand, wind-worked into fluent contour of soft hill and gradual pocket. The Western Desert, where the fighting was, the fighting, Skinner thought, that I won't see, was not, they said, like this. The Western Desert was, they said, harder packed, less yielding to the foot; a car would move over it and not be stuck; men could march on it, fight for it, win it.

The Sinai could never be won; it yielded too readily. On it the feet would sink, the car wheels settle; it yielded, and was therefore unpossessable. Once well within it, the way would be lost, for there was no sort of marker the sand would not cover in a night. It would yield, and in yielding, possess.

Benny's voice said, "Does anyone know why the hell we're going to Syria?"

Either Rod's or Freak's voice, they were almost identically pitched, answered, "To stall around. They haven't room for us out in the blue. There are some rest camps and training outfits up this way that use our ambulances."

Another voice came in, and it was unmistakably Freak's by the slight Southern inflection. "I wish we were going into action." That made the first voice that had answered Benny Rod's. Skinner, still turned away from them, staring out the window, supposed that he couldn't have been listening very carefully. Rod always sounded harder, tireder, less buoyant than Freak did.

Benny, whose voice had a slightly impatient edge to it and was pitched more deeply than either of the others, said, "It's better this way, Freak. We learn the cars, we learn to handle stretchers, that kind of crap. Then we're ready, when we get where it makes a difference."

Yeah, thought Skinner, but that won't be in Africa. The desert war is just about over. The Kiwi's have broken the Mareth line; the Americans are finally clicking on the Northwest side. Everybody says it won't be two more weeks before Jerry is off the continent.

"Steady now," Rod said to Freak. "Don't crowd, ladies and gentlemen. Plenty of war for everyone."

Skinner turned away from the window and looked at them. "It won't be the same war, you know," he said.

"All wars are the same," Benny said.

"No they aren't," Skinner insisted, "this isn't the same war they fought in France in '40. Suppose we invade Greece next? Or Italy? There'll be a different climate, different landscape, different equipment. There'll be towns to fight for instead of desert."

"Sure," said Benny, "but guys wounded in it will bleed the same kind of blood."

"Hell, Napoleon's boys bled the same kind of blood, didn't they?"

"That was the same war, too," Benny said. "They're all the same war. Those who get screwed get sick of it, and fight those who screw them. Only they don't know why they're fighting. So they get even sicker of fighting than they did of the screwing, and when it's all over, they meekly accept the new screwing the bosses are handing out, and call it victory."

"How about Russia in 1917?" Skinner asked. "Was that the same war?"

"Sure," Benny said. "Even more so. Only the people didn't forget what they were after, and their leaders, for once, were out to get it for them."

"And they lived happily ever after," Skinner said. "Benny, you may be right about wars; in fact you are. I was talking from a literary standpoint. But you're dead wrong about the Great Experiment. People are still being screwed."

"Wait, fellows," said Freak, plaintively. "Wait 'til I get to sleep; then you can have this argument and wake me up with it, like you usually do."

"To hell with the argument," Skinner said, "I feel friendly."

"Fine," said Benny, with heavy irony. "We'll all sit here and smile at each other."

"And think beautiful thoughts," Skinner agreed.

From his corner, which was now quite dark, Rod asked, "Who knows a beautiful thought for me to think?"

"I know one," Freak said; he settled back and smiled. "It isn't a female camel, either."

"I'll bet its a male bull-dog," Skinner said.

"Or a neuter rattlesnake," Benny suggested.

"Come to think of it, I do have a beautiful thought," Rod said.

"Thrill us," Skinner urged.

"My thought is that we're a bunch of jerks."

"That is beautiful," said Benny, letting his voice become dreamy.

"Perfectly lovely," Skinner agreed, also dreamily.

"I," Rod went on, "am a musical jerk. Benny is a political jerk. Freak a young jerk. . . ."

"But growing older," Freak broke in, "soon I'll be an old jerk."

"What about me?" Skinner demanded. "What's my adjective?"

"You're a destructive jerk," Rod told him.

"Right. I break things up. Windows, altars, hearts . . ."

"Don't be so eager," Benny said. "You may smash a few hearts and altars for other people, but wait 'til you see what you've done to your own."

"I've thought of that," Skinner said, easily. "That's why I got rid of mine young."

It was night, suddenly, within the minute or two they had been talking.

"Are they arguing or being intelligent this time?" Freak asked Rod.

"They don't know," Rod said. "How would I?"

"I'm making him face himself," Benny said, grouchily.

"A very neat trick," said Skinner, baiting him.

Rod took the issue away from them. "Benny, I wish sometime, when you get tired of working Skinner over, you'd make me face myself."

"You couldn't stand it," Benny said irritably.

Rod chuckled. "What couldn't I stand?"

"I don't know," Benny said. "Anything."

"What's he talking about?" Rod asked Skinner.

"The pictures. Benny's mind is full of pictures. There are four or five of you. Rod the musician and Rod the man. Rod as he is, Rod as others see him, Rod as he sees himself, and Rod as he could be."

"Which is the one that scares hell out of me?"

"The last one," Benny said. "Rod as he could be. The musician. Happy, useful, energetic; maybe great."

"Good, true, beautiful, and bored," Skinner added.

"Shut up," said Benny. "The only trouble with him is he's lazy, and it's guys like you who make it easy for him."

"Not lazy, Benny, indifferent." Rod said.

"That's just a word to make it go down smoothly," Benny accused.

Freak said, apparently enjoying it, "Benny, you've got to get everyone tonight. Don't leave me out."

"Aaah, let it go," Benny said. "You guys never know whether I'm kidding or serious."

"Neither do you, Benny," said Rod, "neither do you."

Skinner turned his head back to the window and looked at the desert again. It was full of mooncast shadows now. It made him think of "The Wasteland," which was a poem he liked, and then of "The Hollow Men," which he liked even better. Then he thought of Cindy, because they had quoted these poems to one another, and because he never went for very long without thinking about her. Finally he thought of how it is only at sea, or at night in the desert, that you can look out at the horizon and perceive that the world actually is round after all, only by visual judgment, not round like a ball, but round and flat, like a coin with one side.

CHAPTER

3

SKINNER, his eyes on the desert, realized that there was present that night, in the antiquated train-compartment, an uneasiness not wholly temperamental, not wholly stemming from uncertainty about the duties and surroundings awaiting them in Syria. It was a different sort of uneasiness, harder to talk about, based on the realization that, in the haphazard business of military assignment, this little group of four might quite probably be separated. and the group spirit, which had grown and strengthened through eighty days on the boat with shore time at Trinidad and Durban, and ten more days in Cairo, might be forever lost. For he knew that each of them, with, perhaps, the exception of Freak who would learn it, knew that group spirit does not survive chance physical separation; that, once it has gone, it is gone, and all the goodwill, the class reunions, the liquor in the world cannot bring it back.

To arrange and fix it in his mind, he began enumerating clockwise in the darkness, beginning with himself:

Thomas Galt, Robert Lacey, Benjamin Berg, Rod (for Rodney or Roderick, we've never known which) Manjac.

Which is the one called Skinner?

Thomas Galt is called Skinner, has been called Skinner

ever since he can remember, though the reason for it has long since been lost. His hair is yellow, partly curly; eyes blue; stands five ten and weighs one-sixty. Looks athletic, which is deceptive, for he has never bothered much with serious sports; but he is quick and well-coordinated.

And the one called Freak?

Robert Lacey, called Freak, has taken sports quite seriously, on the other hand, and was big enough and good enough to get a fair football scholarship to his State University, where he stayed only through his freshman year. The name Freak derives from a complicated joke about arrested physical and mental development, "Six feet tall and only nine years old; see him, feel him, hear him talk."

Benjamin is, of course, called Benny, and Roderick, or Rodney, Rod. They are both dark, and both short, but the resemblance ends there. Benny is stocky, strong, has a pleasant open face. He alone in the group has finished college, holding an A.B. from Columbia. Rod is thin, taut, has deep-socketed eyes and heavy brows. His face is sometimes tired, sometimes tough, occasionally appealing. Dressed for the part, he would fill the Hollywood neurotic thug role to pictorial perfection.

A train, an old, hastily assembled troop-train, carries these four and half a hundred of their colleagues to Syria where they will begin to serve the British Middle East Forces in their capacity as ambulance drivers, a job for which they have all, for varying reasons, volunteered.

The four are friends. They have been knit together from the beginning of the boat trip that brought them out here, Skinner and Benny from a few weeks before the beginning.

What is the basis of this friendship?

Rod, Skinner, and Benny were united, at first, mostly by their dislike for the other members of the ambulance group, though they disliked them for different reasons: Rod because they bored him; Benny because he knew their tolerance for his Jewish heritage and radical politics was superficial. And Skinner because they were, for the most part, the guys he had known and disliked all his life, at prep school, at college, at the beach in summertime: the well-groomed adolescents of all ages who stem from or cluster around the Eastern seaboard colleges. It had always been necessary to hate these ordinarily inoffensive people, simply because there was so much of them in him, and so little of him in them.

Then what drew Freak Lacey into the group? Primarily, his admiration for Skinner, which is an extremely reassuring thing to Skinner, for Freak is quite normal and thoroughly good-natured, and, though in no way intellectual, has the acute perception of the healthy, the intuition which the active develop about people.

Groups have always formed around Skinner, and his personality is probably a sounder basis for this one than a shared dislike. For Skinner's head is full of ideas, full of mischief, full of words, and he was born knowing how to use them compellingly, so that everyone he likes is included, no matter how far outside their customary interests the project or discussion is. Skinner tussles with Freak, and Benny is surprised to find himself down on the floor with his arms wrapped around someone's legs. He talks labor rights with Benny, and Rod will feel drawn to make a point or contribute an illustration. He can stand beside Rod at the piano, listening to Rod's ideas about the blues as they build up in the music, commenting quietly now and then, and Freak, to whom music has always been something to dance to, will join them, and respond to the ideas with understanding and enthusiasm.

And the group, thought Skinner, like all little groups

within groups, has grown to have a personality of its own, which is a composite of the individual personalities, plus a little more: a vocabulary, an understanding, apprecia-tions. A sort of mutuality which is much prized by us all.

Then, returning again to the possibility of separation, he realized that what they faced was what all men face, over and over throughout their lives. That when they reach the ends of the miscellaneous little time compart-ments into which their lives are divided, they sum up the pleasures of the compartment they are leaving, making, each time, a last, futile effort to perpetuate them, forget-ting that there were times when they considered the exist-ence pattern of this particular compartment wearisome and unsupportable, and foreseeing the next compartment with unconfidence and fear.

And Skinner wondered whether, in the endless series of escapes from one compartment to the next, it would not be well and brave were men to ask themselves if they are truly motivated by a desire to find the future, or whether they are struggling rather to regain the pleasures carried over in the mind from past compartments.

Feeling now that he had the situation well-enough summed up, that he had fed himself enough words so that, if he were separated from his friends, he could accept it properly, Skinner glanced again out at the desert, then returned his eyes to the three dim figures in the darkness of the coach for whom he felt so much affection.

Freak, apparently, was asleep. Freak would be all right, Skinner decided. Freak would give himself to whatever came with zest, with sympathy, with unconscious under-standing and conscious appreciation. Why do I like Freak? Skinner asked himself, and answered: first, because every-thing I do is right to him. And because he responds so well. And because he knows my moods, sometimes before I know them myself, but, no matter how depressed I get, he never lets me get him down.

Well, he thought, Rod lets me get him down; in fact, sometimes Rod gets me down. But I like Rod, too, apparently for pretty much the opposite reasons I have for liking Freak. And, of course, because he's such a damn good musician. He thought of the endless kinds and shapes of pianos Rod must have known: the simpering little white ones in the cocktail lounges, the battered uprights in the dives, the concert grands in other people's homes. And yet, he thought, like Benny, I sometimes get annoyed at Rod's indifference, at his willingness to accept everything as inevitable. Because that's what beats him musically. Then, suddenly, he felt that he'd got it about Rod. Rod didn't even believe in music. He lived by it, he gave himself to it, and received from it the fuel to keep living on; but he didn't actually believe in it. Rod, subjectively, got nothing extra from his music; life, yes; breath, yes; but not exultation, not the feeling of extraordinary accomplishment which more conscious artists found in their best creative moments. That was the trouble, Skinner decided; Rod was great, a genius perhaps, but he had nothing bigger than his music—and thus himself—to try for. It was too much a part of him. He couldn't get far enough away from it to realize how good it—and thus he—was. And, summing up, Skinner told himself, "Rod needs music more than it needs him."

And now for Benny, he thought. He supposed that he liked Benny primarily because Benny liked him; and, he surprised himself by adding, because Benny is a lonely guy. All evangelists are lonely; everyone who believes something as zealously as Benny believes is shutting off parts of himself from other human beings. And, since the people who share the belief are similarly cut off, he needs people who will respect without agreeing or disagreeing; people whose minds work differently, who like him without reference to the central belief. And it's funny, he thought, because Benny doesn't even approve of us. Oh, he probably doesn't condemn Freak, because Freak is so elemental, but he must figure Rod for some kind of mildly psychopathic drone, and God knows what he thinks of me. No, that's dishonest. I know what Benny thinks of me. He thinks I'm destructive; he thinks I tear down everything that I set up, and it makes him sad, because he thinks I set things up well. And then sort of turn on them and destroy them.

And what do I think of myself? We've gone over everybody else. Now let's have the word on Thomas Galt, called Skinner.

To avoid the answer, he turned and looked at the figure that would be Benny. It seemed to be asleep, and he felt a surge of warmth towards it: Sleep, Benny, sleep, through the night, through the desert, and wake in the morning in Palestine. And Skinner thought of something Benny had said that he had liked: "Maybe when I see Palestine, and see what's been done, I'll be proud to be a Jew without having to feel aggressive about it."

Skinner slept.

CHAPTER

4

AT TWO in the morning, motion and noise suddenly ceased and the stillness woke them all. Looking out the windows, Skinner saw that they were still in the desert, though he knew from the hour that they must be nearly out of it by now. The moon was almost directly overhead and threw no shadows, making the sand look flat and white. His body, suddenly free of motion, seemed almost capable of flight. His ears, which had long since learned to accept the train noise as normal, strained against the stillness. For a moment after waking, none of them moved or breathed.

Then Skinner quoted softly:

"This is the way the world ends, guys."

Benny, who was against enchantment, got up and stretched. "Where in hell are we?" he asked, in a voice that did not expect an answer.

"Never-never land," said Skinner, laughing, "but you broke the spell."

Freak said, "I feel terrible," stood up, bumped into Benny, said, "Sorry", and sat down.

Rod said, "My mouth tastes like the outhouse in a saw-mill. What did you do with the Arak?"

"Good idea," said Skinner, reaching under the seat and

bringing up the bottle. "Can you open it in the dark?"

"I'll bite it open if I have to." Rod's hand groped for the Arak and Skinner gave it to him. After a minute, there was the gurgle of liquor leaving the bottle. Rod finished, exhaled, and grunted, "You're supposed to have water with this. Who's next?"

Freak said, "What's it like?"

"Its rough," Rod told him. "Take it easy."

More gurgling. "Tastes like liquorice," Freak said, pleasantly.

The bottle came to Skinner. "Its only because I'm desperate," he said, and drank. Benny reached for the bottle and was given it.

"Here's to never-never land," said Benny. "May we never-never return."

"This place frightens him," Rod said. Then, speculatively, "There's probably a camp out here. Do you suppose we could get Benny assigned to it?"

They heard people walking in the corridor, then voices. One voice, close enough to be in the next-door compartment said, "Sorry, we're full in here."

"Bet we get company," Skinner predicted, and, as he said it, there was a knock on the door.

"Come on in," Benny said.

The door opened. Surprisingly, the figure outlined in the doorway was a woman's.

"Iss there room, please?" Her voice was pleasant, a little hesitant, and its accent thickly German.

"Sure," said Freak, "come in." She came in, stepping carefully, and Skinner said,

"Her eyes aren't used to the dark," and lit a match, holding it up. By its light they could see that she was blond, and read the word "Palestine" written on the armband of her A.T.S. uniform. Benny said,

"Sholom."

"Sholom aleichem," she answered. "You speak Hebrew?"

"No," Benny answered. "That's the only word I know. We are Americans."

"So I think," she said. Luggage was piled on the seat that Benny and Skinner occupied, and, as the match went out, she added her musette bag to it and sat down between Freak and Rod.

"I guess you know where the sex appeal is in this crowd," Freak said to the others. "Things are looking up."

"Excuse me?" said the girl.

"I say I am very lucky to have you sit by me," Freak told her.

She said, "I do not know. I do not speak Englisch so good."

"You're doing fine," Skinner said to Freak, "you've wowed her."

"It's the Southern accent," Benny suggested.

"Wait until he starts telling her about the football games," Rod put in.

"What is your name?" Freak asked the girl, speaking slowly.

"My name iss Alma. Yours, please, iss what?"

"Bob," Freak said.

"He's lying," Skinner told her. "Next he'll be claiming he can get you into the movies."

"Look at him leer," Benny said. It was so dark that Freak's face was barely visible.

"The first luminous leer in history," Skinner said.

"Alma and I think you are all cads," said Freak. "Don't we, Alma?"

"Yes?" said the girl, who apparently knew only that she was spoken to.

"Yes," said Freak.

"Why do they make her ride with us?" Rod wanted to know.

"It's the way they run the trains," Benny explained. "Officers and nursing sisters, first class. Enlisted women and sergeants, second-class. All other ranks, third class."

"Which are we?" Skinner asked. "Enlisted women or sergeants?"

"We," said Benny, affecting a cultured British voice, "are Ameddican volunteahs, with the cuhtesy rahnk of warr'nt officah fihst clahss, old boy."

"Well, here's one warrant officer first class who's going to have another drink," Skinner said. "Ask the enlisted woman if she wants one?"

"Drink Arak?" Freak asked her.

"Yes?"

"Try her in French," Freak suggested.

Skinner asked her in French.

"Je ne comprends pas," she said.

"Doesn't anybody know German?" Freak asked. None of them did.

Skinner lit a match and showed her the bottle. "Arac," he said, and offered it to her. She took it, smiled, and drank.

"Danke."

They all smiled back at her. The bottle passed around.

"I go for leave to Dagagnia colony," she volunteered. The bottle came back to her, and she drank. "Now I sleep," she said.

Freak raised his arm, so that it lay across the top of the seat, and patted the shoulder with his other hand. "Like this," he offered.

"It iss all right?"

"It is all right." She settled her head. The match had gone out, but they all heard her sigh sleepily.

"You've trapped yourself," Skinner pointed out to Freak. "Now you can't have another drink without disturbing her."

"Liquor is not everything," Freak said. "You cads are unaware that there are finer things in life."

It was getting chilly. Benny said, "If I weren't such a cad, I'd throw this trench coat over her," and did so.

They heard the engine beginning to work a little faster up ahead, and the train shivered, preparatory to moving. Skinner passed the bottle to Benny.

"Any cad desiring to smoke," said Freak, softly, "will kindly step into the corridor to light his match."

Beside him, Skinner could feel Benny lean forward, passing the bottle to Rod. The train pulled out.

When Skinner woke again, fiinding himself in the same approximate position in which he had been and would be riding, he had a feeling of not having slept at all. Looking out the window and seeing sun-drenched farmland, he decided he had probably been asleep four or five hours. The train must have left the desert, stopped at Gaza without his waking, and was probably well into Palestine by now.

He yawned, stood up, stretched, stepped over Benny who, like the others, was still asleep; got toothbrush, water bottle, and towel out of his musette bag and went down to the washroom at the end of the car. He cleaned up, straightened his clothes, and peered closely into the chipped and grimy mirror above the basin. He smiled at his reflection.

"There was a rumor around a minute ago that you weren't really human," he told himself, aloud. "I just thought I'd better check up."

He went back to the compartment, put his things away, stepped over Benny again, and settled onto his seat. He watched the farms go by. He decided that the ones irrigated by ox-turned wheels were probably Arab; the ones with deeper ditches and streams of water fast enough to come from power wheels were Jewish. He decided Benny wouldn't want to miss any of it, so he woke him.

"Benny, we're in Palestine."

Benny tried to roll away, opened his eyes, and sat up quite suddenly. "What?"

"Palestine, Benny."

Benny looked out and smiled.

"Lo, 'tis the promised land," said Skinner softly, watching him. "Therefore, Israel, rejoice."

"I'll be God damned," said Benny.

By the time Benny was back from the washroom, the others were awake. Rod was putting his shoes on—he claimed he couldn't sleep without taking them off—and Freak and the girl were disentangling their arms and giggling.

"Look," Skinner said to Benny, as he came back in, "the honeymooners."

Benny grinned and sat down. "Did they have a wild night?"

Rod looked up from tying his shoe. "Mr. and Mrs. Freak Lacey wish to announce the conception of a child," he said. "Mr. Rod Manjac wishes to announce a sleepless night due to their thumpings and bumpings."

"Maybe they'll let you be godfather," Benny suggested.

"Shut up, cads," said Freak.

"I hope he won't inherit his father's temper," Skinner said.

"Look, cads," said Freak, patiently. "Mr. Freak Lacey wants you to see his shoulder. On the shoulder, lipstick." His voice grew mournful. "Mr. Freak Lacey also wants you to see his face. On the face, no lipstick."

The girl, who had been watching him, amused, as he

pointed to the light stains on the shoulder of his khaki shirt, where her mouth had brushed against it. Then, when he pointed to his face, she laughed, delighted.

"You are very nice," she said, and, getting one knee under her on the seat, she leaned over, took his face in her hands, and very deliberately kissed him on the lips. She sat back on her ankle and watched him. A blush started from his neck and spread over his whole face.

"More," said Freak, pretending to gasp, and lolling his head from side to side. "More."

Alma laughed again, got up, took her musette bag, and left the compartment.

"Throw some water on him," Skinner said. "There's smoke coming out his nostrils."

The train was pulling slowly across the coastal plain, heading inland slightly, away from the sea. The land was loaded with crops, and there were vineyards and orange groves between the farms. They rearranged themselves in the compartment. Now, Benny and Alma sat opposite one another by the windows, Skinner next to Benny, Freak next to Alma, Rod next to Freak.

Once, passing one of the Arab water-wheels, which were growing less frequent, Benny said, "There. You see how its done? They harness the ox to the wheel with a blinder over his outside eye. That's what makes him keep going around. He's trying to get over to the other side of the wheel where he can see grass."

"I'll bet if you took the blinder off, he'd stop and eat the grass, too," said Freak.

"Sure," Benny agreed. "There's a good political analogy there."

"This is a slow day," Skinner said. "It's taken Benny until ten-thirty to find his first political analogy."

"Nuts," Benny said. "Look. The blinder is ignorance, the wheel is industry, the ox is the worker. Education pulls the blinder off, showing him the whole picture. He stops pulling and the wheel is helpless."

"So he eats up all the grass," Skinner said. "Your analogy falls down."

"Part of it's there," said Benny, frowning.

"You know," said Skinner sadly, to Rod. "Sometimes I think Benny is nothing but a nasty old Red."

"Now wait a minute," Rod said. "Benny's a friend of mine."

"Yeah," said Freak. "You be careful what you say about Benny."

"Nuts," said Benny. "Politically, you guys stink."

"What the hell," said Rod, reasonably. "We know what side we're on. What's the difference if we kid about it? The revolution isn't scheduled for this morning."

"It's all right for you," Benny said. "You can play the piano."

"Benny," said Skinner, knowing what Benny was getting at, and wanting to give him the cue. "Don't be obscure."

"Who's being obscure? Look, Rod plays the piano. Freak is young and eager. I try to think occasionally. And what the hell are you? You stink politically, you're nothing spiritually, you're licked intellectually."

Skinner smiled.

Benny went on. "What the hell have you ever done? Talked sincerely with some good people—turned around and forgotten what they said. Fooled around with the CIO one summer. College-boy crap."

"Benny, what can I say? You're right. So what? So you're right."

"Damn it," Benny said. "The worst of it is that you enjoy it. The more I rave at you, the happier you are. You're proud of being nothing."

Unexpectedly, Alma spoke to Freak. "He is angry?" she asked.

"No," said Freak, "he's always that way."

"He's always either angry, informative, or sentimental," Skinner said. "And we love him very much."

"One of these days," Benny said, moodily, "when the barricades go up, you guys will look across them and see me on the other side. Not because you want to be on the other side, but because you damn well weren't interested enough to find out which side was which."

"Benny, Benny," Skinner said, "there won't be any revolution in America. The middle classes are too well-fed, the working class is too well-fooled into thinking its the middle class, and the intellectuals are too damn tired." When he said "intellectuals", he put the French feminine ending on it, "intellectuelles", accenting the penultimate e sound.

"I know," said Benny, without much spirit. "When it comes to revolutions, you'd rather go on a party."

"Parties is good," Skinner agreed.

"Parties is fine," Freak said.

Rod's tired voice summed up: "If anyone would care to put it in the form of a motion, I think we would find that America's young manhood, as represented by this bright-eyed cross-section with us this morning, would return a landslide vote in favor of parties over revolutions."

"Wait until after the war," Benny said.

"After the war," Freak said, firmly, "we will go on a party."

"We'll go on hundreds," said Benny, gloomily.

"But one special party," Freak insisted. "Right after we get back. In New York. We'll get an apartment and fill it with women."

"And liquor," Rod said. "All kinds of liquor."

"Skinner will have Cindy," Freak said. "And Benny can get Rose. You'll have to get girls for you and me."

"Sure," Rod said. "I'll get you a girl, but you'd better not blush when she kisses you."

"I'll be a man of the world," Freak promised. "She'll do the blushing."

"Not the girl I have in mind; she's been kissed so many times, she does it instead of shaking hands." Thinking of her seemed to amuse him. He smiled. "She's a singer. We'll give her a bottle of gin to cradle in her arms, and she'll sing blues for us all night long."

"It'll have to be a big apartment," Skinner offered. "Four bedrooms. Another room with an piano for Rod, an ice-box, a victrola—and every record Louis ever made."

"We'll keep it going 'til our money runs out," said Freak, pleased.

"It'll last about two weeks," Skinner said. "Then, one Sunday morning, we'll wake up so hung we can't even stand well. We'll all get out of bed, and sort of totter around in our bare-feet, looking for something to drink. We'll find one last bottle of Scotch someone's hidden in the ice-box, and we'll gather on one of the beds and drink it straight."

"It'll be terrible," Freak said, happily.

Skinner went on with enthusiasm. "Really terrible. It just couldn't be worse. We'll be talking over all the awful things about the situation, and the worse it sounds, the more we'll laugh; only that will be bad, too, because we'll feel so awful it'll hurt to laugh."

"A gorgeous feeling," Benny said.

Skinner's prophetic vision grew clearer. "We'll be talking about money at first," he said. "Cindy'll have four dollars left of the dough she got from hocking our engagement ring. Rod will have a counterfeit half. We'll owe a fifty dollar liquor bill, and we'll have talked ourselves a lot of credit with the apartment people which we can't settle. Freak will be due in court Monday morning for some reason. . . ."

"Smashing a plate-glass window," Freak said, "and trying to steal an overcoat."

"Right. Because you traded yours for a bottle of gin to give your singer. And we'll be wondering what the old lady who put up the bail is going to do when she finds out what the charge really is."

"I," said Benny, "will have my arm in a sling."

"And you and Rose will have decided you hate each other."

"This is getting better all the time," Rod observed.

"So finally," Skinner said, "we'll finish off the Scotch. And go out and sell our shoes to buy a couple more bottles—to kill the pain. And the party will break up. My father will want to see me, in Baltimore."

"Rose will forgive Benny," Rod said, "and invite him to stay with her family in Westchester County."

"And I'll have to go," Benny groaned.

"I'll be playing a job in Chicago," Rod added. "And I'll have to borrow train fare from the elevator boy."

"And I'll go to jail," Freak said, eagerly. "Only my old man will buy me out."

The worse the hangover, the better the party. It would be a splendid party. For a while, they were all quiet, thinking about it.

Skinner, opening his book, and pretending to read, watched his friends. He saw Freak, for the fourth time that morning, try to put his arm around Alma, and surprisingly, succeed; which put Freak in any compartment, of any railroad coach, anywhere. Rod, leaning back with his eyes closed, was humming to himself and smiling, so he was probably still in New York; it was Sunday morning, maybe, and he was feeling lousy, and that was a fine thing because it meant it had been a fine party. Only Benny, staring out the window, absorbed, apparently, by what he could see of the agricultural progress made in the smoothly cultivated fields, was in Palestine.

Skinner found his place in the book, which was *Mr. Norris Changes Trains,* and was in pre-war Berlin with Christopher Isherwood and his friend, Norris, investigating the delicacies of flagellation.

The train was slowing, coming into a station.

"Tiberias," the girl said.

"What?"

"Tiberias."

Skinner looked across Benny and out through the window. A huge lake stretched out, alongside the train. Lake Tiberias, the Sea of Galilee.

Alma was gathering her things. "My colony," she told them, "Dagagnia."

The train stopped, and an R.T.O. corporal ran alongside the cars, shouting that they would be there fifteen minutes.

Freak and Benny got off with Alma who, they hoped, could show them where to buy wine if they could make her understand what it was they wanted. Skinner and Rod were alone in the compartment.

"Three or four hours more," Skinner said.

"Right," said Rod. "Then what?"

Skinner shrugged. "Then we drive ambulances, I guess."

They were both silent. Then Rod asked, abruptly: "Why in hell did you join this outfit, Skinner?"

"The same reason you did. Escapism. The quickest trip away."

"Yeah? Then why did Benny join it?"

"I'm not sure. I don't know. I can tell you why Freak joined, though."

"Why?"

"He has something wrong with his knee, from playing football. He couldn't get into the army."

"What about Garry White? And Darian? And Haldemeyer?"

"White's a playboy, and this is a good playboy outfit. Darian's a pretty sincere guy, a conshie; this is a compromise between the army and jail. Haldemeyer brings us back around the circle again. He's almost fifty; he wasn't in the last war, and he's yearned for this one for twenty years, as the finest sort of romantic escape from whatever rut he was in. Escape with honor."

"Yeah."

"Besides which, I think Haldemeyer's a queer. If he is, he'll find plenty of company."

"Yeah," said Rod. "He's a queer, all right. I've had him spotted for a long time, but I didn't want to say anything." Then, after a pause. "And I'm an escapist, huh?"

"You tell me," said Skinner.

"Okay. You don't know what I'm running away from, do you?"

"Sure I do. And so do you."

"Yeah. I guess I do. What's your guess?"

Skinner shrugged. "You're twenty-eight; it's too late to

get the kind of training you need to be a big-time, serious musician."

"That's most of it," Rod agreed. "I think I'll get out of here before you tell me the rest. Or I tell you."

He walked to the door of the compartment, turned, started to say something else, decided not to, and went out.

Skinner thought: okay, brain. So you think you can tell Rod what he's running away from. Now let's go to work on us. This thing has been going on a long time. We changed prep-schools twice. We've never spent two summers in the same place. We just barely lasted two years and a summer term in college before we jumped into this thing. What keeps us moving?

Then, changing persons, he thought: if I hadn't been committed to this thing, maybe I'd still be with Cindy in New York. We'd be married. It would have lasted. Then he asked himself: Yeah? Would we be? Would it have?

Maybe I don't have anything to run from. Maybe I run for the sake of running. Maybe escapism becomes a sort of personal philosophy, or does that make me a romantic?

Or are these the wrong words? Benny and Rod could be right, and, if they are, I'm destructive. Instead of running to escape, I run to destroy. He decided, without much liking it, that they might be right.

But you've got to tear things down, he argued with the accusing images of Benny and Rod, before they fall down and take you with them. You tear them down before they get a chance to fall on you, and you don't get hurt.

And then, suppose, sometime, you got it all built up—a relationship, a religion, a belief, anything that was satisfying emotionally—you got it all built up and you knew in the back of your mind that you would tear it down eventually, but right now it was good, and you wanted to play it for a while. And then suppose, just as you were at the height, really liking it, something you couldn't control beat you to it; tore down your structure while you were still involved in it?

Skinner looked away from the worn spot in the plush of the opposite seat on which his eyes had fastened without his being conscious of it.

"Balls," said Skinner, aloud.

Benny and Freak came buoyantly back into the compartment, flourishing three bottles of red wine. The couplings between the cars started their familiar clatter of preparation for movement. Rod came in and sat down. They left Tiberias.

There was one more stop in Palestine, though none of them knew the name of the town.

It was a little orange growing community, twenty minutes from the Syrian border, and, as the train pulled in, they could see the oranges in bags, sacks, crates, baskets, and plain heaps, lining the platform.

"There's a huge crop this year," Benny told them, "but, with the Mediterranean closed up, there's no way of shipping it out. We can probably get all the oranges we can eat for a cigarette."

They decided to go out and barter for oranges.

They left the compartment and went out on the station platform. Apparently everyone else on the train had the same idea. The platform was swarming with fellow ambulance drivers, Tommies, R.A.F. men on leave, and a scattering of troops who represented governments in exile: Poles, Czechs, Greeks, and French. The crowd broke up into little groups, each crowded around one or two Arab urchins who claimed to have been left to guard the oranges, bargaining with cigarettes and rations.

Skinner was never sure how it started. Perhaps someone,

finding a half-spoiled orange, tried to throw it clear of the platform and underestimated the range.

There was a sudden cry of, " 'Ere, 'oo threw that bloody thing?" and a squash of fruit landing near them.

All along the platform, divided not so much by nationality as by position in the field, men dived behind boxes, grabbed up oranges, and flung them at anybody in sight. All the restless physical energy unexpended during the long trip suddenly found release in a surge of fruit flying through the air.

Arms trained on cricket can throw as hard and as straight as those trained on baseball, and oranges make hard missiles. The platform was a chaos of yelling men. Sacks were overturned, baskets dumped. The little Arab boys, far from resenting the destruction of fruit, were delighted with the general excitement, and skipped about, dodging, shrieking, and supplying oranges to those who ran short.

Finally, as fruit was running low, and the contestants were being reduced to salvaging pieces of oranges thrown by opponents, a tall, fat Rail Transport Sergeant stepped out on the platform between two cars.

"Train's leaving, boys," he shouted, and ducked back as a shower of oranges splattered the sides of the cars between which he stood. Then, docilely, grinning and looking a little sheepish, the soldiers came out from behind their barricades, straightening their clothes and wiping juice off, and loaded back into the train.

Going into Syria, the journey almost over, Benny and Freak opened the wine they had bought in Tiberias, Rod tore their last loaf of bread into four equal hunks, and Skinner opened and divided the can of cheese.

The wine was cool and red, the cheese yellow and strong, the bread tough-crusted. They were so used to the motion of the train by now that they did not notice it; the exercise of the orange fight had given them appetite, and it was not as hot here in the hills as it had been on the plain. They ate happily.

"A real Hemingway meal," said Skinner, mocking their contentment.

"Good Hemingway country," said Rod, looking at the series of steep, sun-crested slopes that rose away from them inland, towards Transjordan. "Those are the kind of hills that make you want to cross them."

"Beyond Damascus there's a valley called the Bekaa," Benny told them.

"Is Damascus where we're going?" asked Freak.

"It's where we get off the train. Then we'll spread around, probably. But I'm telling you about the valley. It's very interesting, because everybody in the history book has conquered it, beginning with the Babylonians and going right through the Persians and Romans and Turks and French, and finally the British." In 1941, Skinner remembered, there had been fighting near Damascus between the British and the Vichy troops. It had been the first Allied victory of the war.

"Where's Beirut?" Rod wanted to know. "I used to know a trumpet player from there."

Benny took out a notebook, and made them a little sketch. "Suppose you stand in Damascus," he said. "You're facing North, towards Turkey. The Mediterranean is on your left, over the mountains, Transjordan and Persia on your right. You're at the lower end of this Bekaa valley which is straight in front of you. A low range of mountains goes right up between the Bekaa and the sea. There are a lot of nice little towns on the sea-coast, on the left side of the range. Marjayoun, Saida—that's where Tyre and Sidon were—then Beirut, and, way up the coast, Latakia.

They're all in the Republic of Lebanon." He made some more dots on the sketch. "Now if you went up the valley instead of the coast, following a roughly parallel line, you'd stay in Syria. You'd leave Damascus and go to Baalbek, where the ruins are and which is about level with Beirut, then Zahle, and then, way up, Aleppo."

"Othello," Skinner murmured.

"What?"

"Othello. He killed a moor in Aleppo, once."

"Yeah," Benny agreed. "Anyway." He referred to his sketch. "Out to the right of Damascus is the Syrian desert. Palmyra is in the middle of it, and there's a pipeline that comes through Palmyra from Iran to Damascus."

"What's up here?" Freak asked, running his finger from Palmyra up the map until it was on an approximate line with Latakia and Aleppo.

"The Euphrates River," Benny told him.

"My God," said Rod. "What a mind."

"A little more than human," Skinner agreed.

"Oh, I'm good," Benny said. "There's no question about that."

"What do you think?" Rod asked Skinner.

"I think he made it all up," Skinner said. "Anyone can take a pencil and a piece of paper and make up a country."

"Sure," Freak agreed.

They took a piece of paper and a pencil and made up a country. Its name was Gloaming.

"It's where you go to roam," Skinner explained.

Its Capital was Inner Labia, and Benny named its principal port Nipple-by-the-sea.

PART THREE

A Young Man at Night in An Old City

CHAPTER

5

THE barracks at Damascus were all but empty. The new men for the ambulance unit had streamed off the train, loaded into trucks, and been driven here. Had scrambled off the trucks, with their luggage, been directed into buildings as assigned, swarmed over the beds depositing bags, overcoats, sweaters and papers in little heaps on top of them, and poured out again to eat. And, now that eating was over, had broken up into little groups to go into the city. The organization made no pretense of discipline or restriction, so that they were free to do what they liked until the morning, when they would learn, at a meeting, what their duties were. Then rumor said, a few classes would familiarize them with the operation and maintenance of their vehicles, and they would be ready for their posts. The new group would take over the posts as the men already there were transferred out to the Western Desert. This much they had learned.

Skinner, refusing Benny, Freak and Rod's urging that he go out with them to see Damascus, was alone in the large, dark, impersonal room, with its untidy row of army cots, each strewn with personal equipment, each topped by an incongruously neat, carefully rolled, mosquito net.

Caught by an impatient longing for order, he had frowningly unpacked and repacked each of his bags, shaken out the clothing and refolded it, arranged the shoes severely under the bunk, and was now laying out toilet articles with rigid precision on the slim shelf above the bed. For no reason, except to have a reason, he placed each unit in the precise order in which he would use it in the morning. Toothbrush, toothpaste, soap, shaving-brush, cream, razor, towel, comb, brush. He finished, looked at what he had done, picked up the razor and put a new blade in it, and put it back again in its place. He looked all around the room for a wastebasket in which to throw the old blade; failed to find one; was annoyed; went out into the hall; found a wastebasket there, and dropped the blade in it, first reading what was written on it. Technocrat, Precision-ground, Double-edged, Finest Surgical Steel, Made in U.S.A.

Back in the room, he sat on the bunk, and began going through his mail. At Cairo, eighty days accumulation had been waiting for him, and there had been over a hundred letters, most of which he had hurried through. Now that he would have time to go over them carefully, he began by taking fifteen minutes to arrange them, by sender and by date, puzzling out the dates from the postmarks where he could, or looking inside the envelopes when necessary. He made three chronologically-arranged piles: the first one consisted of eleven letters, one per week, from his father; there were three letters, bearing Army Air Field postmarks, from his college room-mate, six or seven from a friend of his father's, a breezy lady who made it her duty to write regularly and cheerfully, to the half-dozen boys whom she knew overseas, and nineteen others from miscellaneous friends and well-wishers, all of which made the second pile; all the letters in the third pile were from Cindy.

He went through the miscellaneous pile methodically, making brief notes of the ones he meant to answer, copying the addresses from them into an address book, and re-piling them for later disposal.

He read each of his father's letters. They were amusing, affectionate, and, with one exception, light. The exceptional letter was slightly apologetic: "This is a far different war from ours, son. Without wanting to sound like a rambunctious old goat, I'd like to say that I have tried quite seriously to get over, as a correspondent or something. But the desk has an unanswerable line for bunnies like me. Keep turning out the sports copy, Lou. It keeps morale up. Nobody seems very concerned about my morale, but perhaps that's as it should be." Knowing exactly what he wanted to say to his father, whom he liked, and for whom he had the impersonal respect that the young have for older people whose achievements they admire without any urge towards emulation, Skinner added the letters to the pile for disposal.

He considered the bulk of Cindy's letters, mostly airmail envelopes stuffed with thin paper, closely typed. It represented, not just devotion, but an amazing amount of work. A hundred, a hundred and fifty closely-typed, single-spaced pages. It was a novel. A novel by Cindy about loneliness. About being in love. About being a young woman, victim of a dozen insecurities, alone in New York in wartime. Few days had gone by without her writing, and, on many days, she had written two or three times. Into the letters she had put everything: the fitful, urgent charm of war-driven new acquaintances, and the changes in old friends; the things that silly people said to her, and the things wise people said to one another; how sick the newspapers of the warring republic sounded, and how courageous its leader; how little the stomach was affected and how much the heart, by the rationing of food and love. They had agreed not to try to answer one another's letters, to simply write as the need came, and Cindy's need had been constant.

Skinner, continually meeting new challenges and situations, had felt the need for communication less desperately, and less often; but in the long monotonies of the boat, and the phoniness of Cairo as a headquarters city, and the affection for his friends which could not be expressed directly to them, he, too, had found need to talk to her. Often, too, a simple desire to be writing, for its own sake, had moved him, and he had composed long descriptions of the sea, or committed to paper the intricacies of a new chain of thought, or tried to transcribe the strange mood of Middle Eastern cabarets, with impressionistic glimpses of the tired faces of soldiers and girls at the tables; he had written these out, organized as essays, with "Cindy Darling" at the heads of them, and signed them, "All my love, dear. Skinner."

He began rereading each of Cindy's letters now, and spent two hours with her, taking time to note felicitous turns of phrase, and occasional contradictions, feeling strongly her beloved presence in the sheets of paper.

He finished the last of Cindy's letters, folded it, put it in his wallet, stacked the others neatly together and tied them. He took the other, discarded correspondence out to the wastebasket in the hall, found a piece of wrapping paper, and returned. He wrapped Cindy's letters in it, addressed the parcel to himself in care of his father, and made a note to ask his father by letter to hold it for him.

Then, feeling that the terms of existence-at-the-moment were satisfied, he lay back on the bunk, and, for the first time in ninety days, enjoyed the feeling of being by himself.

He thought of a number of things he would like to say to Cindy, things which couldn't be said in letters because each succeeding statement presupposed the answer to a previous statement, and said them aloud, with the image of her in his mind making the responses. He became interested in the difficulty he had visualizing her precisely. He could close his eyes and yet get no very clear picture of the way she looked, finding instead that the effort reproduced only a sensation faintly like the ones he had felt looking at her.

He wondered why it was, and, experimentally, tried to visualize his father without much more success. Then he tried the clerk in the grocery store near where he and Cindy had been living, and got him clearly—coloring, shape of face, even a slight puffiness he had noticed in one cheek. It seemed quite odd. He thought for a minute, tried one or two other people whom he knew only slightly, and found that his mind could pictorialize them with great clarity. It was only the people about whom he had strong emotions that he couldn't get. He tried breaking the recollection of Cindy up into characteristic poses and expressions, and was only slightly more successful. Finally he found that the only way to get a clear mental image was to isolate a particular event, one of brief duration, and place her in it as she had looked. That way, he did quite well, and he tested it with a dozen recollections.

He opened his eyes, feeling that she was very close to him, and said,

"This is the oldest city in the world, darling. Let us go and see it, now."

He got up, pulled on his battle-dress jacket, and went out onto the parade ground, offering her his arm.

They went out the gate, past the sentry, and onto a wide, uneven street, uneven in an old, worn way, that spoke of countless layers of paving brick, pressed down and beaten smooth. It was not late—eleven o'clock, perhaps—yet there was nothing open in the city. A few lights, lost up side streets, suggested people but as they walked along here, on the thoroughfare, there was no one.

There came a chanting, from somewhere, and she told him to listen and asked him what it was.

"It's a beggar singing, darling," he told her. "Giving alms is one way of attaining heaven." They stopped and listened to the odd, unmelodic song, off on another street in the dark.

The city, Damascus, the oldest city in the world, seemed neither ominous nor friendly. It seemed, rather, a place where people dwelt, had dwelt, would dwell. The mind's sense of the accumulation of history said that this place was as familiar as one's living room, as much a part of one as one's parents. And then the mind began to particularize, and, gradually, the sense of familiarity gave way:

On this street, on feet constructed as ours are, walked a young soldier of Rome, wishing this were no war, wishing he had brought, not a sword, but a bride.

Here, at this very time of night, some exact number of days and years ago, swinging a similarly muscled arm, wandered a young Mede, feeling keenly the absence of his Persian lover, somewhere beyond the rivers.

Against this wall, as we lean on it, so leaned the yearning Greek, the timorous Egyptian, the daunted Crusader, the lonely German, the fearful Briton, and the unbold Turk, each with his human preference for love and home.

And, only two years back, the legionnaire, sick to the heart of bravado and loud jokes, visualized, in the secrecy of this same darkness, hidden by it from his boisterous fellows, the light touch of a beloved hand upon his arm.

The sense of familiarity gave way to awe. The sense of being a part of this gave way to the realization of how small a part. And, somewhere in the giving way, Cindy was gone. And Skinner returned to the barracks by the same street, alone, and, for the moment, humble.

PART FOUR

A Portrait of Jack, Quick

CHAPTER

6

THE assignments hadn't worked out as badly as they might have. Skinner, Rod, and Freak had been assigned together to the car-pool in Beirut. Only Benny had been separated from the group.

Benny's assignment was to a unit which was stationed in a little town called Raqqa, up by the Euphrates, where, they learned, he would share a good deal of hard driving with one other man, getting patients from the remote post over terrible roads to the clearing station at Aleppo.

So they had said so long, Benny's last, mournful observation being, "I memorize every town in Syria and they send me to one that isn't even on the map."

The Beirut car-pool, where Skinner, Rod, and Freak were, consisted of seven ambulances which were on call to various military installations around the city too small to rate permanent ambulances of their own. There was a driver for each car, and, since there were never more than two or three calls a day, they had a great deal of free time. Located just above the old port city, with its theatres, French restaurants, and hotels, it was considered one of the best posts in Syria. The tempo was slow, the life lazy and good.

Of the other drivers, one was a boy named Fred Birch

whom Skinner had known and liked in college. Another was an older man named Heinz, a novelist, who spent all his spare time working on a book which, he said apologetically, would be serialized in the same magazine that had bought his previous stuff, published by a firm that specialized in popular fiction, and make him enough money to keep up alimony payments to his two past wives. The other two were a pair of young homosexuals who spoke of themselves as actors, pleasant, conscientious boys who cheerfully allowed most of the daily routine work to be thrust upon them, and did it efficiently and uncomplainingly. They were thoroughly absorbed in one another, and were hardly noticeable unless they were having one of their periodic fallings out.

When the fallings out occurred, the one named Tommy would go to Heinz, who was nominally in charge of the post, and therefore grateful to them for the amount of painful detail work they relieved him of, and Heinz would lay aside his manuscript, and listen to a recital of how unfair the other was.

Rod was, for some reason, almost immediately singled out for the position of father-confessor to the other, a slight, exceptionally effeminate boy named Billy. Whoever it was to whom Billy had previously told his troubles was one of the drivers whom Skinner, Freak, and Rod had relieved. But Billy's love life seemed, for the time being, quite satisfactory, and they were not much worried with it.

The new members had been on the post six or seven days before an evening came when they were all three free at the same time to investigate the town together. Skinner and Rod had made separate trips. Freak, finding neither of them free on his first night off, and not wanting to go drinking by himself, had gone to see a very old Shirley Temple picture with Fred Birch, since when Freak had been none other than Miss Shirley Temple, the little lady with the great big dimple; and his rendition of "Baby Take a Bow", complete with simper and a little curtsy, was, Skinner said, "The greatest cross I have yet been called upon to bear."

He and Rod agreed that they must take Freak to town and find him a new song to sing.

They left the shack, which they shared with Fred—there were three such shacks on the post, one of which was used as an office—at about five. They were on the lower slope of the mountain which rises behind Beirut, the mountain Benny had described as being between the port and the valley, and it took them five minutes of easy downhill walking to get to the place where the car-line started. While they were waiting for the trolley to come, Freak was approached by a man who was much excited by the word American on his arm-band.

"American? America?"

"Yes?"

"I live for ten years in Lawrence, Mass."

"I'll be darned," said Freak. "How come you're back here?"

"I come to see my family, see. Then the war come, I cannot go back. America is my country, yes."

"Fine," said Freak. "Good country. Have a cigarette?" He offered his pack, and the man took one. Freak lit it for him.

"You have no Lucky Strike? Cigarettes I buy."

Freak had an extra pack of Chesterfields with him. "Okay," he said.

"One pound I give you." A pound, Syrian, was about fifty cents.

"Two pounds is the usual price," Rod said.

"Two pound I give you," the man agreed. He and

Freak completed the transaction. "You got Lucky Strikes, I give you three pound." Where the Syrians derived their curious fixation on Lucky Strikes, they never knew.

"Well, criminal?" Said Skinner to Freak, as the man departed.

"Racketeer," Rod added.

"What did I do?" Freak asked.

"Nothing," said Skinner. "You just pushed Western Civilization that much closer to the brink by dealing in the black market."

"Is that what it means?" Freak asked. "I thought it was something bad."

"Come on, criminal," Rod said. "Here's our street car."

They rode the car into town, standing on the back platform, talking with a boy who was studying at the American University in Beirut, and was glad of a chance to try out his English on them.

They rode through the Midan, where the theatres, and some of the restaurants and bars are, and down to the waterfront which is lined, alternately, with luxurious hotels, first class restaurants, and, for solid blocks in some places, with brothels of all varieties: dance halls, where the girls cannot leave until closing time, and must provide their own rooms; cheap pensions, where only a pretense of dancing is made, and the girls are in and out of the management-owned rooms all evening; more expensive pensions, where decorum requires that the girls sit around and pretend that they live there, and nothing is done without a formal introduction, the sort of place in which French officers could keep mistresses safely; and, finally, traditional brothels, graded, during wartime, by the British, according to rank—some for sergeants, some for officers, some for Other Ranks. And there were still other establishments then, where only civilians were admitted. It was said that, by and large, an officer or civilian brothel would serve the best liquor in town, and would continue serving it after the bars were closed, and this was used as a handy rationalization for dropping down to Lorraine's or Mama Frank's after eleven o'clock for a quick one—meaning drink.

It was, however, not quite six o'clock when they arrived at the waterfront, and Skinner and his friends were intent, for the time being, on drinking and eating. They decided they would begin at the bar in the Hôtel Bonne Chance.

The Bonne Chance was the chic place for afternoon drinking. Officers only, of course, but this was extended, through official courtesy, to include American volunteers.

The bar was a big, shiny room, finished in metal and salmon-pink lacquer, with long, curtained windows along one side, a carpeted floor, cushioned, chrome bar stools, and small tables, set into non-functional nooks along the wall.

They sat at the bar. Rod and Freak ordered gin and lime; Skinner had brandy and plain water. "The only piece of advice my father gave me when I started off to war," he said, "was when you're at a place where Frenchmen drink, always order brandy and you can't go wrong."

"Your father must be a good guy," said Rod.

"My pop gave me some advice, too," Freak said.

"What was that?"

"Well, it was funny. I could feel it coming all week, the week before I left. So one day he said he wanted to talk to me, and I figured, 'Oh, boy. Here it comes. I'm going to hear all about the last war, and staying away from bad women, and everything.' You know what he said?"

"What?"

Freak's voice softened with wonder at the recollection. "All he said to me was, 'Stay close to the ground, son. Learn to love the ground.' "

Rod, who hadn't seen his father in years, said, "I wonder what my old man would have said?" Then he answered his own question. " 'Going to war, eh? Well, my boy, we'd better have a drink on that. Yessir, we'll just go up to Mike's and have a drink. Got any money with you?' "

They ordered another round.

"I'm hungry," Freak announced. "Where do we eat?"

Skinner and Rod discussed the problem of where to eat, and admitted that neither of them had found a very good place. Skinner called the bartender over, and asked in French where they ought to go. The bartender suggested Martin's. They paid their check, walked out through the lobby, took a cab, and drove to Martin's.

It was, as monsieur the bartender had promised, a splendid place.

They were seated at a splendid table by a splendid headwaiter, who whispered that a contraband shipment of vodka had been received, if messieurs would care to try it. Skinner translated the information for the others, somewhat dubiously. To his dismay, Freak was immediately curious and Rod enthusiastic.

"I used to know a Russian girl," said Rod, "who taught me the proper way to drink it. I'll let you guys in."

They ordered the vodka, and, when it came, Rod showed them how to pick up the shot glass and toss the liquid into the throat without having to taste it.

Skinner sniffed his. "It smells like rubbing alcohol and dime store perfume," he said, and tried to drink it as Rod had. He choked. Across the table, Freak choked on his.

"Don't try to swallow," said Rod. "Hold your throat

open and let it go down." He ordered another round and demonstrated. Freak and Skinner were more successful, and a third round was called for to show that it hadn't been an accident.

"Here's to Uncle Rodney's Russian girl," said Freak.

"Uncle Rodney has been around sexually," Skinner said.

"These many years," Rod agreed.

They ordered dinner. Paté de la Maison, Vichysoisse, Filet Mignon, Petit Pois, Salade, and Parfait Môche.

"Tell us about the Russian girl," Freak demanded.

"Nothing to tell," Rod said. "She ran the hat-check thing in a joint in Chicago."

"Get him to tell you about his movie star," Skinner suggested.

"What movie star?" Freak asked, eagerly.

"No one you ever heard of," Rod said. "An aging character part girl who'd saved her dough. I was playing a lounge in Los Angeles. She sent me a note by one of the waiters, 'Would I like a job as her secretary?' I returned it with something insulting on the back."

"What did you say?"

" 'Go peddle your menopause' ". Rod told them. The paté arrived. "The waiter had pointed her out, and I thought she was too damn old. Then, about two weeks later, the lounge went broke and didn't pay the help. So I called her up, and told her I was afraid I'd been a little hasty, and was the job still open? She said, 'Yes', and that was that."

"How was she?" Freak insisted.

"Wonderful," said Rod, ironically. "Just wonderful."

The paté was cleared away.

With dinner, coffee, brandy, and a forty-five pound

check behind them, Skinner said, "I want you guys to meet a friend of mine."

They took a cab and returned to the waterfront.

"Where are we going?" Rod wanted to know.

"Dancing," Skinner said. "I mean really dancing."

He would tell them no more.

They walked along a block full of bars and dance-halls, with low-class pensions on the second and third floors, and turned in at the doorway with a sign on it that said, "Blondie's—English Spoken."

They went down a flight of stairs and were in Blondie's. It was like every other cheap dance-hall in the world. The same huddled interior: tables squashed against the wall to make a space for dancing in the center, a platform at one end with a piano, a piano stool, four chairs, and five musicians, and a window in one wall through which drinks were shoved out, and empty glasses shoved in. It had the same piano, drum, trumpet, accordian, and violin variety of bad music, and the same cast of girls: the young one with a lot of friends, the fat, vulgar one who was too obvious for any but the drunkest customers, the two or three aging, eager, over-made up ones.

The conventions of the place were the same, too. You sat down at a table, you ordered a drink. A girl came over and sat with you, and you ordered a drink for her. Your drink was beer, or eau-de-vie, or so-called whiskey, and cost a quarter; hers was colored water, and cost anything from half-a-dollar up, depending on the quality of the place. Her drink was called, by fixed custom, cherry brandy, and, with each one that she persuaded a customer to buy, she received a colored chip. Her night's pay depended on the number of chips she could collect. There were some girls who considered it cheating not to have a real drink, and they soon lost their youth, lost jobs in the better places, and were reduced to working in the smaller dives like Blondie's.

Having satisfied the conventions of drink-buying, you were then free to dance, neck discreetly—less so as the evening advanced—and make any arrangements you could for "apres vous finissez le travail."

Skinner, Rod, and Freak sat down at a table near the dance floor, and ordered brandy. Two girls came over and offered to sit with them. Freak, on whom gin and lime, vodka, vin ordinaire, and a succession of brandies were beginning to have a decidedly amatory effect, was all for it. Skinner said no.

"Later," he told Freak. "In this establishment, we shall not wallow in sex like the animals you see around you." He indicated a handful of soldiers and sailors of all nations who were embracing girls on the dance floor and at the tables. "We have come here to dance."

"Who with?" Freak asked.

"Why with Blondie, of course," said Skinner, and pointed to a big, lithe, blond woman who was making her way towards their table, a welcoming smile spread over her sensual, friendly face.

"It is the American," cried Blondie, hands on hips. "Who speaks French and does the jitterbug dance." American troops had not arrived in Beirut at the time, and members of the ambulance group still enjoyed the privilege of being accepted as novelties.

"I don't jitterbug well," Skinner said. "But my friend, Monsieur Lacey, is from the South. He will jitterbug."

"Sure," said Freak, grinning at her.

"Your other friend?" She asked, indicating Rod.

"Monsieur Manjac. He is an artiste. He plays the piano."

Then, to Rod. "Blondie is an artiste, too. She is a great dancer. She can do any ballroom step in the world. With any man in the world. To any music in the world. And tirelessly. She has never been tired on the dance-floor. She is a genius."

Blondie laughed. "I can dance a little," she admitted. "But now I am old. In Paris you should have seen me."

"Blondie has a husband," Skinner went on. "And he will kill her if she allows any man to take her home after the closing hour."

"He thinks I make up this husband," Blondie confided. "And who knows? Perhaps I do. It is good for business."

She summoned a waiter, got drinks for them, drank hers off. She rose and took Freak by the arm. "Come, cheri," she said. "We will dance now."

Freak, looking a little embarrassed, stood up and faced her on the floor. The orchestra started playing "In the Mood", which passed for the hottest thing on wheels in the Middle East, and Freak, who loved fast dancing, started to move his feet, standing a little away at first so that she could watch the step. She looked for a moment, nodded, moved into his arms. They whirled away together, Freak grinning, and Blondie throwing back her head to laugh appreciatively whenever he went into a variation.

"She's good," said Rod, watching them, as Freak grabbed her hand, whirled her out to arm's length, turned her around, and moved back next to her. "He's doing all right, too."

"She's tireless," Skinner said again. "She'd go like that all night if Freak could stand it. What do you think of the music?"

"It's awful, isn't it?" Said Rod. He listened. "The violin has some ideas. The drummer holds the beat all right. The rest are hackers."

"The violinist is from Paris," Skinner said. "Blondie

brought him with her. He's worked with Reinhardt and Grappelly."

"Get him over," Rod said.

"He doesn't speak any English."

"I'll talk to him," Rod insisted. He finished his drink, stood up, noticed Freak's glass standing half-full and finished that, too. He walked over to the band.

Skinner saw him smile at the violinist, make motions of playing the piano with his fingers. The violinist smiled back, but shook his head. Rod apparently indicated that he was to ask Blondie, because the violinist took his instrument down from his chin and called out to her on the floor. She nodded and the orchestra trailed off without finishing the piece.

Everyone in the place turned to look at Rod, but he paid no attention to the voices that said, "What's the idea, stopping the music?" and "Who does he bloody-well think he is, Paderewski?" He climbed onto the platform and went to the piano. The musicians talked it over among themselves, the pianist shook hands with Rod, left his stool, and sat down at the musicians' table to have a drink.

Rod moved onto the stool, sat quite still for a brief moment looking at the instrument, ran his fingers up and down the keyboard in arpeggios, listening, touching each key as if it were a nerve. He found a chord he liked, modulated away from it, went back to it, wove it into a bass, and started playing blues. The violinist caught the key, settled his fiddle against his shoulder, and created an obbligato. They played that way for forty-eight bars; then Rod nodded his head, picked up the thread of the obbligato with his right hand in the treble, and the violin took over the blues theme. The drummer, a dark boy who was probably Syrian, had the beat, and was playing it softly with the brushes. It was music.

It was folk music of a kind, folk music for the man who's

been around; what Rod's piano said was, *Life may be a little bit too long this year,* and what the violin replied was, *Paris is a long way off.*

Blondie and Freak came over to the table and sat down with Skinner.

Skinner asked her, "Do you like it?"

Blondie said, "I have heard it like this before." She stared at the glass in front of her, recently refilled, but made no move to drink it.

Skinner reached over and patted her hand. "We'll dance," he said, and they stood up and danced off slowly, Skinner hardly conscious of moving.

Eventually Rod worked out of the blues, and into faster things. He wouldn't satisfy the requests for *Amapola* and *Dark Eyes,* but he played *Sweet Lorraine* and *Sunny Side,* and even played some boogie, which he didn't much care about, for the violinist, who admired it greatly.

Finally he returned to the blues for a couple of minutes, ended with a dozen minor chords, got up, and came back to the table. There was a little applause. Skinner looked at Blondie and saw that her eyes were wet.

They sat down; Rod returned and sat down, and Skinner said they must go. He asked for the check.

Blondie said, "I am sorry I must make you pay for the drinks." She shrugged. "If it was like before, you would not pay." She shrugged again. "It is not like before."

They reclimbed the stairs and went out onto the street.

"I wish Benny were here," Freak said. "He'd have loved that."

"He'd have wept," Skinner said, "and felt wonderful."

"I don't feel wonderful," Rod said. "Let's get a drink."

They went into a bar and had more drinks.

They stood at the bar, and Freak looked at his watch and said, "Ten-thirty. Time to get a woman."

"You don't get a woman over here," Rod told him. "Unmarried women are either whores or virgins. No amateurs."

"That's what I meant," Freak said. "Let's go to a place."

"Freak," said Skinner. "You're brilliant. We'll go to Mama Frank's."

They left the bar and walked two blocks.

"You seem to know the way," Rod said.

"I do," said Skinner. "I do."

Freak, who had never dealt with professionals before, was curious, and therefore enthusiastic. Skinner, remembering the pretty Greek girl of three nights before, was equally charmed. But Rod, who had turned glum since leaving Blondie's, kept wanting to stop off at bars for more drinks.

"We can get drinks at Mama Frank's" Skinner said. "Better and cheaper."

They turned off the well-lighted waterfront street into one which was darker and narrower. Half-way along the first block stood a house with shuttered windows. There was nothing to mark it save for a discreet white card tacked to the door, which said, "Officers Only." Skinner knocked.

The door was opened and a woman put her head out: "You are officers?"

"Nous sommes Americains."

"Bon." She opened the door.

They went in, through vestibule and hallway, to a large, well-lighted room, furnished mostly with chairs and tables, about half of which were occupied by British officers, most of whom were sitting very quietly and self-consciously. There was only one group that seemed to be enjoying itself; it consisted of three very young lieutenants, wearing the patches of one of the good infantry regiments and two girls. The girls were the only ones in the room. They were all drinking and joking together exuberantly, and the other officers, most of them captains and majors, kept casting glances of disapproval towards their table, which was in the corner.

Skinner, Freak, and Rod, sat down and ordered brandy.

"We might as well get a whole bottle," Skinner said. "Then if there's any left, we can take it with us."

There was a burst of loud laughter from the table in the corner of the room, and a major, sitting near the Americans, got up, crossed the room, and spoke to the lieutenants. One of them stood up, apparently wanting to argue. The others pulled him back. They talked it over, with the major standing and glaring at them, and seemed to decide on something. They all three stood up, kissed the girls, put money on the table, and left.

There was a hum of approving comment around the room, and the major, recrossing, got smiles and nods.

"What a gentlemanly whorehouse," said Freak indignantly.

"Sex is a duty to these jokers," Skinner said. "A matter of keeping fit. It won't do at all to get any fun out of it."

Rod, who was growing more and more morose, said nothing.

The brandy came, with glasses and ice, and they drank.

"Well," Skinner said, "This is all very wholesome, but there is work to be done."

Freak and Rod followed him to the next room where the girls were. They were a pretty group, all dressed in evening clothes, and they stopped talking to smile and pose as they saw the door open. They made no attempt to approach the customers as they came in, probably because they had learned that, in dealing with the British, forwardness was felt to be embarrassing. So they assumed poses which attempted to combine discretion with desirability, some stroking their breasts as if absent-mindedly, others patting their stomachs secretively, or moving their hips with covert glances at the men.

Skinner, recognizing his Greek girl, beckoned to her, and she came over and put her arms around him. Freak, who was quite drunk, cried, "I want them all," and flung himself into the midst of a group who were sitting on the sofa. For a moment there was a confusion of arms and legs as they vied for his patronage, he having made the first move; finally, he got to his feet, pulling a plump blonde up with him. "It's love," cried Freak. "True love at last."

The blond was all over him, pinching his cheeks, telling him, in French, what a fine boy he was.

Rod stood, undecided, briefly, then walked over to a rather drab, excessively young-looking girl sitting alone, and said, "You're for me." She got to her feet disinterestedly, making no pretense of caring. She was appallingly thin, breastless, and without color. When she stood up, she looked even younger.

Rod took her by the hand, led her over to where the others were standing, and said, "Let's go."

Skinner looked at the girl. "You can do better than that," he said, frowning slightly.

"Listen," Rod burst out. "This is what I want." His hand went all the way around her thin wrist so that fingers and thumb overlapped to the first joints of each. "She's perfect. Young and thin, and I don't give a damn if she lies still as a board while I do it."

"Okay," Skinner said. "Okay."

But Rod wanted to tell them. "Listen," he said, "I'm so goddamn sick of women who are old and fat and sexy that I'm sick of sex. What the hell do you think it's like being a lousy piano-player? Do you think it's playing the kind of music I was playing back there tonight? It is like hell. Its playing *Stardust* or *Parlez Moi D'Amour* on stupid little pianos in the lounges, and when you can't find a lounge to play in, or a dive, or a band, do you know what it is? It's being at stud, goddamn it, for a lot of fat, sexy women." He started away, pulling the girl after him. "You know what they do?" he asked bitterly, stopping and turning back to them. "They teach you tricks. Cute little sex tricks." He addressed the girl. "If you know any tricks, he said. "I'll choke you. You just lie still, see?"

It was doubtful that she was paying enough attention to him to tell that he was upset. If she was, it is certain that, speaking only French and Arabic, she had no idea what he was talking about. But then, that seemed to be the way Rod wanted it.

Skinner and Freak watched him go, looked at each other and shrugged.

Freak's blonde rolled her eyes and said, "Your friend will feel better soon, n'est-ce pas?"

Freak smiled at her, said, to Skinner, "Be seeing you around," and followed her to the back of the house.

The Greek girl, as a reward for popularity, had one of the desirable front, ground floor rooms, which opened off the parlor in which the clients sat and drank. She and Skinner made their way between the tables and through the door, which she closed quietly.

Physical satisfaction achieved, Skinner rested for a moment, suddenly had an idea which made him smile. He looked at the girl, smiled, and told it to her. She laughed, thought it over, laughed again, and agreed. They got up and made preparations. Then they went to the door, which Skinner opened a crack, and peered out at the officers sitting by the tables.

They saw Rod come back. Apparently the blonde's prediction had been accurate, for there was no trace of the recent bitterness in his face, and he seemed relaxed as he poured out three fingers of brandy and drank it off, smacking lips.

His arrival had been greeted by looks and whispered remarks from the room at large. The officers here gathered seemed to check comings and goings avidly, getting up their own desire, perhaps, by observing that of others; or, to be kinder, overcoming their own shyness by observing how others overcame theirs. Skinner could imagine that they were saying of Rod, "Dashed quick, wasn't he?" but it annoyed him less than he thought it would. Then he happened to notice the major, sitting at the table next to theirs, the one who had spoken to the happy young lieutenants, and he allowed it to annoy him a little more.

Freak came back, grinning, and Rod smiled at him. "How was it, kid?"

"Wonderful," said Freak, exuberantly. "It was love at first bite." Then, as heads turned all over the room to look at him, he sat down, grinning and said something to Rod in a whisper which made Rod grin back.

Skinner closed the door and nodded to the girl. They went into the middle of the room, and Skinner screamed, a high, shrill, male scream. As he did it, the girl toppled a heavy wooden chair onto the floor with a great clatter, and laughed crazily. Skinner counted three under his breath and screamed again. The girl began shouting excitedly in Greek, hitting the floor violently with a heavy leather belt. Skinner screamed for the third time, and shouted, "No, no," breaking it off into an insane chuckle. She kept on beating the floor, he groaned loudly; then they were silent.

He could imagine the buzz of conversation around the tables, the chairs being turned to watch the door, the conferences as to whether interference might be advisable. He screamed again. The girl laughed wildly, broke again into a fierce stream of Greek, kicked the side of the dresser violently, Skinner groaning and thumping his feet on the floor. He signalled her, and they stopped abruptly. They let a moment pass. Then Skinner crept over to the door, and, letting his body sag, opened it very slowly.

He stood for a moment, teetering in the doorway, holding himself erect by clutching the knob. Long, bloody streaks ran from the lobes of his ears down the side of his neck and into his shirt, and red welts marked his face. He fell forward, lost his grip on the knob, managed to land on his hands and knees, and began to crawl painfully across the room towards the table where his friends sat, moaning and fighting for breath.

They stared at him in silence. Painfully, doggedly, gasping, he crawled along until he reached the table next his own, where sat the major who had spoken to the lieutenants. Then, heaving himself with great effort to his knees, he pointed an accusing finger at the major. "What have you taught that girl?" he demanded hoarsely, and fell backwards, hitting the floor full-length at Rod's feet.

Stunned silence.

Then Rod arose. "Poor fellow," he said, addressing the room at large. "He's been on these orgies before. But," he added, looking accusingly at the dumbfounded major, "it's never been this bad."

With a thoughtful frown, Rod picked up the brandy bottle, corked it, and slipped it into his shirt front.

"You get his feet," he said to Freak, and, together, they lifted Skinner and carried him out of the room.

They barely made the street before Freak burst into uncontrollable laughter. Skinner was allowed to stand,

and they whooped and pounded him on the back. Then they helped wipe off the lipstick that ran from his ears to his neck, and the rouge that mottled his face.

Freak, overcome with liquor, the excitement of the evening, and Skinner's triumphant performance, got a little hysterical. He laughed until he had to sit down on the curb, and, finally, to lie down and roll in the street before he could stop. Then, too exhausted to laugh any longer, he stopped, lay still, and, regaining strength, sat up and reached for the brandy bottle.

All three sat on the curb together for half an hour, finishing the brandy. They tossed the empty bottle across the street, listening to it crash, decided they were drunk, decided that they didn't care, decided that they had better go back to camp. They wandered up the alley to the main street, along which the street-car ran.

A dim memory struggled through to the surface of Skinner's consciousness.

"You know something?" he asked Freak.

"Good 'r bad?"

"Awful. Wait a minute. What is it?" He thought. "Oh yeah." He laughed. "Stree'car stops running 'leven-thirry. Gotta walk to camp."

"Gotta walk to camp," Freak sang, merrily. "Gotta walk to camp. Gotta walk to camp." He sobered a little. "Gotta walk to camp?" he asked incredulously. "Can't. Can't walk to camp. Gotta getta stree'car."

"No stree'car. Stopped running," Skinner insisted.

"Getta car, then."

"Thas ri'," Rod agreed. "Gotta getta car."

They took a few steps along the street, looking for a car. They saw one, parked across the street; a staff-car, whose officer was probably down at Mama Frank's.

They crossed the street with exaggerated caution.

"Prob'ly gotta driver in it," said Skinner, cautiously. "Gotta look."

Luck was with them. The driver was not there, had probably left for a few minutes to get a drink somewhere, knowing that his officer would not be back for some time. He had left an old man to watch the car for him.

"Here," Rod said to the old man, handing him a pound note. "You scram. Shoo."

The man, asking no questions of those who paid him twice for a dull job, slipped away.

"The keys in it?" Freak asked.

"Don' need keys. Milit'ry vehicle." Skinner said. "Quick. Get in." He climbed into the driver's seat, turned on the switch, and stepped on the starter.

"We shouldn't," he heard Freak say.

"Get in," said Rod. The back door was opened, and Rod added, "Gotta make it fast."

Skinner stepped on the starter again and the engine caught.

" 'Ere," shouted a voice out in front of them, "that's my car." Skinner snapped on the lights to blind the owner of the voice so that they wouldn't be recognized, caught a brief glimpse of a big Britisher running towards them, not thirty yards away. Savagely, he pulled the shift lever down, spurted gas through the engine with the accelerator, and swung forward and out into the street. Picking up as much speed as he dared, he followed the car line, hoping desperately that it was the right one.

In the back, Freak was saying, "Wrong thing to do. Wrong thing to do," and Rod was laughing, and urging Skinner to go faster.

With relief, Skinner found that they were tearing through the darkened Midan, and knew that he had hit on the right set of car tracks to follow. He made a left turn off the Midan, glanced into the mirror, and saw that there were no pursuing headlights. He made himself slow down. No sense being picked up for speeding. They'd gotten away with it.

Feeling quite sober, he said, "We've gotten away with it."

Rod, also soberly, said, "Yeah. I guess we have."

Freak's voice was dubious. "I guess so." Then, apparently relaxing and accepting it, "Might as well enjoy it. Beats walking."

They came to the end of the car tracks and began to climb the hill.

"He didn't see us," Skinner said. Then, "We'll go about half a mile above camp, leave the car, and walk back."

They drove on through the dark, passed their camp, reached a place where there was a clearing beside the road, and left the car in it. Freak was anxious to get away from the car, but Skinner made them wait until they had wiped off the steering wheel, gear-shift lever handle, ignition and light switches, and doorhandles.

"If we're going to be car thieves, we might as well do it right," he said.

They decided to work their way back down the hill without going onto the road, and, after five minutes of rough going, had reason to be glad. Two cars with the red-glazed headlights which indicated M.P.'s came into sight below them, and toiled up the hill while they lay flat in the underbrush. They saw the cars stop up above at the clearing; they took off down the hill at a dead run.

When they made camp and looked back, they could see that the M.P.'s had probably left someone with the car, and the M.P. cars had split, one going up the hill and one down, swinging their spotlights from side to side.

"They work fast," Rod said.

"We're plenty lucky," said Freak.

They were all completely sober now. "Anyway you look at it," Skinner said, "that was a dumb thing to do."

The next morning, waking and feeling logey, they reiterated: it had been a dumb thing to do.

"What would Benny say?" Freak asked.

"He'd say that it didn't matter about the car, but we had no right to get the driver into trouble," Skinner guessed. "And he'd be right."

"What about the girl?" Rod asked.

"What do you mean?"

"Won't that stuff we pulled at Mama Frank's get her in bad?"

"Oh," said Skinner. "No. It was partly her idea. She'd been telling me that she had a chance to go to work in a civilian place if she could get in Dutch with Mama Frank."

Fred Birch came in. "Heinz wants one of you guys to take a run," he said.

Rod offered to go. "Where to?"

"The docks. Probably more sun stroke." Fred and Rod went out.

Freak, who had been very quiet, said, "Skinner?"

"Yes?"

"Do you think that driver will get into much trouble?"

"Not if he's smart," Skinner said. "The officer won't want to take it into a court-martial because of where he was himself. So he'll let the driver get away with saying that we overpowered him." He was not really convinced that it was as easy as he made it sound, but he wanted Freak to feel better.

"Good," Freak said. "But listen, Skinner."

"Yeah?"

"What about Rod?"

"What do you mean?"

"The way he acted about the girl and everything?"

"I don't know. There's something wrong with him, I think. Has been ever since we've got here. And playing at Blondie's really seemed to upset him."

"I've never seen him act like that," Freak said. "It isn't just being depressed, or a couple of drinks would fix everything, the way they always do."

"I know," said Skinner. "Well, he'll come out of it."

Billy, the little fairy, knocked on the door and came in. "Good morning," he said. He had a delicate, musical voice, with no trace of the simper and lisp which amateur and professional funny men insist is an attribute of all homosexuals.

"Good morning," Skinner said. He and Freak were stretched out on their beds, and neither of them got up.

Billy came over to Skinner, holding out half a dozen letters. "I brought you your mail." He gave four of the letters to Skinner, turned and gave the other two to Freak. Skinner thanked him.

Billy moved back to the center of the room, turned, leaned lightly against the edge of the table, clearly posing but doing so with great poise. "How do you like our city?"

"Good town," said Skinner.

"Sure is," Freak agreed, apparently wanting to say something to prove that he felt no constraint in Billy's presence.

"It really is too gay," said Billy, tossing his close-cropped blond curls back, to display the fine white skin of his throat, and laughing.

"It's gay all right," Skinner said.

"Well," said Billy, straightening away from the table edge, "I just wanted to come by and bring the mail. I have to run along."

He did a half-turn, and skipped towards the door.

"Thanks a lot," Skinner said.

"So long," said Freak.

Billy turned, gave them a dazzling smile, and left.

"Gee, he's pretty," Freak said, with honest admiration.

"Yeah. Different from most of them. He really looks like a girl."

"He acts like one, too." Freak raised himself on one elbow, started to open his mail. "You know," he said, interrupting himself and looking up from the letters, "I can see how, if you were off someplace, away from women, you might really go for him."

"Right," said Skinner. "You really might."

They opened their mail, and forgot about Billy. Freak had a letter from his mother and one from a girl named Margie, the latter, most of which he insisted on reading aloud, a triumph which made him forget his depression completely. All four of Skinner's were from Cindy.

CHAPTER

7

THE runs they made took them to all sorts of installations. Port Companies, Labor Companies, workshops, the docks, and other small or detached units where they would collect patients as cases arose that required hospitalization. Occasionally they would have to go to the local prison camp, across the mountain, which the Tommies called the "Glass House." Another run consisted of taking a medical officer around to the brothels to inspect, only, as one M.O. complained, the girls always knew when they were coming, and, in preparation, would use alum to dry themselves up, so that seldom was anything found wrong. Occasionally, too, there would be an emergency trip somewhere, or a two day stay at one of the permanent posts to relieve a car due back at Headquarters for a workshop check.

This is from a letter of Skinner's to Cindy. ". . . the only run we really hate is the one to the glass house. The casual callousness of the medical orderlies, the ineffectualness of the medical officer, the official attitude which accepts brutality as an amusing commonplace, are infinitely depressing. Most of the wounds and ailments for which we remove prisoners to the hospital are self-inflicted.

"Army punishment is, we are told, necessarily harsh.

You've got to whip them into shape, kill their spirits, crush that hateful streak of individuality. Stámp out their spunk, boys, that's the idea; kick them, beat them, take the sparkle out of their eyes, and we, their officer gods will be looking the other way, drinking native liquors. Make them mind their betters, their capable corporals, their wise and experienced sergeants, and their officer gods. Make them mind, God dammit.

"So I'll tell you what we'll do. There are bound to be a certain number of fellows crop up in the army who are just naturally beastly. Sadists, see? Well, we'll put these sadists in the M.P.'s, see. Show them how every soldier hates them, make it a semi-official policy to get any bit of decency they happen to have left out of them, and put them in charge of the punishment camps. Then we'll get some officer whom even other officers can't stand. Some guy who doesn't bathe often enough, and stuffs greasy food into his mouth with dirty fingers all day long, and laughs when he sees hurt animals; we'll put him in charge of the place. Then when some lively lad steps over the line a little bit, we'll send him down to the glass house and see what a little kicking, beating, double-time, starving, insufficient sleep, sweating, swearing at, rubber hose work, and just all-around bullying will do for him. We'll take his smokes away, and give him one razor blade a week—and cuff him when he isn't clean shaven. Of course, we'll have to have regulations in the books against making the prisoners lick their commanding officer's boots clean of dung before each meal, but those regulations will be to fool the public. We have plenty of colonels and brigadiers to put in charge of areas who know how to overlook things properly.

"You think, perhaps, that this is only the British Army talking? No, honey. This is every army in the world. The

British, Russian, Armenian, German, French, Scandanavian, Mongolian, and Congolian armies. And the American army. The nice, clean, right-thinking, democratic American Army, which, with its smug pretense that it runs things differently, is the most vicious of all. We've asked Yanks about it; you might ask a guy that's been there.

"Prisoners in these pleasant institutions will adopt any painful method to get into the hospital, and, thus, away from the camp. They'll cut themselves dangerously, if they can find anything sharp. They'll crush their feet with shovels and pick-axes if the guard isn't looking. They'll go on sick-call, steal adhesive tape, stick it to their genitals with sand between tape and skin, and then, by a quick ripping off, simulate syphilis lesions. If one is sick, the others will crowd around him, trying to catch his fever. They will slyly enlarge the holes in their mosquito netting to let the blessed malaria in.

"Anything is better than the glass house. Anything. . . ."

It was on a run from the glass house to the hospital that Skinner lost his first patient. Later, working in the line, there would be others who would bleed to death, or die of shock, but none of those was ever quite so bad.

A Field Punishment Camp, that was the name of the establishment, and you got there through a double barbed-wire gate, attended by a man who hated you because your ambulance might take one of his victims away.

So there was unpleasantness at the gate.

The man who came out to challenge Skinner when his ambulance drove up snarled, "What are you after, Yank?"

And Skinner said, "I'd hoped I was after you. Aren't you dead yet?" As coldly as he could, and produced the paper authorizing him to enter.

"Watch your bloody tongue," the guard said, and opened the gate.

Skinner drove to the Aid Room, parked the car, and went inside.

The patient lay on a stretcher, groaning, breathing in gasps, shouting a curse whenever he could save up enough breath.

The Medical Officer said, "Took your time getting here. This one's for the hospital, quick."

Skinner said, "Right. Got a ticket for him?"

"Orderly'll give it to you." The M.O. glanced at his patient. "Blasted appendix burst. No ice here, you know. Short on morphine, too."

"Oh."

The Medical Officer wanted to excuse himself. "Not my fault at all. They all come in the same way, or want to. Run up a fever, say they've got pains inside. Guards give 'em salts and put 'em back to work. Blasted malingerers, most of them. I've tried to stop them from giving salts. Pig of a commandant won't let me. Won't let me send 'em to the hospital when they should go. Wants me to hold 'em, see if the fever goes down."

The patient wrenched himself around, stared at the doctor's face, and gurgled something.

"You'll be all right, old man," the docter said, unconvincingly.

Two orderlies appeared from an inner room, laughing at something one of them had said. One knelt by the head of the stretcher, and tied a ticket to one handle. The other went to the foot of the stretcher, and they picked it up.

"The car's right over there," Skinner said, opening the door for them. The M.O. came over and stood by him in the doorway, watching the orderlies carry the man to the ambulance and load him in.

"Not my fault," he said again. "They all come in the same way. Fever, pains inside. That blighter should have been out of here three days ago. Commandant won't let me send them. Bloody pig."

The doctor turned, agitated, and walked away. He was a thin little man, past middle age. Skinner had heard his story. A failure in private practice, an insurance doctor, a ship's doctor, a hotel doctor; joined the army for a soft spot, drank too much; the prison camp was his last refuge professionally. The only lower step would be abortionist. The prison camp job grouped him with the other drinkers, the other failures. In this job the pressure worked quite differently: he was here to catch malingering. If he let the prisoners get away with anything, he was through; to lose a patient was pardonable error. To let one put it over on him was the crime.

The orderlies were settling the stretcher in the rear of the car, and Skinner walked over to it quickly, got in, and started the engine so that he could pull away the second the back doors were closed.

"No use hurrying," one of the orderlies said, climbing out of the rear end, and apparently not a bit concerned with whether or not the sick man could hear him. "This one's gone."

The rear doors slammed, but didn't latch. Skinner had to jump out of the seat, run around to the back, and close the door again. He fought down an impulse to pick up a rock and hurl it at the head of the man who had spoken and was now walking back to the Aid Room.

He got back into the car, wrenched it into gear, and said, over his shoulder, "I'll get you there, mate." But he knew that, in all probability, it was already too late.

He started forward in a quick jerk. The patient groaned

loudly. Biting his lips, Skinner slowed down, and made his next shift more smoothly. He came to the gate, and had to stop while the guard got up and came over to the window.

"Let me see your papers," the guard demanded.

"You've seen my papers, God damn it," Skinner said. "Open the gate. I'm in a hurry."

"Got one with you, eh?" The guard said, peering into the back. "Got a slip to take him out?"

Skinner had to reach around, untie the ticket from the stretcher-handle, and show it to him. "You know damn well I've got a slip," he said, bitterly.

The guard, apparently intent on being as annoying as possible, took the slip and began to read it, very slowly, aloud. Skinner lost his temper.

He pressed down the door handle, freed the latch, and swung the door out violently. It caught the man in the chest, throwing him back a step, and before he could recover, Skinner was outside facing him, had grabbed the slip and was shouting, "Are you going to open that God damn gate, or am I going to kick your stinking teeth down your throat?"

The guard jumped back, pulled his gun out of his holster, and said, threateningly, "All right, my lad, you take it easy or there will be trouble." But he turned, walked to the gate, and opened it.

Skinner, feeling his knees go weak with rage, got back into the seat, closed the door, and remembered, somehow, to start the ambulance slowly. He rolled through the gate, braked slightly as he came even with the guard, enunciated the foulest curse he knew, very carefully and savagely, picked up speed, and turned onto the main road.

Within ten minutes, the patient died.

Skinner knew he was dead because the groaning, the

gasping, the attempts to curse and scream, all stopped, all culminated in a choking sigh. He stopped the car and looked back. He had never seen a dead man before, but he felt that this was one.

He started again and drove slowly on. The reason for speed was gone now. He wondered if he could really blame guys like the one at the gate, and decided he couldn't. The guy didn't know the score; he'd been given a nasty job and did it nastily. You can't blame any of them, Skinner thought; the M. O., the orderlies, the guards, even the pig-commandant. You couldn't blame them. You could only blame the men who searched for their qualities and put them there.

Maybe you couldn't even blame the ones who put them there, the stupid little pigs who ran armies. Or blame armies or their generals for being stupid and pigs, or even wars for creating armies. Maybe they all operated on a general mandate from mankind, a stinking little group of mammals whose wretched wills drove them to create these unspeakable perversions: these wars, these cities, this civilization.

And nothing to blame exists, he thought, because it all arises from the nature of the creature. And, he thought with a shudder, there are even those whose minds are so distorted that they conceive of an all-powerful, all-evil thing called God on whom they shift responsibility for the whole lousy mess.

Coming suddenly full circle, he thought, if I'm looking for someone to blame, why look any farther than myself? Maybe that guy back there is the Tommy who was supposed to drive the car I stole. Maybe they court-martialled him, and locked him up, and his appendix burst. It's possible. It's possible that I'm the murderer. It could have happened that way.

He tortured himself with the idea as he drove along up the mountain, until finally he was half-convinced that this was the man whose car they had taken. Finally, fearfully, he had to stop the ambulance and look at the man's face to be sure. He could remember the face of the Tommy who had been driver of the stolen car, could remember seeing it clearly in the blaze of the headlights as he cut them on.

He looked into the back, moved the blanket away. It was not the same face.

Skinner got out of the car. He'd had to cross the mountain to get to the camp, which was near a little town named Chtaura at the foot of the inland slope. Now he was half-way up, still on the inland side, headed back towards Beirut. He looked at the Bekaa valley, lying quietly away from the foot of the mountain, let his eyes rest on a green field, lit a cigarette, and got himself in hand.

"I am not responsible," he told himself. "But could have been."

He realized that he was very tired physically. He got back in the car and started it.

"Mea culpa, boys," he said, aloud, as he drove on up the hill. *"Mea* plenty damn *culpa."*

He wondered whether, if he were drunk, and in Beirut, and wanting a car, he would do it again. That's the trouble, he thought. When the time came, it wouldn't matter. I'd do it again.

When he got back to the post he wanted to talk to someone about it, and tried to find Rod. He went to the shack, but Rod wasn't there. Rod was seldom there anymore for some reason. Freak was there, sleeping, but Skinner didn't want Freak to be oppressed by the thing, so he closed the door quietly, and went up to the shack that was used for an office to turn in his trip papers.

Heinz wasn't there, but Fred Birch, the guy Skinner had known in college, was. Fred was sitting at the desk, reading, taking care of the place.

"Where's Heinz?"

"Working on his book."

"Rod go on a trip?"

"No. He's around somewhere."

"Want to hear a sad story?"

"Sure," said Fred, putting down his book and grinning. "Who'd you knock up this time?"

Skinner told him about the trip to the prison camp, about the car, about his feeling of guilt. Fred listened sympathetically.

"You'd better not take any more runs to the glass house 'til they've had a chance to forget you," he said.

Skinner agreed, gratefully.

"And don't let that big guilt complex get you," Fred went on. "Hell, we all pull stinks. We pulled them back in college, we pull them here, we'll pull them wherever we go."

"Sure," said Skinner.

"I'm a great believer in taking things easy," Fred went on. "So take it easy, will you?"

"Yeah, but how do you square it with yourself when things go screwy?" Skinner asked. "How do you get along with yourself then?"

"Nothing to it," Fred said, smiling. "You just say, sure, it's a lousy world and I personally stink, but why let it get me. So you go along, and try to get a few laughs, and try not to hurt anybody."

"It's not that simple," Skinner objected.

"Of course it isn't," Fred agreed. "But if you act on the assumption that it is that simple, you get along all right."

"The old philosopher," Skinner said, cheering up a little. "Consciences and complexes painlessly removed."

"It's just that I'm against intensity," Fred said.

"You always used to talk well to me this way in college."

"You were a neurotic bastard then, too," Fred said, picking up his book.

PART FIVE

The Old Gag

CHAPTER

8

FROM time to time, lying in bed in the shack, Skinner would find himself half-awake around four or five in the morning, hearing, as clearly as though it were actually being played in the room, Benny Goodman's version of *I Got It Bad and That Ain't Good.*

He would lie there, not quite wanting to wake up, and not wanting to go back to sleep, and hear Peggy Lee's voice come in, in the middle of the third chorus:

"Though folks with good intentions
Tell me to save my tears,
I'm glad I'm mad about him,
I can't live without him."

with a strong beat in back, and Goodman's clarinet doing plaintive figures.

"Lord above me, make him love me
The way he should.
I got it bad and that ain't good."

It was wish-fulfillment.

Because one night, months before he had sailed for Middle East, he had woken up on the sofa in the game room of his fraternity house, and the record had been on the automatic record-player—the last of the stack, so that it played over and over. With him on the sofa was a girl, who must have been somebody else's houseparty date, for he had no date himself. Her arm was across his side, and her face nuzzled into his chest. Some of her makeup had come off on the white bar-jacket he was wearing.

He moved his arm carefully, so as not to disturb her, and peered at his watch. Only one lamp was burning, over in the far corner of the room, but he could make out that it was around five o'clock.

He didn't feel at all badly, though he knew he would if he stayed awake very much longer. Peggy Lee's voice on the record trailed into Goodman's clarinet, which picked up the line and rose into a lonely, soaring variation of the melody, in which each note expressed the clarinet's judgment: yes, you're right, to have it bad ain't good.

The girl had on a bar-jacket, too, over her sweater—it was customary, when the formal dance ended at one o'clock, for the girls to change into short skirts and rugged shoes for the informal drinking which followed. As he looked at her, he gradually remembered that he had been tending bar down here, in the game room, and that there had been a very noisy party on. The reason he was bartender was because he had no date, and he decided that he must have served drinks for two or three hours, probably until after three o'clock.

Sometime during the party, when things were rushed and everybody was fairly drunk, this girl had come behind the bar to help him—put on a bar-jacket, and cracked ice and opened soda bottles for him. And between mixing batches of drinks, they had had drinks together; gotten into one another's ways, laughed, and kissed by way of apology; shouted jokes at friends, when they came up to be served; talked excitedly about who was how drunk; and evolved a private joke about bombs and hand-grenades, stored beneath the bar, with which they proposed, when the right moment came, to blow the whole roomful, including themselves, to Kingdom Come. Each time one of them would reach for a bomb, there would be a dramatic speech by the other, recommending "one last, long kiss before eternity sets in", and they would go into a clinch while impatient customers shouted for more service and less romance; then they would break, and mix the drink, saying to each other, "Ah, if they but knew," and patting the bombs affectionately.

Then, finally, the bar quieted down. Couples drifted off, stags went over to the dormitories to sleep, girls, who, having lost their dates, had compensated for it by drinking up all the dates' liquor, were taken to bed by soberer girls.

At last, Skinner and the girl were alone amid the wreckage. Her name was something like Elizabeth or Mary or Peggy, but it didn't matter what her name was, because he called her Cindy—Cinderella, the bartender's daughter who, not having been approached with a glass slipper, found that a Scotch bottle fitted her just as well.

They stood there, quite drunk, behind the bar, and looked at the mess in the game room, and she said, wistfully:

"Time to clean up, Skinner?"

And he said, decisively, "No, no. Time to pass out."

She said, "That's an excellent idea, Skinner. An excellent, excellent, excellent idea."

He frowned. "Excellent?"

It was her turn to be decisive. "Excellent, excellent, excellent. . . ."

"All right," he said. "You pass out over there." He

pointed to the sofa. "And I'll come pass out with you in a minute." Obediently, she went over to the sofa, took off her shoes, and lay down. She lay on her side, laughing at him as he went around the room turning off all the lights but one.

"Got to put some records on," he said, "never go to sleep without music." He put a new batch of records on the machine, and started it going. Probably, he decided, he had meant to try to make her, but as he lay down beside her on the sofa, she tucked her arm around him, put her face against his chest, and went immediately to sleep. He slipped an arm around her shoulders, let the other hang off the sofa with the fingers trailing on the floor, and realized that he was very tired himself.

As his eyes closed, the record on the machine was Louis' *West End Blues,* and the soft scat voice echoing the tenor sax phrases in the middle of the record was their lullaby.

Now he was awake and the machine clicked as the record changer went through the motions of putting a new disc on and, coming to the end of the fruitless sequence, began to play over again:

> "Never treats me sweet and gentle,
> The way he should . . ."

He wondered if he ought to get up and put on new records before he went back to sleep, so that something else would be playing when he woke up again; no, he liked this one. He decided Cindy would like it. He put his other arm around her and shifted his body to wake her. She opened her eyes, lifted her head, looked at him, smiled, and rested her head on his chest again.

He moved her body up until her ear was against his lips, and whispered, "Listen to the music, Cindy."

Her answer was a noise, somewhere between a purr and a sigh; she turned her head slowly, not raising it, so that her cheek brushed across his lips, and stopped moving it when her mouth reached his. Holding her head still, in that position, she said, "It's beautiful," and he could feel her lips move against his, forming the syllables. Then she kissed him.

Their arms tightened, and her body pressed his tightly; he could feel the pulse in her breast against his chest. He moved his hand along her back. Their breathing quickened.

They were only half-awake, and Skinner's feelings were of warmth and infinite tenderness. Some detached part of his mind recorded the thought that this was the way it ought always to be: gentle, warm, without tenseness.

When they woke again it was morning. Daylight was harsh; they avoided one another's eyes. Trying to break the constraint, he got up, turned off the record player, and took the Goodman record off the turntable. He gave it to her. "Keep it or break it," he said, "no one else hears it."

"I think I'll break it," she said, unsteadily, but she held it against her, crossing her arms over it.

At houseparty time, the guys who slept in the fraternity houses found rooms outside, so that girls could have the rooms in the House. Cindy went upstairs to sleep a while longer; Skinner, who, as a sophomore, lived in the dormitory, went over to his room and also went to bed.

He slept until noon.

When he got up he felt fairly well. He took his clothes to the shower-room, had a shower, brushed his teeth, shaved and dressed. He found his room-mate, Jeff, back in the room with a half-full bottle of Scotch in front of him on the desk.

"You hung, kid?" Jeff asked.

"Not much."

"Drink?"

"Naturally." Skinner had a drink out of the bottle, made a face. "I'm hungry as hell."

"Let's go over to the house and get some lunch." They had another drink and put the bottle away in the desk. "How'd you make out with Kellerman's girl?" Jeff wanted to know.

Skinner decided he felt like playing it cagey, so he said, shrugging, "She disappeared. Went to bed, I guess. Kellerman sore?"

"He would have been if he'd seen the ball you were throwing behind the bar. But he got extra drunk and went to Boston with Moody and Fred, so he'll probably be grateful to you."

"Were we that bad behind the bar?"

"Listen, towards the end we had to reach over and mix our own."

"Nuts," said Skinner, "I wasn't making that much time."

"Remember the Eternity Special you made me?"

"No."

"Two ice cubes, a jigger and a half of soda, and fill up the glass with Scotch."

"God," said Skinner, remembering it, "let's get lunch."

On their way over the fraternity, he asked, as casually as he could, "Is this babe Kellerman's idea of heaven or anything?"

"No. Hell, no. Just some girl he dates in New York. Very frigid young woman to hear him tell it. He was fed with her last night because she didn't want to play house."

"Yeah," said Skinner, vaguely, "house probably isn't her game."

When they arrived, Jeff went to find his date and Skinner went to the dining room. Lunch hadn't been served yet, but Cindy was standing there with another girl, drinking tomato juice.

"That looks awfully good," he said.

"Have some." Cindy handed him her glass, and they smiled at one another. "Nancy Roseman, this is Skinner. I don't know his last name, and he's drinking up all my tomato juice."

Skinner handed the glass back. "It's nice to meet you, my last name is Galt, and I didn't take more than a swallow," he said.

"You belong here?" Nancy asked.

"Sure."

"Oh, yes. You were the bartender, weren't you? God, what kind of dynamite were you mixing last night?"

"Feeling tough?" Skinner tried to sound sympathetic, though he didn't feel it. He was very anxious for Nancy to go away so that he could talk to Cindy.

"God," said Nancy, "am I?"

"Look, aren't you Dave's girl?"

"Yes, have you seen the brute?"

"He's looking for you," lied Skinner. "I think he's in the library."

"Thanks," Nancy said. She finished her tomato juice and went out.

Skinner took a deep breath, looked at Cindy, and couldn't think of anything to say.

She helped him out. "Speaking of dates, have you seen anything of mine?"

"He's in Boston. Are you glad?"

She wouldn't answer him, and he decided that he felt like a fool.

"I woke up this morning and couldn't remember what

you looked like," he said, feeling even more of a fool. "What do you look like?"

"I'm thin and intense," said Cindy. She was thin. Not much shorter than he, with hip bones that made little knobs under her skirt. But intense was the wrong word, he thought; she was too slight, too leggy, too young-looking, and her brown eyes were big and set wide apart, which somehow made her look good-humored. A round face, with very clear light skin, and a great deal of black hair. Good ankles, thought Skinner, good, small breasts, and fine shoulders. "I'll never launch a thousand ships," said Cindy.

"You are by no means the way I have claimed to like them," said Skinner, reflectively, sitting on the table, "but that only goes to show a man never knows his own mind."

"I have many good points," said Cindy, mocking his tone of voice, "and am, on the whole, very intelligent for a girl."

"I'm very intelligent for a girl, too," said Skinner; he reached over and put a hand beneath each of her elbows. He pulled her gently towards him and tried to kiss her. She turned her face, and slipped away.

"Rather have tomato juice," she said, and finished the glass.

Others came into the room. Lunch was served. It was warm and cheerful, and people were being funny about their hangovers. The smell of lamb chops and French fries was reviving; food in the stomach killed butterflies. The medicinal drinking of the morning was replaced by the first, tentative rounds of sociable, afternoon drinking.

After the tables were cleared, Skinner and Cindy sat with Jeff and his girl, talking, and drinking canned beer.

Somewhere around three o'clock, Jeff's girl, whose name

was Doris, broke up what promised to be a close foursome, by remarking: "I can't see it at all. My father says the whole thing is run by Jews."

Immediately, invisibly, there was a hard little group of three against her.

Cindy said, "I'm sure you're very broad minded. Probably some of your best friends are Jews."

"Whole countries run by them, though," Jeff added. "Europe, too. Planning to take over Mars as soon as the war's over."

Skinner said, "Niggers, Jews, and radicals, eh, Doris?"

Doris, not quite sure what was happening to her, said defensively, "Well, look at the movies."

"Right," said Jeff, "the movies."

"Do you know," said Cindy, confidentially, "that when you go in to ask for a screen test, you have to have a card from the High Council?"

"No kidding?" said Skinner, "The High Council, eh?"

"Sure," said Jeff, "they live in High Point, Michigan."

"And they'd better get down off their high horse," Cindy added.

"High time something was done," Skinner agreed.

Doris said, uncomfortably, "Well, if they know about it, why don't they do something about it?"

"They're highly subtle," Skinner told her.

"Fiendishly subtle," Cindy agreed.

"They move subtly," Jeff said, darkly.

"And with subtlety," said Skinner.

It began to dawn on Doris that she was being taken for a ride. She got up indignantly. "You can all go to hell," she said. And then, to Cindy, "I ought to slap your face." She walked out.

"She's a feminist," Cindy said, "she thinks I ought to have stuck by her."

The three looked at each other, and Jeff burst out laughing. "Last night she said I was the nicest man she knew," he told them.

They had more beers, and Jeff said: "I ought to go out and make peace; after all, she's just a silly little girl."

"With a silly little body," Skinner pointed out, "that you're feeling kind of silly about."

"Me too," said Cindy. "I'm a silly little girl."

"You too," Jeff told her, and went out to find Doris.

Skinner was glad they were alone. He was anxious, had been since he had seen her before lunch for the first time that day, to find out how Cindy felt about the previous night. As soon as Jeff was out of the room, he reached over and took her hand, trying to think of a good way to lead up to it.

But before he could figure out the right angle of approach, Fred Birch came into the room, looking for him. Fred, who belonged to a different fraternity, had a redhead with him, and they were both quite drunk.

"Thomas Galt," he said. "Thomas Skinner Galt. Skinner Thomas Galt. All over your house we have been looking for you. Under chairs. Upchairs and downchairs, and in my lady's chamber."

"The chaperon didn't want us to look in my lady's chamber," said the redhead, pushing Fred into a chair and sitting on his lap. She twined her arms around Fred's neck. "She called my Fred a peeping Tom."

"Didn' know my name," said Fred. "Peeping Fred, that's me."

"How's the party over at your place?" Skinner asked.

"Dead, dead, ever'body's dead," said Fred.

"Freddy killed 'em," said the redhead, pinching his cheek. "Didn't you, dear?"

"Skinner," said Fred. "Got something to tell you. Something to tell Skinner." His mind veered off onto another track. "Hey," he said to his redhead, "ever tell you about Skinner? Took a young girl out to dinner. . . ."

"No," said Skinner. "Not that, Fred. Not that again."

"Tell me," said the redhead.

"Later," Skinner pleaded, afraid of the effect the old dirty limerick might have on Cindy, and realizing that neither he nor she had had enough to drink to find Fred or his girl very amusing. "Make him tell you later."

"All right," said the redhead. "Don't forget. Won't forget."

"What were you going to tell me?" Skinner asked Fred.

"Going to drive nambulance," Fred said. "Volunteered yes'rday 'n Boston."

"No kidding?" Skinner asked. "You quitting college?"

"Takin' off," Fred said. "See the war. Pass out 'na shadow of the Sphinx."

"Good enough," Skinner said. "When do you leave?"

"Month. Six weeks." Fred said.

"That's pretty quick," said Cindy.

"Pretty quick fella, me," said Fred. "Gotta see Middle East pretty quick. Landa mystery 'n' history. Cradle civilization. Fertile crescent."

"Fertile crescent," the redhead repeated, proud of her man's knowledge.

"Great thing, fertile crescent," Fred said; then, peering with the false shrewdness of the very drunk at Cindy. "You got a fertile crescent?"

"Not with me," Cindy said rather primly, apparently not sure just what symbolism Fred attached to the phrase.

"She's got one," Fred said, patting his redhead on the shoulder. "You got a fertile crescent, haven't you, dear?"

"Ticklish subject, Freddy," said the redhead. "Prefer not discuss it in front of strangers."

"Ticklish subject?" Fred repeated. Then he laughed. "Les go tickle the ticklish subject, dear," he said. He pushed her off his lap, convulsed with laughter at his own joke. "Gotta tickle ticklish subject," he gasped, struggled to his feet, and dragging the redhead after him, left the room.

There was a silence.

"That wasn't so good," said Skinner, soberly.

She didn't say anything.

"It wouldn't have been so bad if we'd had as much to drink as they have," he said. "But this way, it wasn't very good."

"No," said Cindy. "It wasn't."

Then she said the thing he was afraid she might be thinking: "Is that what we were like, Skinner? Last night before . . . I mean, while we were behind the bar?"

"No," he said. "We weren't like that."

"We were silly, though, and drunk."

"We weren't like that," Skinner repeated. "We were silly and drunk, but we had a marvelous time; we felt good, we looked good, we were good to each other."

"Were we?" She didn't look at him. There was an empty beer can on its side on the table; she began to roll it back and forth under her palm.

"Look, Cindy," he said. "That guy's name is Fred Birch. He's a very smart guy, and he's kind, and he's sympathetic. But right now he's a pretty drunk guy, and the two things he knows are that he's going overseas to drive an ambulance, and he's got a redhead and a bottle of liquor."

"Fine," she said, keeping her eyes fixed on the beer can. "That's fine."

"Look, Cindy, there's a party on. Fred's having a lovely time. Everybody's having a lovely time. How is Fred to guess that we're sitting here, mulling over problems, while there's a party on?"

"Problems?" There was no inflection in her voice. "What problems, Skinner?"

He reached over, and gently took the beer can away from her. "Hey," he said, softly and urgently. "Remember me? This is Skinner. Old Skinner Galt."

She looked up. He smiled, looked at her, put his hand over hers. The tightness went out of her face, was replaced momentarily by a sort of sadness; then, slowly, the answering smile broke through. She turned her hand under his, palm up, and squeezed his fingers.

"Hi, Skinner," she said. "Hi, pal. Nice to see you."

They went to get a drink.

Late that night, the last night of the party, Cindy, of her own accord, answered the question Skinner had found himself unable to ask.

They had borrowed a car, and driven out to a bluff, overlooking the bay. They sat for a long time, watching the sea and trying to get one another to talk.

And, after an hour, Skinner decided that he still didn't know very much. He knew that she came from the West, that she wanted to be an actress, that she had some training but not enough. She could be kidded a little about the stage, but it had to be done gently; she was very serious about it. They seemed to agree on a great many things: people, books, labor, that parties were good, that it was best to be casual, that the important thing was to laugh, that Scott Fitzgerald was underrated, that the final state of beatitude was not to give a damn. She quoted Gibran; he talked jazz and blues. He quoted Eliot; she talked Debussy and Ravel.

They probed for gaps in one another's poise. He found

that she couldn't talk about her family with any detachment, which was a gap, and that she was afraid of money, which was another. He carefully let her find none of his.

It was one o'clock before he tried again to kiss her.

"Look, Skinner, please don't kiss me."

"Sorry," he said, and then, after a moment: "Why not?"

It was then that she answered the question. "I'm still fighting for my self-respect, after last night."

"I'm sorry," he said.

"I've been trying to persuade myself ever since that I'm not that easy."

"Hell," said Skinner. "I didn't seduce you. It was Benny Goodman."

"The cad," said Cindy, smiling. Then, because she probably realized that it had cost him something to say it: "As long as it was Goodman and Johnny Walker who betrayed me, I'm glad you were the guy on the sofa."

"Thanks. You know, its a very fine paradox, if you like paradoxes. If last night hadn't happened, we'd have gotten to know one another quite easily. The way it is, instead of being friends, we've spent the whole day fencing."

"I don't guess I like paradoxes," she said. She thought for a little. Then she said, very carefully: "Don't think I regret last night, Skinner. It's just that I don't want to feel it's got anything to do with us as individuals."

"I think I get it," Skinner said. "Tell me, if I'm right. You don't want to base what may be a human relationship on something that happened on sort of an animal level. You'd rather we forgot about it, and started in all over again."

"That's close," she said.

"If you hadn't had to see me again today," he said, getting interested in the idea, and half-forgetting that it was more than an idea to her, "you could be perfectly contented about last night. If you were never going to see the other individual again, it would be a neat little secret between you and your pillow, and you'd like it that way."

"We're talking like a couple of text books," she said.

"Right," said Skinner. "Time for me to shut up."

The next time he saw her, he was in uniform.

Once, during the two intervening months, he wrote the beginning line of a letter to her. It went:

> Dear Cindy: In all the theorizing about love we have read and discussed since we were kids, the factor of need has been outrageously minimized.

He stopped writing, read the line, told himself that that was hardly the smart way to play it, and wrote a little note instead, with a few cracks about houseparties in it.

Her answer was just as impersonal.

There were six weeks left, then, of the summer session, and the days were sixty hours long. The whole world was stalled. Montgomery and Rommel faced each other at Alamein, said the newspapers, and the front was quiet; in the Pacific, there was some naval stuff, which was interesting, if you were interested in naval stuff. Skinner Galt, and his room-mate Jeff, were stalled on the second floor of the sophomore dormitory. It was too damned hot.

They were sitting in their room one day in their underwear. Some guys stuck their heads in and asked if they wanted to play bridge. It was too hot.

Supper was hours away.

"We might get drunk," Jeff said, lazily.

"Or play a nice, cooling set of tennis," Skinner suggested.

"Or study." The most unlikely thought of all.

Skinner got up and went over to sit on the window sill. "Jeff?"

"What?"

"What the hell are we doing here?"

"Having a good time?"

"Not particularly."

"Getting a liberal education?"

"A likely story."

"Dodging the draft?"

"Aren't we all?" They had signed up for a scheme whereby they would, perhaps, be allowed to finish college and get degrees, conditional on their becoming flyers after graduation, so that the draft problem didn't affect their stay. Skinner left the window, suddenly restless, and began to sort through the heap of papers on his desk, with the vague intention of cleaning it up. "Jeff," he said. "What the hell use is a degree? And don't give me that crap about needing it to get a job."

"A lot of businesses blackball guys without 'em," Jeff said.

"Sure. And I hear that they're making bullets now that will turn aside when they approach a man with education."

"That's true," said Jeff.

"Damn it," Skinner said. "An education should prepare you either to live with other people, or to live with yourself. After two and a half years of college, I don't like other people, and I can't stand myself."

"Nice healthy outlook."

"Colleges are all wrong, Jeff. I'm not interested in the things they want to teach me here, and I'm less interested in their standards as to whether I've learned them."

"So what are you going to do? Found a new college?"

"No, but I'm going to get the hell out of this one."

"Air Corps?"

"Jeff, midsummer madness has got me. The only picture

I get when you say Air Corps is of thousands of products of these delightful old Eastern colleges, smoothing around in beautiful uniforms with bars on their shoulders, having a merry, campus time being officers. Because they had dough enough to go to a place like this one."

"There are some fairly good guys flying planes."

"I know, Jeff, but I'll never make a decent pilot."

"I thought you liked flying."

"I do. Love to be in a plane. But I'm just not sold on the war." Then, thinking about it, he said, "I could have flown well in Spain."

"Skinner, what the hell do you want? It's not 1937, and you can't go to Spain. This is our war, for better or for worse."

"Until death do us join. I want a nice, small war; Jeff, with clearcut issues. There should be more than just a villain you can hate. There should be a side you can love, too."

"I don't think so," said Jeff. "I think it's enough just to love the guys you're fighting beside."

"Sure. That's enough, subjectively, to carry you through the actual fighting. But you need something else to get you into it in the first place."

"They've got a law."

"They damn well need it."

"Why don't you have a nice, long struggle with your soul, and decide you're a conshie?"

"Not a good enough guy."

"So what do you want?"

"I want to do something decisive. It's too damn hot for indecision." He sat down, stretched his legs, and looked at the ceiling. "I want to see this war, just out of curiosity, and to say I've been. And I'd like to be with the guys in it

—you're right. That feeling of fighting side by side must be good. And . . . I don't know." He gestured around the room. "I'd like to get all this crap out of my system."

"Skinner Galt in search of reality, huh?"

"Skinner Galt in search of a nice, thorough escape."

"What about this thing Fred joined? This ambulance deal?"

"It's been on my mind," Skinner said.

Forty-eight hours later, having gotten the details from Fred, he mailed his application off to the ambulance people, and, shortly thereafter, was instructed to buy his uniforms and told that he would be notified when to report to New York, preliminary to sailing.

From what he could learn he had a couple of months. He went to New York and bought uniforms. He went on from there to Baltimore, and spent a couple of weeks with his father. He had not yet been told to report, and, though he understood there would be two or three weeks between notification and sailing, he decided he wanted to be in New York.

After he had been there three days, he called Cindy.

He called her in the evening and they agreed to have lunch the next day. She had gotten a job in a small bookstore in the forties, and she was waiting for him in front of it. He saw her as he turned the corner from Madison Avenue.

He had an impulse to run to meet her, but the street was crowded. Then she saw him coming, and smiled, and came towards him. When they met they both laughed, for some reason, and he took her hands, and looked at her, and said,

"You've no idea how good it is to see you."

They walked west, towards Broadway, keeping on the sunny side of the street; she kidded him about how well he looked in uniform; people passing them on the street smiled, and they were conscious of looking well together.

"We're appropriate to the season," Skinner said.

They went to a little restaurant where the sun came in through a plate glass window, and ordered Old Fashioneds.

Cindy said, "I feel very sophisticated, taking a drink at noon."

"Right," Skinner said. "Have another, and you'll feel twice as sophisticated."

They ate a big lunch, and talked and laughed a lot. The waiter asked them if they were just married, and Skinner said, "Sure," and Cindy threw a piece of bread at him.

After lunch they talked about the war.

He tried to explain what he was doing. "It's a clear case of itching feet. This is a fine, fast way of getting overseas."

He hoped she would disbelieve him. She did. "You're an idealist."

"Because I'll be picking them up instead of knocking them down?"

"That's the way it looks."

"It's nice to be thought well of."

"You just don't want to sound soft."

"Ever know a guy twenty-two who did?"

"No. Nor a girl, either."

He grinned at her. "What soft feelings are you hiding?"

"Traditional feminine excitement that you're in uniform, and going off to war. I never figured I was the type."

"I'm glad you are."

"So am I. It makes me feel ten years younger, and much less emancipated."

They smiled at each other.

Skinner said, "I wish you didn't have to go back to work."

"Oh, my God. I'd forgotten about it. What time is it, Skinner?"

He looked at his watch. "Two-thirty. Are you late?"

She moaned. "Oh, Skinner, I'm forty-five minutes late. I'll be fired."

"Cinderella," he said. "Don't go back to work. Look. It's a beautiful day. It's early autumn. New York is the finest city in the world. I'm going to war and you're having traditional feelings."

She smiled. "What are we waiting for?"

They decided they would go to Fifth Avenue and ride on the bus. They walked slowly, holding hands, liking the feel of the sun on them. They crossed Sixth Avenue, and Skinner asked,

"Were you here when the el' was up?"

She hadn't been.

"It was better then. Nice and unrespectable."

"I've never been on an el'," she said.

"Want to?"

"Sure."

They forgot about the bus, and went down to Second Avenue. They took the el', and rode all the way downtown. They were at the Staten Island ferry slip, and Skinner looked at Cindy's palm and predicted a voyage to a fabulous island.

They took the ferry. On the way over to Staten Island, they met a sailor named Mack, who said he was just home, for the first time in three years, and that he was going to the best bar in the world. Mack had been in the Navy for quite a while, and had seen a lot of bars, but even the ones in Rio couldn't beat the bar in Staten Island, right around the corner from where he was brought up. It was a great occasion. Would Skinner and Cindy accompany him?

They would.

It was a small place, comfortable and old-fashioned. There was no one there except the bartender, who had his back turned. Mack put his finger to his lips, and walked to the bar on tiptoe. Then he said, to the bartender's back, "Hello, Tiny." The bartender turned around. "Oh, my God. It's not Tiny."

"No, sailor, Tiny quit work here a year ago."

"Oh." He was disappointed. "I was raised around here. Right around the corner."

"Yeah? What are you in, the Navy or the Coast Guard?"

"Navy."

"I got a brother in the Coast Guard."

"Yeah? Hey, have you still got Michelob beer?" He turned to Skinner and Cindy. "What'll you have?"

They asked for beer.

They sat down at a booth together, and Mack said, "Gee. I wish someone was around."

"Have you been home yet?" Cindy asked him.

"No. Mom wrote me that they'd moved away, but she forgot to write the address that they moved to. I'll have to go around and see if I can get it from our old landlady, or one of the neighbors."

"Give me a nickel, Skinner," Cindy said. "Let's have some music."

She and the sailor went over to the juke box.

"How about *White Christmas,*" Skinner heard Mack suggest, as they read over the titles. "I just love that piece."

"It's my favorite," lied Cindy, who didn't like it at all.

They started *White Christmas* playing, and came back to the table. Mack was looking glum, and they tried, without much success, to cheer him up.

Skinner tried him on baseball, first. Who did Mack like for the National League pennant? Mack didn't much care.

Cindy asked him about his ship. He didn't like the transport he was on, wanted to transfer to submarine duty, but probably couldn't make the physical.

They had another round of beers, and Mack had a

double Rye straight with his. While he was at the bar, Cindy said to Skinner:

"He's having an awful homecoming. Can't we do something?"

Skinner, who had been wondering what to do, said, "I'll try." Mack came back with the drinks, and Skinner drank his off quickly, and asked them to excuse him for a minute.

"Couple of things I want to get, while I think about it," he said. He got up and left the bar. He walked halfway down the block, and out into the middle of the street. On the far corner was a candy store, and he decided that would be the logical place. He went in and looked around. There were some girls sitting at the counter, but they all looked too young.

He decided to try anyway, so he stood at the end of the counter, rapped on it with a half-dollar, and asked, loudly, "Anyone here know a guy named Mack who joined the Navy?"

There were some giggles, a couple of voices said, "Not me," and one asked, "Young, blond fella?"

"No. Sorry."

A girl sitting near him said, coyly, "I got a brother in the Navy."

"Good," Skinner told her. "Tell him not to get his feet wet." And left.

"Well, of all the nerve," he heard the girl say, as he went out.

Across the street was a drug-store, and he decided to try it next. The people inside seemed a little older. It ought to be the place. There was no one at the counter, but the dozen tables in the rear were filled with girls, dressed in business and factory clothes, sipping malteds or cokes.

He tried again. "Does anyone here know a guy named

Mack who lived on this block until he joined the Navy?"

They looked up. Most of them looked down again. He decided to put the pressure on. He walked over to the nearest table, where three girls were sitting, rested his palms flat on it, and leaned towards them.

"You're sure you don't know Mack?" He asked, with his most charming smile. "He's been away about three years, and his family moved a year ago. He's short, with curly hair and brown eyes."

"I don't think we know him," one of the girls said, doubtfully.

"He looks pretty nice in his sailor suit," Skinner said. "If you don't know him, you ought to."

They giggled.

A voice behind him, at another table, said, "You don't mean Jimmy Mackanski, do you?"

"Sure," said Skinner, turning to the girl who had spoken with a big smile, "Maybe I do. Do you know him?"

"Yeah. Only we called him Jimmy. I went to school with him." She turned to her girl friend. "You remember the fella Harriet used to talk about? The one she had the pitcha of?"

"Sure," said the girl friend, "I remember."

"Is he the one?" The first girl asked.

"Did his family move away about a year ago?"

"Sure. To Jersey City. My mom got a letter from his mom."

"Hey, well, listen. Mack's just gotten in from sea duty. He's over in Kelsey's bar. Want to go see him?"

"Sure. Let's go see him, Caroline."

"Okay," said the girl friend. "Suits me."

They got up and accompanied Skinner out, along the street, and to the bar. Skinner was still a little dubious as to whether it would turn out to be the right sailor, but he figured this was the best he could do.

They went into the bar. Mack and Cindy were laughing together, and Skinner thought: Nice work, honey.

To the first girl, he said, "Is that him?"

"Yeah," said the girl, "that's him all right." At the same time, the sailor looked around and recognized her.

"Marion!"

"Jimmy Mackanski!"

He jumped out of his seat and came running over to them. "I've just gotta kiss you," he said, and kissed her on the cheek.

"This is my girl friend, Caroline."

"Swell," said Jimmy—or Mack.

He led them over to the booth and introduced them to Cindy. Marion sat on one side of him, and Caroline on the other. Skinner got three beers, a double rye for Mack, and Cuba Libres for the girls, and sat down beside Cindy.

"You did fine," she whispered to him.

"You were pretty good yourself," he whispered back, and she squeezed his hand under the table.

The conversation across from them was of old times, of Mack's experiences with U-boats, of Marion's and Caroline's struggles with the supervisor at the local plant, where their shift ended at noon.

Skinner and Cindy stayed for another round of beers, and, though they were pressed to stay longer, decided that they'd like to be back in Manhattan before dark. They shook hands all around, and Mack said to Cindy:

"Honey, if he don't treat you good, look me up," which seemed to please her very much.

They walked back to the ferry, and Cindy said: "That was a pretty nice thing you did."

"I was just showing off," said Skinner.

She picked him up on it again when they were on the ferry, riding back towards Manhattan.

"You weren't showing off at all. You were being a good guy."

"I was trying to impress a good girl."

Sunset filled the sky over the city with unreal color. Lights began to come on in the silhouetted buildings. The slap of little dark waves against the sides of the boat was the only sound. The air was clean and salty.

They leaned against the rail, watching the city creep nearer, and Skinner said, "It's a stage set." He put an arm around her shoulder, and she settled against him.

"Are we in the play, or are we spectators?" she asked.

"We are the play."

"Is it a comedy or a tragedy?"

"Both."

"How?"

"It's a comedy if you listen to the dialogue. It's a tragedy if you're waiting around for it to prove anything."

"Why won't it prove anything, Skinner?"

"Because there's nothing for it to prove."

"Nothing?"

"Nothing. No principals, no truths, no ethics, no stand ards."

"What is there?"

"Nothing. Just people you like, and people you don't like; people you love and people you hate."

"Is that the philosophy of Skinner Galt?"

"No, honey, that's his lack of it."

"I'd like to try to talk you out of it," she said.

"You're welcome to try."

"But you know so much more than I do."

"Only more words, Cindy. You know your best bet?"

"What?"

"Just stick around and be yourself. Knowing there's someone like you is the greatest shaking my theory's had yet."

They went farther forward to watch the boat jockey into the slip.

They rode back uptown and had dinner at Skinner's hotel.

They walked over to 42nd Street, where you could see a double feature for twenty-two cents, men in uniform, tax only. They walked up and down the street, reading the nostalgic names of six and seven year old movies on the marquees. They walked up from Fifth Avenue to the Square, to Seventh, and half-way back, before they decided. Then they stood on the West Side of the Square for a moment, and Skinner said,

"If you weren't such an intelligent girl, I'd say let's see the Marx brothers in *Horsefeathers.*"

"We can pretend we really wanted to see the other feature," she suggested.

They went in to see *Horsefeathers.* Twenty-two cents for one ticket, and say, what kind of uniform is that? Ambulances, huh? British Army—well, I'll be darned. You just have to pay the tax.

The Marx Brothers were terrific; they left before the other feature started.

When they came out, Cindy made him buy her a hot dog at Nedick's. "I'm a girl of vulgar tastes," she said.

"Well," he told her, "When a fella picks up a girl on Staten Island, he don't expect her to wanta eat at the Sherry-Netherlands."

"Hey waita minute. Who picked up who?"

"Well, you did kinda give me the eye."

"I'll say."

"Our dialect stinks," said Skinner.

"Yours is pretty bad," she agreed. "I thought mine was good."

"Pulling your profession on me?"

"I'll say."

They wandered out of Nedick's, back onto the street.

"How'd you like to hear the most beautiful trombone music in the world?" He asked her.

"I'd love it."

They took a cab down to Nick's, in the Village. Those were the days when George Brunies led the group at Nick's, and the music was old, and good, and from the heart.

They sat at a small table in the corner, next to the bandstand, where they could talk to the trumpeter, and watch Brunies, leaning against the piano, playing his trombone.

They were there for hours, and the band played almost everything they wanted to hear: *Baby Won't You Please Come Home,* and *Farewell Blues,* and *Sister Kate,* and *Ugly Chile* and a lot of others. Every two or three numbers, the band would leave the stand, and Cliff Jackson would come in and play the piano. A guy Skinner knew came over to the table, had a drink with them, and drifted away.

Skinner got Cindy to talk about the stage:

"I pretend I'm just selling books to pass the time until the season opens—correction, was selling books." She grimaced. She had decided she would call the bookstore first thing in the morning and quit before they had a chance to fire her; jobs were easy to find around New York, then. "I'll hang around the casting offices, as I did last winter. Only this time I'll do better than a walk-on in a flop. I'll get something good, you know the way the dream goes, a bit part with one big scene. And everybody will be nuts about me."

"You'll turn down Hollywood offers right and left. . . ."

"The critics will ask angrily if somebody can't write a play worthy of my talent . . ."

"The Sunday *Times* will run your biography."

"That's the dream, all right."

"My father knows a couple of people," Skinner said. "I'll ask him to get in touch with you when he gets to New York."

"What's your father like?"

"He's a pretty nice guy. Sports' writer, unpublicised. But a damn good one. He's writing service team football, now. He'll be in town around Thanksgiving."

"You'll have sailed by then."

"I know. I've just come from spending a couple of weeks with him. He had to take off."

"Does your mother make the trips with him?"

"She's dead."

"Sorry."

"It's okay. She's been dead for years. I don't even remember her, but Dad says she was a nice lady."

"Sorry again."

"It's okay. Tell me about your family."

"They're ranchers. Dad works pretty hard. Makes money in the good years, breaks even in the bad ones. They were swell about my coming to New York. I spent a year in State College first. You know that story, too. Did well in dramatics, teachers said I ought to come here and study."

"And you came last winter?"

"Last fall. I spent a few months going to classes. We'd under-estimated what it would cost to live, so, when I found I was running out of money, I began working days and going to class nights."

"What about the show you were in?"

"That was luck. Both kinds. A girl I know got me in. We got paid for rehearsal time, but never opened. The backers took their money out. That's the kind of a show it was."

"Since then?"

"I'd work for a while, then go to school for a while; or take night classes. I was with a summer company in July, but they closed early. I sound like an awfully footloose girl, don't I?"

"Practically fly-by-night."

"I don't really like it, Skinner."

"It's the way it's done though, isn't it?"

"I haven't found any other."

They got up and danced, though Skinner claimed it was sacrilegious to use consecrated trombone music for so profane a purpose.

On the dance floor, Cindy said, "This is the first time we've ever danced together."

"That's right," said Skinner. "I hadn't realized it."

"It would be awfully trite to say that I felt we'd danced this way before," she said.

"Awfully trite and awfully true."

She pressed her cheek hard against his.

"I think of the tritest things," she said. "I was almost ready to say, 'I feel as if we'd always known each other'."

"Trite sprite, be my delight," Skinner murmured.

"I must be very young, and not too clever," said Cindy.

"No," said Skinner. "It's just that as two people get closer to falling in love, they get closer to feeling the way that everybody else who's ever been that way has felt, and they use the same words. They're nice old words."

She moved her cheek away from his so she could look at him. "Did you say falling in love?"

"More nice old words, Cindy."

She put her cheek against his again. "I know some other words, Skinner. Want to hear them?"

"Sure."

"But Mr. Galt, I hardly know you," she said, letting her voice count the old phrases gently, without coyness. "It doesn't happen this way, it's all happened so quickly, we hardly know each other."

"I know an old gag to parry your old words," he said.

"What is it?"

"Let us love today, sweetheart, for tomorrow I'll be gone. War is my new mistress, let me rest but briefly with you. I could not love thee half so much."

"Is it an old gag, Skinner?"

"As old as war."

"And just as certain," she said, pressing his hand. "It doesn't miss, Skinner."

The music stopped, and they went back to their table.

They had another drink, and decided to leave. They got their coats, and went out onto the street. They found a little place where the music was not so good, but they liked it because every other number was a waltz.

They danced to the waltz music, conscious of dancing well together, and Cindy said:

"Waltzes and the old gag fit fine."

"Made for each other."

They had the dance floor almost to themselves, and they did a series of slow turns, covering the length of it.

"Skinner?"

"Yes, Cinderella?"

"Is the old gag to make you laugh?"

"No. It's to make you cry."

They left the little joint and found a cab.

As soon as the door closed, and she had given the address of her apartment building, thirty-odd blocks away, he kissed her.

And just after he kissed her, the cab driver said:

"Here's your address."

The apartment, which she shared with another girl, was on the third floor of a brownstone in the East Thirties. They walked up three flights, and stood in the hallway, just outside the door.

"I can't ask you in," Cindy said. "It's just one room, and Jane's probably in there, sleeping."

"Look, Cindy," he said, putting his arms around her and holding her lightly against him. "It's been a wonderful day, hasn't it?"

"A wonderful day, Skinner."

"Well, here goes everything, sweet. I'm going to pull the dumbest trick a guy can pull."

"What, Skinner?" She looked at him; he could see that she held her breath, waiting for what he was about to say, and her eyes were excited.

"The dumbest trick a guy can pull, or a girl either, is to be honest when he falls in love. Love is promises and lies, Cindy, that's the way it's done. If you want to be a big success romantically, you keep your mouth shut and play it cagey."

"Yes, Skinner."

"We haven't time for that. We've got just two weeks, honey, maybe three. Then off I go. I think I've been in love with you all summer, Cindy."

She turned her cheek and pressed it against his chest, tightening her arms around him.

"I could keep taking you out," he went on, "trying to

lure you into my hotel room, and maybe you would, and maybe you wouldn't, and either way it wouldn't be any good. I'd offer to marry you, but I don't think you'd do it, and I'm not even sure I'd mean it. There's only one way, Cindy."

He waited, but she said nothing.

"I've got some money," he said. "Enough to take a little apartment in the Village, if you'll come and stay with me there, until I sail."

Still she said nothing.

"Time's running out, Cindy. Perhaps we'll both live fifty years, but it's as if we only had three weeks. This is the old gag again, honey, with the pressure on; the cards on the table; the cold turkey proposition. I'd tell any lie to get you to do it. Instead, I've told you the truth."

He was finished talking now, and he waited a long time for her to answer.

Finally she disengaged herself, walked a step away, and turned to face him. Then she said, very seriously, "I don't trust myself to answer right away, darling. I've known all evening that you'd ask me, this or something like it. I thought maybe you'd wait a few days first, but I see what you mean about the time. And I've been wondering what I'd tell you." She came back to him, and leaned against him, looking down. "I don't even know if I love you, Skinner—I don't even know whether it matters whether I do or don't. It's like I said before, I'm awfully young, and not very clever."

She stopped talking, and he waited.

Suddenly she moved her head, and looked up at him. "Skinner," she said, as if the thought worried her very much, "If I say no, you won't think I'm just being coy?"

"Right," he said. She put her face back where it had

been while he was talking, against his chest. He looked at the cloth of her dress, where it stretched tightly, just below her shoulder, and, lightly, drew a pattern on it with his thumbnail. It was a circle with two arms on it, and there was a smaller circle at the end of each arm.

"Look," Cindy said, without raising her head. "Is this all right? Is it all right if I call you up in the morning, when I've stopped feeling traditional?" She looked up now, and repeated, "Is it all right if I call you at ten o'clock in the morning?"

He looked away from the circle, which now had a square inside it, and into her eyes. "Of course," he said, gratefully. "And if the answer is no, thanks for considering it."

He kissed her on the forehead, and turned to go. She caught his arm.

"Skinner?"

"Yes?"

"Have you ever done . . . made this sort of arrangement before?"

He smiled. "No," he said, "But I've read about it in books."

She put up her lips to be kissed, and he kissed her hard. He could tell by the way she responded that it was all set.

The apartment was really a big room, with two closets in it. One of the closets had a refrigerator and a tiny stove in it, and was therefore called the kitchen. The other closet was very narrow and deep. When they had cleared away the boxes and papers which were piled in it, they found an oil painting of a great yellow arm reaching down from the left-hand corner, holding a red tree. In the background were things which, they agreed, should be called

Shapes. Cindy insisted that it was a portrait of Skinner, so they hung it in the middle of one wall, the right hand wall as you came in the door.

The next day, Skinner bought a picture which contained a grotesque mandolin, with a little man jumping angrily on the strings, and more Shapes, on a grey background. This was a portrait of Cindy, and was hung by the first picture.

"Oh, darling," Cindy said. "Suppose we were to have four children and we all sat for a family portrait."

The Shapes were very important. They became the *Lares* and *Penates* of the apartment, and were consulted on such decisions as where to go for dinner. There was a very uncomfortable straight chair of dark, carved wood, which was kept beside the piano—on the left hand wall as you came in the door—and in which it was forbidden to sit lest you sit on a Shape.

The rest of the furnishings were a couple of daybeds, one on each side of the room, at the end near the window, which looked out on the backyard four stories down; a very comfortable chair, covered with what Skinner insisted was surplus overall material; three or four straight chairs, a chest of drawers, and a drawing board which doubled as dining table and desk.

Skinner had packed his books and records in boxes, and left them with Jeff's family, and, on the morning of the second day in the apartment, he went to get them. Cindy made a trip to her place to get the few things she couldn't bear to be without—she had told her room-mate that she was going home for a few weeks. When they assembled the things they had about twenty or thirty volumes, not really enough to make a good showing, in the bookshelves: Skinner's things from college which were a few text-books, most of Hemingway and Fitzgerald, some Modern Library stuff; the things Cindy had had to have were *The Prophet,* Eliot, Yeats, Housman, Tagore, a battered copy of *Winnie the Pooh;* finally, there were three books of Henry Miller's, which they had found in the closet.

There was a piano, too, an upright, of course, with a fairly respectable tone, which neither of them could play. Cindy said the Shapes could play it at night. Skinner said they couldn't, because, by and large, they ran to an average of two fingers per hand, and therefore couldn't get the chords. Cindy said that was all right, five of them could get together at the keyboard any time they wanted to.

They stood in the center of the room and looked around.

"It doesn't look anything like us," said Skinner.

"No," Cindy agreed, "except that we're all three miscellaneous."

"Anyway, we've got Venetian blinds." Solemnly, they went over to the window and worked the blinds.

They went out and bought a victrola. They lugged it back, and Skinner made her carry it up the last flight of stairs. "I'm saving my strength for battle," he maintained, keeping a few steps below her, and pinching her ankles as she hurried up, laughing, trying not to drop the machine, and begging him to stop with what breath she had left. They went into the apartment, and plugged in the record-player, and agreed that now it looked like Skinner and Cindy's place.

"I can't wait for you to go away," said Cindy. "I'll have a victrola, and sixty-one records, and three books by Henry Miller, all for my very own." It was supposed to sound light, but the last words faltered some.

Then she made him go into the kitchen and wait, while she put on a record that she had hidden, and the record, of course, was Benny Goodman's *I've God It Bad and That Ain't Good.* And he came out of the kitchen, grinning, and kissed her, and showed her what he had hidden, which was a bottle of Dewar's White Label Scotch.

They opened the bottle and had a drink, and decided the thing to do was have a house-warming party, for which Cindy made out the guest list:

Mr. Thomas Kendrick Galt
Cinderella
The Shapes

Every morning, Skinner would have to go down to the Ambulance Corps office, to get the latest information on when the ship was due. He would return about noon, stop in at the delicatessen on the corner, and buy half a roast chicken, or a couple of big liverwurst sandwiches, or some cheese, and fruit, and milk or beer. And anything else that looked good. Usually he would call her up on the phone behind the counter, to see if she had thought of anything she particularly wanted to eat.

Cindy always woke when he did in the morning, and talked sleepily to him while he ate breakfast, but the phone conversation between delicatessen and apartment was the first actual coherent discourse of the day.

"Hello."

"Hello, darling."

"Hello, lover, where are you?"

"In the delicatessen, behind the counter talking over the phone to a girl named Cindy."

"What's she like?"

"Rather silly."

"Probably she's just light-headed from hunger. Her man doesn't give her enough to eat."

"Listen, darling, Mr. Schultzer and I have a problem."

Schultzer was the old man who ran the store, and had become a staunch friend.

"What's the problem?"

"Whether I should get potato salad or Russian salad."

"Is there any difference?"

"Well, one's got potatoes in it, and the other's got Russians."

"How do the Russians taste?"

Skinner would ask Mr. Schultzer for a taste of the Russian salad, and report, with his mouth full, "They taste amazing."

"We've got to be careful, Skinner. Make sure they aren't White Russians."

"They're comrades."

"Okay, darling. Hurry up."

"Well, there are a couple of movies I wanted to see, but I'll drop in if I get a minute afterward," Skinner would say.

He'd hang up, collect his purchases and pay for them, and dash out of the store.

"What's de rush?" Mr. Schultzer would ask, beaming at him as he went out.

"No rush," Skinner would call back over his shoulder, "I always walk this way."

Usually he would arrive to find Cindy practicing boogie basses on the piano, doing exercises intended to give her timing and stage presence, or working with her voice.

He would wait outside the door for a moment, getting his breath back from running up the stairs, and try to guess what she was doing, from the sounds on the other side of the door. If it was piano or voice, it was easy; if there was no sound, he usually figured exercises, though she might be reading. He would picture her doing whatever it was, and feel his face dissolve into a thoroughly uncontrollable smile, which he was sure made him look very foolish. He would picture her doing whatever it was, and, along with the picture would come feelings of warmth, and the expanding list of words he had for her: tender, young, glowing, curious, eager, affectionate, wonderful.

And sometimes she would open the door and catch him standing there, claiming to have heard him, and he'd drop the things he was carrying, and they'd cling together in the doorway, laughing. Usually, though, he managed to unlock the door without her hearing him, and catch her in the middle of a backbend, or a passage of rhetoric; but he could never get very far into the room without her seeing him, and, the second she did, she would stop whatever it was she was doing, and fly across the apartment and into his arms.

"What a constructive hussy," he'd tease. "What miracles of self-improvement have gone on around here this morning?"

"You're just gullible. I didn't start until I heard you coming up."

The apartment would be spotless, and he would plead with her to wait until he got home after this, and let him help clean up.

She'd say, "My mother kept a twelve-room ranch house clean single-handed for twenty-four years. She won't let any Mexican women any farther than the kitchen. You're just a dirty old Mexican woman and you can't come in."

"Keep me out."

"Try and get in."

And they'd fight and wrestle around like kids.

They were always frantically glad to see one another. While they ate the things Skinner had bought at the delicatessen, he would invent and embellish things that had supposedly happened at the ambulance office to amuse her.

"They had a real ambulance down there this morning for us to practice with."

"Really, Skinner?"

"Sure. They shot one of the guys through the hip, so we'd have a real patient to drive around, too."

She'd stick out her tongue.

"First Aid Class tomorrow. I volunteered to let them slash my wrists, so we could get in some practical tourniquet work."

Usually, after lunch, they would sit together in the big chair, smoking and playing records, until one of them said:

"Let's get out of this love nest."

And they would play their exit music, which was Bessie Smith's *Buggie Ride,* say goodbye to the Shapes, and go somewhere. Somewhere as often as not, meant the Modern Art Museum, where they would see the showings of old films, or Central Park, or a bus ride if the day was nice, or gallery seats at a matinee. It didn't seem to matter where they went; the big thing was that they went there together. They talked to everybody who would talk to them, went any place that caught their eyes, and were as easily enthralled as tourists in a new country.

In the evenings they ate in restaurants—little places, mostly, because Cindy wanted Skinner to have some money left over to take with him—and went afterwards to 52nd Street for the music, or Nick's, or the Vanguard, or got seats for a concert or a play. Twice they went out to Brooklyn to hear the Brooklyn Opera Company, where to be in the audience is to be part of the show, which was the way they liked opera.

One night they bought steaks, and cooked their own

dinner in the apartment. It was the first cooking they'd done, except for the coffee and bacon Skinner fixed in the morning. Everything tasted fine, and they washed the dishes, and felt very domestic.

"What shall we do with our long evenings at home?" Skinner asked.

"I'll lie around and eat chocolates and get fat," said Cindy, settling herself on one of the daybeds. "And you'll bring me glasses of warm milk and read to me and listen to my symptoms."

"Read Scotch for warm milk," said Skinner, "And your dream comes true."

"I'll read Scotch for chocolate, too."

"Right," he said, and brought her a drink. "Now, which comes first, reading or symptoms?"

She considered. "Read to me," she commanded.

He went to the bookshelf and got the copy of Eliot.

"Here we are," he said. "The soul of Cinderella." And he read the piece called "Portrait of a Lady".

"You're mean," she said, when he had finished. "I'll never be like that."

"What will you be like, love?"

"You tell me."

"Well," he said, matter of factly, "As you grow older, you'll have more defenses and fewer illusions."

"Will that be good?"

"No, it will be the same."

"The same?"

"Every time you lose an illusion, darling, you acquire a defense. The great Twentieth Century error is to confuse the process with growth."

"And it's not?"

"No, darling, that's where we've gone off the road. We've figured that as soon as we replaced all the illusions with defenses, we'd be mature. Instead, we're just lost."

"Can't one get back on the road, ever?"

"No. Because, without the illusions, there is no road."

It was a trick he had for whenever he talked seriously, a trick which, he had noticed, she was catching from him: picking up a word that occurred in the conversation, and making a symbol out of it arbitrarily, letting the word stand for a whole area of feeling and belief that, it was assumed, was mutually understood. Now "road" was the symbol, and, in the game of being serious, one could let its meaning change with one's phrases, redefining it as arbitrarily as one selected it. But the game, Skinner admitted to himself, wasn't quite fair, because to Cindy it wasn't a game at all.

So they talked about the road, and Skinner said you had your choice between believing in the road and being happy, or disbelieving and being right.

"There isn't much to be said, either for the road or for the underbrush," he said. "In the underbrush, you tear your clothes. On the road, you keep going, even though you're tired, but you never find an end. If you walk the road, you walk it for its own sake, because you feel safe on it, and you are wrong if you think you are walking on it because of what is at the end."

"I think there's something at the end."

"Once you get away from it, into the underbrush, you can see that there isn't."

He was better at the game than she was, for he had no scruples about words.

Liking the negation of the mood he was working into, he read her "The Hollow Men."

When he had finished, she asked, "Is that the way it is, Skinner?"

"That's the way it is, darling. The old story: no faith, nothing worth believing in."

"Don't you mind it, Skinner?"

"Sometimes. Sometimes I mind like hell. Sometimes I think I must be inadequate. Mostly, though, I think the faiths they're offering around are inadequate, and I mind that worse."

"They aren't really, darling. It's just that the world's spent twenty-some years telling you how fine it is to be cynical about morals and patriotism and God. And now, when it has more use for you as a devotee than as a skeptic, it wants you to toss all the skepticism aside."

"We're having a swell time wasting tears on Skinner Galt."

"He's worth them."

"Maybe. Or maybe the tears just aren't worth saving."

"You're really licked, aren't you, Skinner?"

"Sure." Then, in a different tone. "Do you love me?"

"Of course."

"Then I'm not licked, am I?"

"Sometimes," she said, "I think I'm beginning to understand you. And every time, just as I think I'm getting somewhere, you say something or do something that makes me wrong."

"I'm sorry," he said. "I'll try to be more predictable in the future."

"You're stubborn," she accused. "You're afraid of being understood."

He realized that she was close to being right, and he thought about it for a minute. "I guess you may be right," he said, no longer playing. "But I don't think there's much fear behind it. I think it's more like pride. Pride in being an enigma. One of the last and strongest of the defenses we trade illusion for. Do you like the theory?"

"Pretty well."

"I'll think about it, honey. If it is right, I'll have to

stop being enigmatic. That's one of the rules. As soon as you discover what your defenses consist of, they automatically join the illusion class, and you've got to get rid of them."

"Skinner, darling," she said. "Stop talking circles around me, and kiss me."

He kissed her.

"Your rules don't work for me," she said. "I'm a normal little girl. I'm not even rebellious. Thirty years ago it would have been rebellion for me to want to come to New York and be an actress. Now it's the accepted thing to do." She paused. "Nowadays I guess I'd be rebelling if I wanted to get married, and make a home for my man."

"Is that what you want?"

"Damn the war," said Cindy.

"Look, darling," said Skinner. "I won't be anything but perfectly honest with you. We can just as easily be married tomorrow as not. That's the trouble with it. All it would mean would be that I'd go off to war a married man, and you'd sit around here, a married girl with a year or two or three to face without your husband. And then, when I got back, there we'd be, with all those differences in experience and personal change between us."

"I know," said Cindy. "But what we're doing is so much like having your cake and eating it, that I can't make myself trust it."

"Probably we will be married," Skinner said. "I think maybe we'll stick. But we have nothing to gain by marrying now, and we might suddenly come face to face with the fact, when I got back, that instead of us having marriage, marriage had us. Look, darling, I don't want to talk you out of it, if it's something you really want. But it would be terrifically irresponsible on my part if I married you now, because it wouldn't make any difference to me. I'd simply be saying what's the difference, it doesn't matter enough to me to be worth making a fuss about, one way or the other."

"Damn the war," said Cindy.

He realized that her need to confirm her belief in some source of affirmation outside their relationship was much greater than his. He was the one who was going away—to action, to excitement, to new and soulfilling experience. She was the guy who had to stay behind, facing the soul-drain of the familiar.

But he had based his integrity on disbelief for too long to retrench, and he perceived that it was hard for her to resist him. Their physical and social surrender to one another was so complete that it would be, by Cindy's code, almost disloyal not to give in to him intellectually, too, and share his outlook. And he was quite sure there was nothing.

Still, she tried occasionally to fight it, probably feeling that it was as much for his sake as for her own, realizing that there is one final and unavoidable conclusion at which those who hold that life is basically intolerable must arrive to be consistent.

Still, as long as she played his game, tried to argue with symbols, he could always defeat her.

"Skinner," she said, one day. "I know a riddle."

"Okay, Sphinx, what?"

"Look," she said. "In movies and books and plays and everything, people are always striking these sort of John Garfield poses, and saying, 'When you get it all added up, it always comes out nothing.' What I want to know is, what do they add up?"

They were standing by the window in the apartment, holding hands and looking half at one another, half at the courtyard below. He thought it over, and laid a trap for her. "That's easy, honey. Two and two."

"I'm a silly little girl," she said. "But why wouldn't it come out four?"

"That's not a riddle," said Skinner, pretending to be stalling for time, "that's a challenge."

"Don't duck out," she pressed him. "Why doesn't it come out four?"

"It's because of the obligation," Skinner said, "imposed on us by our educations and the books we've read, and everything we've ever seen or done." He frowned down at the little courtyard, four flights below. "Look, friend, here's the way it goes. You scurry around, you look everywhere, you talk to people, you scrape stuff together. Finally, you've collected two and two. So you're pretty pleased. You run off by yourself. You take your two and two and put them together. They make four. Fine. Swell. You're getting somewhere at last." He paused. "Then you go on to the second part of the problem. Maybe it will work out differently this time. So you divide by infinity." He shrugged. "Zero again."

"But Skinner," she argued. "Do you always have to go on to the second part of the problem?"

"Don't you?"

"There are plenty of people who don't, and they get along all right."

"Sure, darling. They get along fine. Because they don't realize that there is a second part. They never got far enough in arithmetic to know about infinity. Or, if they did get far enough, infinity scares them and they get ingenious. They work out these vast, elaborate, and highly logical answers, and call them religions and philosophies. But they're all based on a false premise."

She was under the spell now, he knew. The words were

too certain, the eyes too sincere, the faintly frowning brow too patently on the level, for her to hold out. Submissively, she gave the cue: "What's the false premise, Skinner?"

"The refusal to admit that when you have infinity on one side, of an equation, you've got to have zero on the other."

They were only words, but they came surely and sounded well.

Once she tried to argue with him on terms she could use.

"Darling," she said. "If there were only something you loved it wouldn't matter whether you believed in it or not."

"I love you," he pointed out.

"Yes, darling, but I mean something impersonal, like the theatre."

"Perhaps I could, if this were Elizabethan London, or Athens. The theatre had importance then—it was part of everyone's life. It had magnificence."

"It still does."

"Yes," he agreed, "but in an awfully limited way. It's so localized and its people are so kind of small town, isolated from the main current. The closest thing we have to a theatre like the one in Elizabethan London is professional sport. You like to think of the crowd at one of Ben Johnson's plays getting into it, the way a good baseball crowd gets into the game."

"Well, what about the movies?" Cindy urged. "People get awfully enthusiastic and excited about the movies, don't they?"

"A few intellectuals do, in the right way," Skinner said. "The members of great movie-going public go to the movies to lose themselves."

"But they go. It's an important part of their lives."

"Darling, the movies are too tasteless. They're too obsessed with the necessity of being second rate. First-rate art is arrogant: the artist creates in a spirit of 'I'm doing this, and if the public wants anything from me, they'll damn well take what I give them; and like it, too.' Out in Hollywood they're afraid. The movies don't create mass taste and opinion, they cater to it. Movies aren't made in magnificence, they're made in fear."

"What about writing?"

"What would I write—if I could write? Novels are too routine. I'd be another amateur in a field whose professionals make dough out of standard models, and whose amateurs are supposed to be terrific if they produce one good scene out of every four. Poetry's too esoteric. So's painting, too, for that matter. So's sculpture and dancing. That leaves music, I guess."

She bit. "What's wrong with music?"

Skinner grinned his most infuriating grin. "Too musical, darling."

If Skinner would not give way to her in being serious, they always gave way to each other when the moods were of tenderness and emotion—and they gave in completely to being silly together.

One evening they went home right after supper, because Skinner had some customs papers to fill out. He should have done them in the afternoon, but there had been an old Duse film scheduled at the Modern Museum, and they had decided they simply couldn't miss it.

After the picture, they had eaten quickly and hurried home.

Skinner settled down with his papers immediately, wanting to get them out of the way. He noticed Cindy watching him for a moment or two; then she sat down across the drawing board from him, and became absorbed in something. He assumed that she was writing a letter.

For half an hour neither of them said anything, and then, finishing his papers much more quickly than he'd hoped to, Skinner asked: "Letter, darling?"

"Hush," she said, without looking up, "I've almost got it."

He decided that he wasn't supposed to know what it was she'd almost got, so he got out of bed, went into the kitchen, fixed a couple of drinks, and came back with them. She was still figuring. He sat down and waited, curiously.

Cindy sighed, smiled, turned the paper over and wrote something quickly on the other side. She looked up and said, triumphantly, "Here."

He took the paper she offered him, and read what she had written on it:

Now the sexy typing typing teacher found Thomas B. Tizdale a very queer jerk.

"Darling," he said, "it's wonderful. It's the best thing since Beowulf. But what is it?"

"All the letters," she said, very pleased with herself.

"Huh?"

"You know. Like that thing about the quick brown fox they make you type in school."

"Yeah," he said, still puzzling over it. "Oh. You mean all the letters in the alphabet in one sentence?"

"Yes, darling. I've always hated the one about the fox, and I thought there should be a new one."

"Cinderella," he said. "You are the smartest girl in the world."

She got up, came over, and sat on his lap.

"The smartest in the world?" she asked.

"Yes," he told her, solemnly.

She kissed him. "The prettiest, too?"

"The very prettiest."

She kissed him again. "What else?"

"The nicest, the worst, the lightest, the heaviest."

She kissed him four times, once on each cheek, once on the forehead, once on the tip of the nose.

"But your sentence," he said, firmly, "is not fair."

She jumped off his lap, and said, "Thomas Galt, you're a nasty thing. What isn't fair about it?"

"You can't do it with names," he said, decisively. "You'd never have gotten z or d or b or anything without this Tizdale fellow."

"You're mean," she said.

"Tizdale is an interloper."

"No he isn't. He's a friend of mine."

"Tizdale must go."

"All right," she said. "I'll banish Tizdale when you do a better one."

"Right," he said. "You fix the drinks, and I'll have one before you're back."

It took him considerably longer than the time required to fix two Bourbon and waters. Cindy was out for vengeance, and she wouldn't leave him alone.

She pulled his hair, jiggled his writing arm, blew in his ear, and recited the alphabet backwards. She covered his face with kisses. She untied his shoes. At one point, catching him off guard, she snatched the paper he was writing on and ran away with it. It required an ice-cube held against the back of the neck, and dire threats of letting it slip down, to get the manuscript back.

Finally, he barricaded himself in the kitchen to finish his sentence.

At last he went back to the big room, said, "Here, wench," and gave it to her to read.

Skinner's sentence was:

Barnacle Bill vexatiously quacked, "Gimme that fuzzy wimple, Joe."

"Oh, Skinner," she said in horror, "it's full of flaws. Two names, and gimme isn't a word, and I'll bet you don't even know what a wimple is."

"My names are all right," he said, stoutly. "Good common names, and gimme is a good common word, and a wimple is a good common. . . ."

He didn't know.

Barnacle Bill, Joe, and their fuzzy wimple were sent to join Thomas B. Tizdale in a special Siberia presided over by Shapes.

They declared a truce then, and sat down, each on one side of the drawing board, to create the perfect sentence with which to replace the quick brown fox, who, as everyone knows, jumps over the lazy dog a million times a month.

They worked in perfect concentration for twenty minutes or so. Skinner got his first, read it over, and said: "It's not really fair. There's a name in it, but I'm damned if I'll change it."

She finished, and they traded papers.

"Mine is an injunction to you," he said. "And I'll beat you to it by admitting that it isn't fair. Besides the name, it's got one of the same words that's in the fox sentence."

His was:

Move quickly in juxtaposition with dozens of young Bernhardts.

"Oh, Skinner," she said. "It's lovely. It even makes sense. But it isn't fair. And mine's fair, but it doesn't make sense."

He read hers:

Quixotic zebras have faked damp jungle ways.

"Yours is closest," he admitted. "No names. None of the same words . . . hey, you know what?"

"What?"

"I don't think it's any longer than the fox one."

"Oh, Skinner. Count the letters. Quick. I'll count the fox."

He counted. "Thirty-seven," he said.

Her face fell. "Thirty-five in the fox. Oh, Skinner, they've got us beaten."

They decided to abandon the typing students of America to their quick brown fate, and concentrate on Bourbon.

Only once, in three weeks, did things go really wrong between them.

It happened on an afternoon which was like any other afternoon in the beginning. They had lunch; they smoked; they played records. Then Cindy said,

"Darling, you worry me."

"Right," said Skinner. "Pretty bothersome fellow."

She hadn't meant it lightly, for she went on: "When you're away, I'll be afraid for you."

"The chances aren't so bad, honey. The percentages are all with me."

"It isn't the war," she told him. "Every girl has to live with the percentages; if the others can take it, I can. You'll be as safe as the percentages can make you from the guns, Skinner. I worry whether you'll be safe from yourself."

"Don't worry, honey. That part of it isn't your fight."

"Oh, but it is, darling. Anything that concerns you is my fight, now."

"You're worried that I might knock myself off? Or get

careless, and let myself get knocked off because I didn't care?"

"Yes, if it's got to be put into words."

"There's nothing you can do about it, Cindy. Everything is okay right now. I'm in love, and I like it. And I'm not going to get depressed and hurt myself. Do you believe me?"

"Yes, darling."

He was unconvinced. Suddenly he had an impulse to test it, to test her belief in the meaning of their love to him, and he said: "Look, Cindy, We'll prove it. I'll walk over to the window, and climb up on the sill. You'll know I'm not going to jump. If you really know it, you ought to get a laugh out of my pretending."

"That's not necessary," she said quickly.

He got up.

"Don't Skinner."

He walked over to the window. It was about five feet high, and hinged at the sides, the two halves swinging together and clasping in the middle. He undid the clasp, and swung the halves open. He stepped out onto the sill, grasped the edge of the frame with one hand, and looked down at the brick courtyard, four stories below. I should be far enough up, he thought, smiling down at a fading deck chair someone had left in the court. He wondered how it would feel; marvelous, he thought, the two seconds you were in the air. The feeling, for two seconds, that you had, at last, of your own volition, achieved a kind of perfection for once.

He imagined how it would be, falling. He hung one foot out to see if he could get part of the sensation that way, at the same time letting go of the frame with his left hand and grabbing the other side with his right as he started to go; he was pleased with the shiver that ran . . .

Suddenly he realized that, behind him in the room, someone was crying.

He turned. He had never seen anyone so pale.

He jumped down from the window sill, and ran across the room to where she was sitting, in the big chair. She didn't move her eyes away from the window, kept staring at it as if unaware that sobs, half of fear and half of sorrow, were forcing themselves out through her clenched lips.

He picked her up out of the chair, carried her to the closer of the two beds, and put her down. He stretched out beside her, and held her tightly against him.

"What a rotten thing to do, darling," he said. "What a rotten thing to do."

The sobs were coming more easily now.

"I'm frightfully sorry, darling," he soothed. "I don't know how I could have done it."

It was several minutes before she was well-controlled again.

Then she said, quietly, and almost tonelessly: "I know why you did it, Skinner, and so do you."

"No, darling, honestly I don't."

Pensively, then, she told him. "I understand you, now, darling, better than I ever thought I would."

"Tell me, Cindy."

"What happens when you take a guy with a big capacity for love, and persuade him that there's nothing worth loving?"

"It turns to hate, darling. Do you mean I'm a hater?"

"No. I'm making an analogy." She paused. "Skinner, what happens if you take a guy with a big capacity for creation, and he persuades himself that there's nothing worth creating?"

He wouldn't answer her.

She answered herself. "It turns to destruction," she said,

and the tight, flat way she said it made him shiver.

After that they were silent for a long while and held each other tightly.

One night they had company.

Skinner had spoken once or twice of Benny Berg, who was the one guy he had met in the group up until then who had made much of an impression on him.

"What's he like?" Cindy asked.

"He's a communist." Skinner said. "I'm not sure whether he's a party member but I imagine he is. He's very nice, sort of amusing in a savage way. He's got a good, analytical mind—has read everything there is to read. And he rather surprises me because he doesn't let his politics interfere with his literary taste."

"That's odd," said Cindy.

"I think it's a sort of conflict for him," Skinner said. "He'd like to look at a picture, and say 'Is it Marxian?' first, and 'Is it good?' second. But his honesty won't let him. I'm a conflict, too. He likes me, but he doesn't approve of me."

"Can you kid him about his politics?"

"As long as you aren't trying to use kidding in the middle of an argument to detract from one of his points, or something like that."

"He's not very close to type," Cindy said.

"I'd like you to meet him," Skinner said.

"Swell, darling, I'd love it."

"He could get a girl, maybe, and we'll all go out together."

"Why don't you ask him up here?"

"I'd like that a lot, sweet, but I didn't want to suggest it myself."

"Why not?"

"Afraid it might embarrass you."

"Because we're living in sin?" She smiled at him. "He probably won't even notice it, darling, and besides, I'm proud of being a hussy."

Benny came up for dinner the next evening.

"Cindy, this is Benny Berg."

"How do you do?"

"Fine, Cindy. How are you?"

"I've been fighting for you all day."

"How come?"

"Well, Skinner said either we should have black bread and hang a red flag on the wall, or we should have squabs and sparkling burgundy and be patronizing."

Benny laughed. "There's no red flag," he said, "are you going to patronize me?"

"Nope. I won. We're having fried chicken and beer."

"Good," said Benny, "I've never had any black bread, but I'm sure I'd hate it."

They moved over towards the window and found seats.

"You have a wide choice of drinks," Skinner said. "We have two bottles of bourbon and a bottle of gin."

"What do you do with the gin?" Benny asked.

"We drink it late at night with grapefruit juice."

Benny shuddered. "Remind me to leave early," he said. "I'll take bourbon."

"Right," said Skinner, "water, soda or ginger ale."

Benny asked for soda, and Cindy for plain water. Skinner went to fix the drinks.

Benny and Cindy discovered a couple of mutual acquaintances whom Benny insisted were young communists who acted for a living, and Cindy maintained were actors who went to party meetings on the side.

Skinner came back with three glasses.

"They're young actors." Cindy said. "It's just that they

get cold sometimes and they go to your old meetings to get warmed up because they know the halls are heated."

They got up to eat. "You're worse than he is," Benny told her, holding her chair. "At least I don't have to convert him from anything else."

Cindy's fried chicken was a big success.

They were still talking theatre, and Benny said he'd always though he'd like to write a play.

"Oh, do," said Cindy, "and put a big fat part in it for me."

"Sure," Skinner teased, "you could be the White Russian countess who gets shot just before the play opens."

"Yeah," said Benny, "and I'll give her another appearance as a ghost, just after the last act curtain."

"Humph," said Cindy, "I don't think you're smart enough to write a play, anyway."

"Smart?" said Benny, "who said anything about being smart? All you have to do to write a play is put a lot of jerks on the stage and let 'em scintillate."

They were finished eating.

"Okay, Benny," said Skinner, "we'll clear the table. You write it."

"I would," said Benny, "but my pen's out of ink."

"Here's a pencil," said Cindy, getting up to help Skinner clear. "Now go ahead."

"Hmm," said Benny, "how do you start?"

"Just put down 'Act One'," said Skinner, coming back for another load, "then hit 'em with everything. A bucket of laughs, a bucket of tears, and some of the old songs."

"And an interpretive ballet," called Cindy from the kitchen.

When they had the table cleared, Benny had written his play for them on a paper napkin. It was called *A Pox on The Master of This House,* and went:

Act One

First Jerk: Ever hear of Skinner Galt?
Second Jerk: No.
(Song: Seeing Nellie Home.)

Act Two

First Jerk: Want to hear about him?
Second Jerk: No.
(Song: Seeing Nellie Home.)

Act Three

First Jerk: Neither do I.
(Interpretive ballet: To Hell with Cindy, too.)
CURTAIN

They came back from the kitchen with more drinks, and read it.

"Let that be a lesson to us," said Skinner, "no more hospitality."

"I don't know," said Cindy, "the characterization is pretty good. You could really get your teeth into that First Jerk part."

"Sure," said Skinner, "but the plot is old."

"How about the message?" Benny insisted. "That's the important thing."

They moved Benny into the comfortable chair, and Skinner and Cindy sat facing him on the daybed. They didn't hold hands, or even sit close, but Skinner knew that looking at them, it would be plain that they were sitting together, and not just two people sitting on the same piece of furniture.

"Nothing I'd rather watch than young love," said Benny.

"Next time you come," said Cindy, "bring a girl and we'll watch you."

"Something awful would happen if I did," Benny said, "I am the world's most star-crossed lover. Nothing ever works out right for me. If I'm in a car, about to get kissed, kids drive by and blow their horns. If I'm in a dimly lit room, holding hands and talking earnestly, somebody turns on the light."

"If you're in the back row at the movies," Cindy suggested, "the film breaks?"

"Exactly."

"If you got a girl into a bathosphere, twelve fathoms down," Skinner said, "the airline would clog."

"And now," said Benny. "Now that I'm in uniform about to sail away. Now that I find myself for the first and only time in a position to be irresistible, I have to be interested in a girl named Rose who cries every time I kiss her."

"You mean literally?" Cindy asked.

"Absolutely. When every other soldier in the world is filling his last moments with unforgettable caresses, Benjamin Berg is saying, 'There, there, little girl!' "

"Why don't you get another girl?" Skinner asked.

"Because I can't get it out of my head that Rose is what I want. Cindy, tell me what to do."

"I'm a very prim and proper girl," said Cindy, "but if I weren't, I'd say the thing to do was pick her up and carry her to bed weeping."

"Sure," said Skinner, "she'd either stop crying or start screaming, and either way, she'd be dry-eyed for a while."

Skinner and Cindy matched to see who'd go for drinks. Cindy lost.

"She's terrific," Benny said, as she headed for the kitchen with the glasses. "How'd she ever happen to go for a stinker like you?"

"It's my madcap manner," said Skinner. "She's a sucker for a madcap manner."

"Nuts," Cindy called, overhearing them. "I'm one of these girls you read about who can't resist a heel."

"I'm a heel," Benny said, "I kicked five dogs on my way up here."

"He'd have kicked seven," said Cindy, coming back.

"Besides," said Skinner, "you haven't got a madcap manner."

"I'll trade you girls," Benny offered. "Wouldn't you like one you could make cry?"

"I like this one," Skinner said, "she makes me cry."

"I'll throw in a jack-knife and a bicycle tire," Benny said.

"How about your red aggie?"

"Oh, no. Nobody gets my red aggie."

"Not even for me?" Cindy pleaded.

"Not even for you."

Cindy had been smart and brought the bottle, soda, water, and ice-cubes with her. They were on the floor, now, where anyone could reach them.

The level of bourbon in the bottle went steadily down.

Skinner made a trip to the kitchen for more soda.

The last of the ice cubes had melted to a translucent wafer floating on the surface of an inch of water in the bottom of the glass bowl.

Benny noticed their pictures. "Love abstract art," he said, "you like these?"

"Sure," said Skinner. They were all talking a little thickly.

"Portrait of Skinner onna right. Portrait of Cindy onna left," said Cindy.

Benny got up to look at them more closely. "Won't tell you what they mean; very lewd symbolism; very lewd."

"Good portrait," Skinner said, "I'm a very lewd fella."

"Not me," said Cindy, "prim 'n' proper. Prim little Cindy."

"Love abstract art," Benny said. They were all standing, looking at the pictures now. Benny went to the drawing board, found a pen and some paper. "Make a nice portrait of Cindy," he said. "Very abstract."

Skinner joined him, took out his own pen. "Me too. Nice abstract of Cindy."

Cindy got a pen out of her pocket book, and sat down with them. "Self-portrait," she explained.

Benny already had his completed. It was a cleverly drawn pair of hands offering a heart, the sort that appears on valentines.

"Not fair," Skinner said, "you can draw."

"I can't," said Cindy, who was happily making a series of smudges and messy lines.

"Not abstract enough," said Benny, considering his drawing and frowning. "Trouble with abstract art. Not abstract enough."

"Got to have a new school," said Cindy, exhibiting her scrawl, "so I can get mine in."

"New school," said Benny. "I know. Draw with our eyes shut."

They closed their eyes.

"Same subject?" asked Skinner.

"Yeah," Benny said.

With their eyes closed, they drew. Then they looked. Meaningless blobs, curves, and pen scratches marred the surfaces of three sheets of white bond paper.

" 'Swonderful" said Cindy, admiring all three. " 'Swonderful."

"Non-ocular art," Skinner suggested. "Name of new school. Non-ocular."

They had more bourbon, and tried other subjects, until each of them had covered half a dozen sheets of paper.

"Gotta save 'em," said Cindy. "Some day be worth millions."

"Right," said Benny. "Origin here tonight of great new art school."

"Non-ocular," said Skinner, holding up one of the drawings. "Look, Mom, no eyes."

The eighteen sheets of paper, each labelled with the title, subject, and name of artist, were scotch-taped on the blank wall above the piano.

"Three man show," said Skinner, happily.

Benny looked at his watch. "Stwo-thirrrry," he said. "Gotta go."

They said goodnight to him.

"Come back and see us every day," Cindy said.

"Every day," Skinner agreed.

"Move in tomorrow," Benny promised, and left.

Benny did come back, every day or so, usually for an hour in the afternoon, occasionally for lunch when Skinner could persuade him to.

The non-ocular art stayed on the wall. They agreed the next day that it was a good thing they had labelled the drawings; otherwise they wouldn't have been able to tell one from another. But Cindy said:

"The Shapes like them." So they stayed up.

Late one night, when they had been trying to sleep for over an hour, and couldn't because Cindy was restless and blue over the prospect of his having to leave soon, Skinner said, to take her mind away from it: "I know a rude question, darling, but it would satisfy my curiosity if you wanted to answer it."

"Go ahead," she said. "Be rude. What's the question?"

"Remember the second day I saw you at the house-party, how much you minded what had happened?"

"Yes."

"Did you mind it so much because it was the first time for you?"

"No. Because it was the second."

"Oh." He decided he'd better not let himself ask about the first time.

She told him anyway.

"I'd like you to know about it, darling," she said. "The reason I minded so much was because it was like the first time, in a way, undeliberate and uncontrollable. Or, not uncontrollable, but it just didn't occur to me to control myself at the time. Would you like to hear about it?"

"Yes, I would."

"You mind it, don't you?"

"Yes," he said, honestly, a little surprised at himself. "I do. I didn't think I would."

"I want to tell you," Cindy said. "It was this summer, four or five weeks before I met you. When I was in stock in Connecticut. We'd been working terribly hard, and we were all tired. It was like all stock—while you're doing one show, you're rehearsing the next. Our new show started on a Wednesday, and I had my first really big part in it. I'd been pretty bad in rehearsal, and I was sure I'd be terrible; I think everyone else was afraid I would be, too. And then, just before the performance, I suddenly felt so tired that I didn't even give a damn whether I was good or not. And, the minute I hit the stage, it was all changed. I went through it like a breeze. It was the best performance I'd ever given in anything and everybody loved me for it. And after the show, I was sort of intoxicated with success, and everybody being so grand to me. We had some liquor backstage, and I took one drink and went off my head with joy. Practically the next thing I knew, I was in one of the dressing rooms with a boy I'd seen around once or twice, just a nice kid who was staying around there somewhere for the summer, and we were on a sort of chaise-lounge thing together. And that was it, darling. It didn't even occur to me not to until it was over. Afterwards, I was awfully surprised at myself, and I think the boy was even more surprised than I was. I didn't feel guilty or anything, in fact, I sort of liked it; but I decided next time it would be someone I cared about. That's why I was so worried at the houseparty. Because I thought maybe I was just a pushover after all."

"And you weren't?"

"You mean between college and when I saw you again? No, I wasn't darling. I had a few opportunities, and was relieved to find that I didn't want any part of them. You know why?"

"Why, Cindy?"

"Partly because I was proving something to myself, but mostly because I wanted you."

"You're very honest with me, darling. Wouldn't most girls sort of lie, and claim that they'd been virgins until you came along?"

"Yes, darling, they would. But you once said that love was mostly lies, and I decided that ours wouldn't be. I was willing to tell you, anytime you asked."

"Thanks," said Skinner. "In a way, it's none of my business, but I'm glad you told me. And I'm very surprised at my own reactions. I'm supposed to be a very uncaring young fellow but, just for a second, when you were describing the guy, I had a completely uncivilized impulse to try to find him and kill him."

"Really, darling? Maybe I shouldn't have told you."

"Oh, that's okay. I'm all over it now. It was just one of those things that shoots through your mind. Proof that we're not very far removed from animals, yet, as far as our bodies go."

"Is it proof that men, basically, want their women innocent?"

"No. It doesn't prove it. Innocence is an attractive thing, but it doesn't make any kind of a rational damn. There's an old superstition around that the way for a girl to get a man is to hold out on him until he offers to marry her, but I think that's kind of exploded by now."

"I don't think I'd want a man I had to get that way," said Cindy.

"Well, darling, by and large, the other way's surer—if the guy you want has been around at all."

"What's the other way?"

"Most guys I know who've gotten themselves married have had the girl first. As often as not, they aren't really in love with them until then. I think the reason is that the guys are sort of constantly wondering whether the girl really loves them, or whether she's primarily interested in being married to someone. And when the girl surrenders, without even having marriage promised, he figures that's proof; she loves him so much she's willing to say to hell with all the things she's been taught by prudes about sex. So he reciprocates by falling for her."

"Yes," said Cindy. "It takes an awfully cynical girl to plan it out like that, though."

"And what's your method?" He teased her.

She ran her fingers into his hair and tugged gently at it. "Fall in love and keep your fingers crossed," she said. "If your luck holds, it may work out all right."

One Sunday morning while Skinner was eating his breakfast, preparatory to making his morning trip to the ambulance office, Cindy suddenly sat up in bed.

"Darling," she said. "Come here a minute."

Skinner picked up his coffee cup, and went over and sat beside her.

"Skinner, it's Sunday, isn't it?"

"I think so."

"Listen, darling . . . may I have a sip of your coffee?"

He held the cup to her lips, and tilted it so that some would run into her mouth. She nodded when she had had enough, and he took the cup away. She sat straight up, looked at him very seriously, and said, "Skinner, ever since I heard you get up, I've been lying awake trying to get up nerve enough to ask you to do something for me."

"What, sweetheart?"

"Listen, would it be all right if you didn't go down to the office this morning?"

"Sure. Benny will call up if anything happens."

"Listen, darling, I want you to take me to church."

Skinner smiled. "Sure, darling, why not?"

"This is our third Sunday, darling, and it might be our last. Will you take me?"

"Of course."

"You're wonderful," she said, and kissed him.

It took her only twenty minutes to wash, and dress, and drink the orange juice and coffee that Skinner made for her while she was getting ready.

They went to the ten o'clock service at the church which stands at Broadway and Eleventh Street. They sat in the rear pew, on the left, and Skinner, deciding that he would do it right for her, watched her carefully, and stood up and knelt when she did.

He had forgotten more of it than he'd realized. He supposed he had been twelve or thirteen when he attended his last service, but he couldn't even be sure where it had been.

He looked around. The atmosphere was familiar. The dimness, the coolness, the colored air. The hushed people. The droning voice of the robed man in front. Cindy slipped a prayer-book into his hand, and indicated with her finger what the man was saying. Skinner followed it for a few minutes, got ahead, turned some pages, and lost his place. He looked at her book to see where he ought to be, and found the place again. He decided he would feel silly reading the responses with the rest of the people, so he didn't try.

It became time to sing a hymn, and they rose, sharing the same hymnal, and joined in it. The boy-soprano choir was very good.

During the sermon, he read the Service for the Burial of the Dead.

After the sermon, there was some more reading, which he didn't try to follow. Instead he thought about Fred Birch, already overseas, and wondered whether Fred had gotten to where the shooting was yet. He thought about the little his father had told him about the last war, and wondered whether this would be the same. He didn't suppose it would. He wondered if he had gone to Church with his mother when he was very young, and decided he probably had.

Cindy whispered in his ear, "I don't have my purse, darling."

He looked up and saw that a man was standing at the end of the pew they were in, waiting for a bowl with a felt bottom to pass in and back to him, and remembered that you were supposed to give money. He wasn't sure how much, so he dug out his change and offered it to Cindy to choose the coins she thought proper. She selected two quarters; he put the rest of the money away; she handed one of the coins back to him and, when the collection plate reached them, they each dropped a quarter into it.

The organist was playing something he recognized. He listened for a minute, and asked her, "Hindemith?"

She nodded.

"It's very good," he whispered.

After the collection, the service lasted only a few minutes. He was getting restless, but he didn't want her to know it, so he made himself sit very still and kept his eyes on the hat of the woman in front of him. They knelt once more, and he thought, I feel like a jerk, but I suppose I'd feel more like one if I sat still and made everybody aware that I was refusing to get down. He kept watching her knees, so that he could tell the second she was ready to get up.

Finally, they got off their knees, and she found another hymn in the book. The tune was unfamiliar, and not particularly pretty, and the key wrong for him, but he hummed along with the choir which was filing out through a side door up front, relieved that they would be able to leave soon. The minister followed the choir out, and Cindy closed the hymnbook and put it in the rack. The choir sang "Amen", and he figured it must be all over, but, as he started to turn and walk over to the aisle, she took his arm and held him still a little longer. As if from a great distance—it was probably done with doors, he thought—the choir sang "Amen" again.

Then it was over, and they went out into the street and into the sunlight.

They walked back to the apartment, and, on the way, she said,

"Were you terribly bored, darling?"

"No. I kept remembering things about it; and that Hindemith thing he played was fine."

"Did you like the choir?"

"Very much. They sound sort of disembodied, don't they?"

She smiled. "I don't think either one of us listened to the sermon."

"Nope. I read."

"I watched you," she said. "And kept wanting to touch you. The first part of the service always gets me, though."

"Do you go often?"

"Every month or so. I like it, Skinner. It quiets me."

"Does it have any meaning to you? Do you believe in it?"

"The little girl in me does."

"What does the big girl believe in?"

"You. And the stage. And that life is kind of nice."

He squeezed her arm. "Easy to please, aren't you?"

"Very," she said.

They arrived at the apartment, and found Benny waiting for them. He was sitting on the front steps in the sun, reading the Sunday paper.

They stopped in front of him, and Cindy said, "Doesn't Benny look nice in the sunlight?"

"Like a statue," Skinner said. "Well-Adjusted Young Man Reading Newspaper."

Benny looked up at them. "I don't know you," he said, and looked down again at his paper.

Cindy said, "He doesn't know us."

"I could have sworn it was old Benny Berg."

"At least we know he's not a statue. He spoke."

Benny got up with an exaggerated sigh, and folded his paper. "It's an awful thing," he remarked to a nearby lamppost, "When a man can't sit in the sun on Sunday morning and read his paper, without a bunch of gawking tourists gathering to stare at him." Then, to them, "What do you people want?"

"We live here," said Cindy. "And it's an awful thing when self-respecting house-holders can't go to church on Sunday morning, without coming back to find bums sitting on their steps, reading newspapers."

"Church?" asked Benny, incredulously. "Did you say church?"

"Naturally," said Skinner.

"Oh," moaned Benny. "Lenin, thou shouldst be living at this hour."

"Benny hath need of thee," finished Skinner. "Let's go up."

They went up to the apartment. Cindy said she was hungry, and made Benny admit that he hadn't had breakfast. She cooked eggs and bacon and made fresh coffee. Skinner declared that church had made him abstemious, that he would change his sinful ways, and, forsaking all food, fix himself a drink.

"The reaction," he explained.

They gathered around the table, and Benny and Cindy ate.

Benny said, "No kidding. Have you two been to church?"

"Sure," said Skinner.

"How did you get him to go?" Benny asked Cindy.

"He wants me to choose between him and God," Cindy said. "And he thought he'd give God a fair chance."

"I'll get you for that," Skinner threatened.

"Which do you think I ought to choose?" Cindy wanted Benny to tell her.

"It's a meaningless choice," Benny said. "Substitution of one petty bourgeois symbol for another."

Cindy was enjoying herself. "Which do you think I ought to choose, darling?" she asked Skinner.

"Young lady," said Skinner, "my advice to you is to count ten, have a drink, and say to hell with both of them."

"I'll take two-thirds of your advice," said Cindy. She counted ten rapidly, and went to get herself a drink.

She brought a drink for Benny, too, while Skinner cleared away the dishes. They sat around the drawing board and talked.

"Benny," Cindy said. "You have a nice, reassuringly affirmative answer to this question of whether life is a worthwhile way to spend a few years; is it all based on Communism?"

"Pretty much," Benny said. "Most of the people who say 'Yes', if they think about it enough so that they have to say yes or no, base it on one central belief. There are even some people who think the whole thing through, and can't find a central belief, who say yes anyway, just for the joy of saying it. They do all right."

"But what are the other things you could base it on?" she asked.

"Oh, religion. Art. Belief in mankind. Lots of things. If your belief is political, it probably boils down to belief in mankind."

"But why don't any of those things work for Skinner?" she wanted to know.

"Nothing I like better," said Skinner, plaintively, "than being discussed as if I weren't around."

"Hush, darling," said Cindy. "Tell me why those things don't work for guys like Skinner."

"Well," said Benny. "You can take the simple explanation, and say he's a masochist, and doesn't want any of them to work. But that's too easy. I figure with those guys, it's a case of there being two ways of believing. If you're an objective believer, if you have to be sure something is true first, before you believe it, you'll never find anything that will satisfy you for long. You have to believe subjectively, believe because you find it satisfying, believe by faith without requiring proof. A cause or principle is just as true as the amount of devotion you give it. If you wait for it to become true because it's undeniable, you wait forever."

"That's pretty good, Benny," Skinner said.

"I'll bet there've been a dozen things," Benny said, "that made you want to say yes, until you went into them objectively, trying to find a sort of absolute truth basis for them."

"At least a dozen," Skinner said. "And a dozen of the other kind that made me want to say no. It's mostly in stuff you read—or people who are right people, or the other kind, who sell out. You think about Lincoln, and the answer is yes; you read Voltaire, and the answer is no."

"See," said Benny to Cindy. "Does that explain him?"

"Yes," said Cindy. "It's like a game. The Yes boys make a few yards, then the No boys make a few the other way. And Skinner's the ball."

"It's the big game," Skinner said. "Lawrence plays center for the Yes team, Marx is right guard, Christ is left guard."

"Who are your tackles?" Benny asked.

"Let's see. A couple of good big boys," Skinner said. "How about Falstaff, for one?"

"Tom Wolfe for the other," Benny suggested.

"Sure."

"And Roosevelt playing end," Cindy urged.

"Good man," said Skinner. "A defensive end's got to be able to spill a lot of interference. And Heywood Broun for the other end." They got a piece of paper, and began diagramming the football game.

"Lenin's calling signals," said Benny. "And young Mark Twain can handle the reverses."

"Lincoln for a good steady fullback," Skinner said. "And . . . I don't know. Who for the other half? Saroyan? Koestler?"

"They're both tiring," Benny said.

"How about putting me in, coach?" Cindy asked.

"Yeah," said Skinner. "Put her in. She may be new around here, but she can play a hell of a lot of ball."

Then they arranged the No team.

There was some question about using Scott Fitzgerald. Skinner said he could almost make the Yes team, because of his belief in the magic of women. Benny wanted him on the No's, because of his life. Cindy agreed that he should be on the No's, and they put him in at half.

There was great question about using Eliot.

"He's the best man the No's have got," Skinner said.

"That's the early stuff," Benny argued.

"It's the only stuff I read," Skinner said. "And besides. When those guys who are so negative when they're young get religion, you feel sold out. You figure they did it because they got scared. So it may make them feel nice and affirmative, but it makes you feel more negative than ever."

When they had finished the wrangling, and agreed on the officials, Benny drew them out a neat copy of the game. The Yes team had the ball—Cindy had just recovered a fumble, Skinner said—deep in their own territory. It went like this:

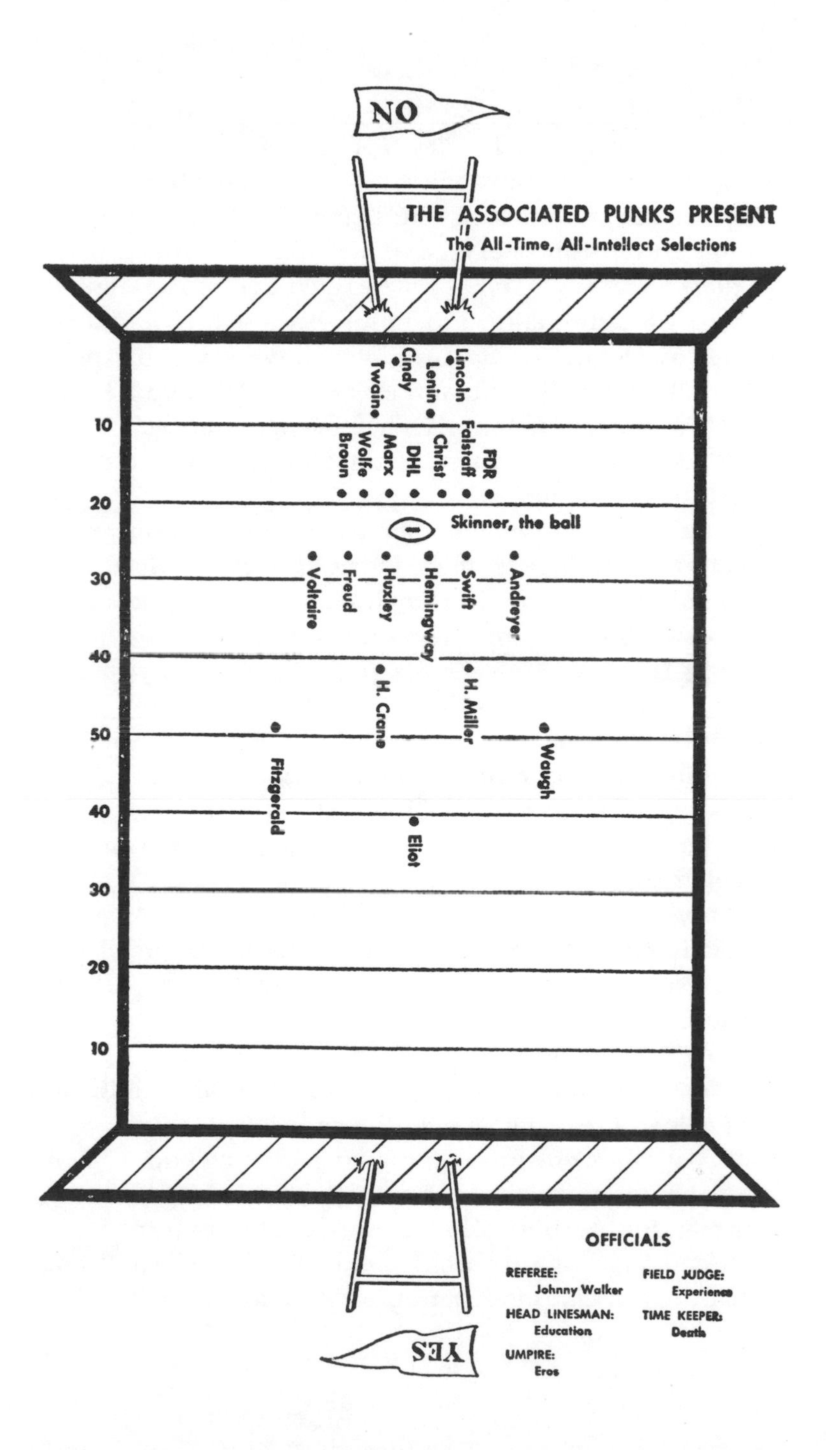
NO
THE ASSOCIATED PUNKS PRESENT
The All-Time, All-Intellect Selections
Lincoln
Lenin
Cindy
Twaine
FDR
Falstaff
Christ
DHL
Marx
Wolfe
Broun
Skinner, the ball
Andreyev
Swift
Hemingway
Huxley
Freud
Voltaire
H. Miller
H. Crane
Waugh
Fitzgerald
Eliot
10
20
30
40
50
40
30
20
10
YES
OFFICIALS
REFEREE:
Johnny Walker
HEAD LINESMAN:
Education
UMPIRE:
Eros
FIELD JUDGE:
Experience
TIME KEEPER:
Death

They looked it over, and Benny pointed out that Waugh was a Catholic now, Huxley a mystic; Hemingway's last book had had political affirmation in it, and Freud was only negative if you took him that way.

"It's all the same story," Skinner said. "It's which parts of them affect you. And as for the guys that grab religious straws, if you disqualified them just because they lose their energy and grow afraid, it wouldn't leave you many players. Hell, look at Twain on the Yes team. He died a bitter old man, but Huck Finn is what I judge him by."

"I look wrong in there," said Cindy. "I don't really think it's my league."

"You're a good symbol," Skinner told her. "You know, there are two sides to the Cinderella legend. Mostly we think of it from the girl's angle—Cinderella going up in the world. But the person who really gets the break in the story is the prince. He knows all kinds of girls, rich and poor, but he spends his time hunting around with a glass slipper in his hand, looking for the particular girl who will fit it; and he's lucky enough to find her."

"Sure," said Benny. "All Cinderella wanted was a prince, but the prince wanted the one, unique girl who would fit his glass slipper."

They abandoned the football game.

Cindy said, "Benny, I'm getting a lot more out of you than I've ever been able to get out of him. Can you tell me what makes him like he is?"

"Get him analyzed," said Benny.

"You mean terrible things happened in his childhood, and he's still reacting to them?" Cindy asked.

"That's only one way of answering," Benny said. "There probably are things in his unconscious mind that account for him, but it would take a trained analyst to ferret them out, and I'm not sure what they'd prove. I can tell you what the conscious motivation is, though."

"Look," said Skinner. "I can balance a knife on my nose." He attempted it and failed.

"He's trying to change the subject," Cindy said. "Tell me what's wrong with him."

"Well," said Benny, "Remember the phrase they used about the lost-generation group after the last war? Postwar neurotics?"

"Sure," said Cindy.

"He," said Benny, pointing at Skinner, "Is a pre-war neurotic. Same symptoms, world-weariness, enlarged death-wish, tendency towards self-pity. . . ."

"Exhibitionism," said Skinner, being a pre-war neurotic for them. "Look. I can put ink on my nose." He thrust a finger into the ink-bottle, brought it out, and touched it to his nose, leaving a big spot.

"You see," said Benny, continuing his explanation. "We've all been involved in this war unconsciously, ever since we were old enough to know what the word inevitable meant. It was so clear that it was coming. All of us are pre-war neurotics to some extent—Skinner almost a perfect one. The pressure was terrific, Cindy. Every time we read a book about the last war, we were fighting this one."

"I see," said Cindy, thoughtfully.

"Look," said Skinner. "Bullet holes in my forehead." He dotted his forehead with a series of ink-spots.

"A lot of the time," Benny went on. "We weren't conscious of what it was we were reacting against. And, since we all had individual conditioning factors in our backgrounds, we didn't all take the pressure the same way. But the pattern of reaction was taking chances, being amoral, doing anything for a laugh."

"Anything," said Skinner, looking around for something he could do for a laugh.

"Mostly," said Benny, "We've been after thrills and

chills. Tickle the nerve ends and to hell with the consequences."

"I know lots of guys like that," Cindy said.

"Look, friends," Skinner said, suddenly, in a very serious voice. They both turned to look at him. He stood up. He picked up the glass in front of him, with part of a drink left in it. "For once and for all," said Skinner, with great sincerity, "I am not a neurotic." And, with exquisite care, he emptied the contents of the glass over the top of his head.

It was completely effective. Benny's mouth dropped open, then he began to laugh. Cindy half-shrieked, half-whooped, sprang out of her chair, and threw her arms around him.

"You aren't neurotic either, are you, darling?" Skinner shouted, his hair matted with whisky, his face running with ink.

"No," she said. "It's my masculine protest." and she fastened her fingers around his neck and began to choke him. Skinner sank to his knees, and spread his arms.

"Crucified again," he moaned, and collapsed on the floor.

Benny grabbed the empty glass from the table, dropped to his knees beside Skinner, and began to hammer at Skinner's hand with it. "Racial guilt," he cried. "Again we kill Christ."

Cindy knelt at his feet and began to stroke them. "I'll wash them," she said, "Little Mary Magdalene will wash them."

"The thorns," Skinner insisted. "I will have my crown of thorns."

Cindy kicked off her shoes, and stepped onto Skinner's back. "I'm superior," she announced. "I'm queen of the Amazons."

"Enslave us, beat us," begged Benny, kneeling.

"I'm inferior," Skinner began to wriggle. "I'm low. Lower than a snake."

"He's a snake," screamed Cindy, running to hide behind the corner of the piano, "I hate snakes."

"There, there, mother," said Benny, running to her, and putting his arms around her. "I won't let him hurt you, mother. I love you too much."

"That's not mother," Skinner shouted, rising. "I killed mother. I killed her, I tell you." He picked up the piano stool. "Here's mother's piano stool," he said, caressing it. "Mother's beautiful piano stool. She used to sit on it." He sat on the floor, fondling the piano stool.

"Here's mother's metronome," Benny said, sweeping the metronome off the top of the piano. "I locked her heart in it." He started it ticking. "Listen," he said, reverently. "It's mother's heart beating."

"Here's father's face," said Cindy, grabbing a victrola record and covering it with frantic kisses. "I skinned it off and dried it."

A little red vase stood on a small table at one end of the piano. Skinner abandoned the stool, leapt to his feet, and snatched it up. "I told you never to have anything red in the house," he stormed at Cindy. "You know I can't stand red." He took a step towards the window, and hurled the vase out of it.

The record Cindy held had a red label on it. "Nothing red," she shrieked, and, running to the window, flipped the record out.

There was a red cushion on one of the day-beds. Benny dove for it, and held it up. "Nothing red?" he demanded.

"Nothing," said Skinner.

The cushion followed vase and record. A salt shaker with a red top, an ashtray, and a pair of Skinner's socks all sailed out the window.

Benny picked up the bourbon bottle dramatically. "I'm

jaded," he announced. "Think I'll try laudanum."

"Cocaine," said Skinner, picking up the fountain pen, aiming it at his forearm, and working the lever so that ink spurted over his wrist.

"Save some for me," pleaded Cindy, and holding out her arm, received a huge dose.

"Still jaded," Benny bemoaned, dropping listlessly into a chair with a great lolling of the head.

"Try a new sensation," cried Skinner, grabbing him by the shirt-front.

"Velocity," said Cindy, "that will do it."

Benny leapt out of his chair, and all three raced across the room.

They raced back. "My car will go faster than yours," Benny yelled.

"Collision," Skinner shouted, and crashed into them, spilling all three onto the floor.

Benny jumped to his feet at once. "More sensation," he cried. "I crave more."

"Try a parachute jump," Skinner said.

Benny crossed to the piano. "How high will this plane go?"

"Ten miles," said Cindy, getting to her feet.

"I'll do it," Benny said, climbing onto the stool, and hoisting himself from it to the top of the piano.

"Don't forget to count ten before you pull the ripcord," Skinner called.

"I'm in it for thrills," Benny answered, "I'm only going to count five."

"He'll be killed," Cindy wept. "I can't bear to watch," and she put her hands over her eyes, looking through the gaps between her fingers.

"One, two, three, four, five," said Benny, tugging at his necktie. "The ripcord's stuck. The 'chute won't open. But

I don't care." And he leapt from the piano to the floor, letting himself sprawl forward as he landed, and lying still.

"He's dead," said Skinner, "We'll burn the body." He lighted a piece of newspaper and danced around Benny. Cindy lighted another piece of paper and joined him.

"Fire," said Skinner. "I love fire," and he dashed to the window and dropped his torch out of it. Benny came to life, and all three scurried around the apartment, gathering up all the loose paper, lighting it, and letting it drift, flaming, out of the window.

Skinner crawled under the table. "The womb," he announced. "Back to the womb."

They joined him. All three curled up on the floor.

"Feel the warm womb juice," said Skinner.

"We'll stay here always," Cindy said.

"No," said Benny, struggling out from the womb. "We'll lose ourselves in the cult of athletics." He crouched in a runner's start.

"Clean-limbed youth," said Skinner, lining up beside him. "The thrill of physical endeavor."

"I'll cheer," said Cindy. "The vicarious thrill of being a spectator."

They ran the mile, the half-mile, the quarter-mile, and the twenty-ninth of a mile. They had the broad jump, the high jump, and, with Cindy as the shot, a sort of two-handed shot-put. Then, running low hurdles over overturned chairs, Benny barked his shin, sat down on the floor, looked up at them, and said, very matter-of-factly, "Ouch."

They rushed over to him, helped him to his feet, and took him over to the nearest of the day-beds. Benny shook them off. "It's okay", he said. He sank into the day-bed

Skinner and Cindy collapsed beside him, exhausted.

They quieted down. They considered the wreckage.

They rested. They decided to clean up and go out for dinner.

Early one afternoon, Skinner came into the apartment with his hands behind his back.

"What have you got, darling?" Cindy asked him.

"Just things for lunch."

"What kind of things, darling?"

"Oh, some crab-meat and stuff."

He walked over to the table, keeping his back turned from her so that she couldn't see what he had. Then he made her turn away while he spread the things out. When he let her look, there was food and two bottles of champagne.

Immediately she knew that this was to be their last lunch.

He came to her, and took her in his arms, and she buried her face in his shoulder, and said: "I'm not going to cry. The Shapes would never approve."

Later, he gave her a ring. A small diamond in a plain setting.

"I have traditional feelings, too," he said.

PART SIX

A Portrait of Jack on the Other Side of the Candlestick

CHAPTER

9

ROD'S mood became the central problem of life in Beirut.

Skinner, Freak, and Fred had felt him withdrawing, going steadily away from the closeness of their friendship. They couldn't figure it out. He was seldom in the shack which they all shared, even when off duty. He came in late to sleep; was silent and frowning at meals; refused their invitations to join them on trips to town.

It had started—or, at least first been noticeable—with the evening at Mama Frank's brothel, where Rod's extraordinary outburst against the women in his life had occurred. It was so uncharacteristic for Rod to go into a long speech about anything. Normally, he talked in short sentences and wisecracks, and you had to feel out the mood behind the meaning, for the mood itself was seldom expressed directly.

But there was no trick to feeling out Rod's mood these days. Everything he said was expressive of depression and irritability.

"He's fighting himself about something," Skinner said. "And he hasn't got anything left over to be pleasant with."

"I don't mind so much when he's griped," Freak said. "It's when he sounds so damn tired and discouraged that I get worried."

Then, as suddenly and unaccountably, Rod reversed himself, came joyfully into the shack one night with a set of Arab pipes, talked and laughed with them, and caught them all in a spiral of exhilaration which had Skinner breathless until its climax, two days later.

The Arab pipes were the beginning. Rod came into the shack waving them, and insisted that Skinner and Freak drop what they were doing and listen.

"It's on the willow whistle principal," he said, showing them how the mouthpiece was split and then tied. He blew into the pipes, producing a rather mournful note, ran his fingers over the stops to show them how the scale was played.

"It's a screwy scale," Rod said. "I think it's all whole tones, but I can't be sure." He played it again.

"I think it's quarter tones," Skinner groaned.

"I just think it's awful," Freak said.

Skinner agreed.

"Wait until I learn to play it." Rod went on experimenting.

Because they didn't want to dishearten him, Skinner and Freak stood it for almost half an hour. Then they looked at one another, and Skinner nodded.

Freak, who had been trying to write a letter, stood up. "Rod," he said, "we've been friends a long time."

"Right," said Skinner, also rising. "Thick and thin."

Rod stopped playing, and watched them warily from the chair in which he was sitting. Skinner was approaching on the right, Freak on the left.

"I'd cut off a hand for you," Freak said, lugubriously, coming a step closer.

"A leg." Skinner took a step.

"A nipple." Another step.

"A bollick." They were closing in.

"Stop, false friends," Rod cried. He jumped up and away from them, Freak made a dive for him and Rod dodged behind the table. "I'm going," he said, "and my pipes are going with me."

Rod went out, and they followed him to the door.

"Don't come back until you can play *Easter Bonnet,*" Freak called after him.

"In four part harmony," Skinner added.

They watched him go over to where his ambulance was parked, and get into the front seat, where he settled himself. The thin, eerie tone of the pipes could be heard, seeping through the thick glass window of the cab. Going back into the shack, they agreed that they were pleased. "Uncle Rodney's a new man," Freak said, hopefully.

At five the next morning, Skinner, Freak, and Fred, were awakened by a haggard but triumphant Rod, playing a minor version of *Easter Bonnet* on his Arab pipes, moving from bed to bed.

"Jesus," said Skinner. "Doomsday."

But Rod was too overjoyed to be dismayed by a sleepy reception. "Listen," he crowed, "I've got it. Mind-finger coordination, like a trumpeter. I can play anything."

"In a minor key," Fred observed, yawning and putting his pillow over his head.

"Sure," Rod said. "It transposes everything. Name a tune, any tune at all."

"I'll be Glad When You're Dead," Freak suggested. Rod played it.

Skinner, trying to think of a piece that Rod didn't like, asked for *South of the Border.* It came out sounding like Debussy.

Finally Skinner sat up in bed, looked at his watch, and said, "Rodney. It's five A. M."

"One more piece," Rod pleaded. "Just to prove I can do

it." And, without waiting for permission, launched into, *When Johnny Comes Marching Home.*

Then, smiling, he kicked his shoes off, and fell into his bed. He went immediately to sleep without bothering to get between the covers, and Skinner noticed, just before he went to sleep himself, that Rod was holding the pipes tight against his chest, clutching them as a scolded child clutches the doll which comforts him.

Rod woke up, hungry, at about two o'clock. Skinner was at the table, reading. He had bought a paper-bound, French edition of *Journey to the End of the Night* in town, and was trying to get through it, though he seemed to be spending more time with the dictionary than he was with the novel. Fred was on a run. Freak had gone up to the University to play tennis with a British sergeant whom he had met at the hospital.

Rod sat up, put the pipes to his lips, and played a weird version of *Old Black Joe.* Skinner, watching out of the corners of his eyes, registered a wince, and pretended that he was absorbed in the book. Rod played *Tuxedo Junction.* Skinner decided he was tired of the book anyway, and put it down.

"Good morning, soloist," he said.

Rod played *Reveille.*

Skinner said, "I had great difficulty in persuading Brother Lacey not to tear that thing out of your hands and destroy it while you slept."

"He'd have had to cut my hands off to get it."

"We thought about it, but couldn't find a knife."

"Let's go down-town," said Rod, swinging his legs off the bed; then, noticing that he had his clothes on, said, pleased, "Look. I'm dressed already."

Rod put on his shoes, they left the shack, and walked

down the hill. They stopped at a place at the edge of town, and ate eggs and chips. They took the streetcar.

"What do we do in town?" Skinner asked, as they rode.

"Music lesson," Rod said.

At the Midan, Rod got off the car, and Skinner followed him.

"Where are we going?" Skinner asked.

"See that yellow sign, that says 'Out of Bounds to Allied Troops'?"

"Yes."

"We can't go past it, can we?"

"Nope."

"The hell we can't," said Rod, happily.

The yellow sign marked the limit of the tough part of Beirut's native section: beyond it lived Beirut's poor. Most of them were Moslems, back in there, and in there were their stores, their restaurants, their coffee shops, and their homes. It was Hell's Kitchen, the Lower East Side, the heart of the city. There were stories of soldiers who had gone into the district and never come back: others of those who had crawled back, robbed and beaten; there was one gruesome yarn about a soldier who had followed a girl into the section late one night, and been found unconscious under the yellow sign the next morning, his testicles cut off and stuffed into his mouth and the lips stitched together.

They looked around to make sure there were no M.P.'s in the Midan, walked quickly past the yellow sign, and turned into the first alley they came to. They stopped and looked around. The transition was unbelievable.

"Two thousand years in two blocks," Skinner said.

They stood in a sunny little street, with white-washed walls on either side. Wooden doors in the walls would lead to dwellings. A few men, robed and wearing khefirs on their heads, squatted in the sun, talking among themselves, paying no attention to Rod and Skinner.

"I wonder where the women are?" Rod said.

"Inside, mending their veils," Skinner said.

They walked on.

"What are we looking for?" Skinner asked him.

"You'll see," Rod said.

It took them about ten minutes to find it.

They heard it first, rather than saw it: thin, tuneless music, played on pipes like Rod's, around the corner a block away. They stopped and listened, Rod frowning and concentrated, Skinner not understanding.

The music stopped. "That's it," said Rod, softly, and getting out his own instrument from his shirt front, he repeated the last three phrases they had heard.

The music began again, and they walked towards it, Rod humming with it, a note behind the pipes. "I get it," he said excited. "I get it."

"I don't," Skinner said.

"Look," Rod told him, stopping for a second to make the explanation. "An instrument is made to play its own kind of music. Music is made to fit instruments. There's only one kind of music you can really play with these, and that's it."

A singing voice joined the pipes:

"Ya salaam, ya salaam,
Salaam aleik."

It repeated the phrase over and over again, changing the emphasis, the tune, the accents—now dwelling on the a's for several notes, now cutting them short. It ended by running up and down a minor scale on the last word, then half-way up again and leaving it there, agonizingly unresolved to Skinner's ear.

"Marvelous," said Rod. He hurried Skinner along toward the music, as the pipes took up the tune again by themselves.

Skinner thought: It's all just as unfamiliar to him as it is to me, but he gets it already.

They came around the corner and saw the musicians. There were two of them, both old men, sitting on the curb. A little crowd stood around them, and there was some loose money in the skirts of the singer's robe. One or two of the group looked around at Skinner and Rod, and immediately turned their eyes back to the musicians; whether it was hostility or indifference was hard to tell.

They stood on the outer edge of the group until the instrumentalist had finished the thing he was playing. Then Rod took out his pipes, which he had held concealed, and carefully played the ending, note for note, just as the Syrian had. The old man looked up and smiled.

The Arabic-speaking people are warm people, with a long tradition of hospitality. They offer enmity where enmity is offered them; they respond to friendliness with friendliness; they are, except when angered, or when one tampers with their customs or ceremonies, humorous, humble, and wise. When the old musician smiled at Rod, the coldness of the group towards the Americans evaporated; there were smiles, there was laughter, and one, who could read Western characters, spelled out the magic word, "American", on Skinner's arm.

The Middle East had not yet had American troops in great numbers, and the illusion, born of the memory of Woodrow Wilson, the reputation of Franklin Roosevelt, and the nineteenth-century dream of America as the land of opportunity, still held. Rod and Skinner were made very welcome and, at the general insistence, Rod played again the phrases of music he had picked up.

They sat in the sun on the curb, one on each side of the musicians, and Rod was given a lesson.

Skinner, listening to him repeat phrases, memorize fingering, achieve effects, wondered what it was in Rod that made him so completely receptive, gave him his immediate grasp of all things musical. He thought of the tag-lines he had heard used about musicians: "a good ear", "knows his chords", "a lot of ideas". But it was more than these. What Rod had might have been learned, but it had been learned so thoroughly, was so much a part of him, that it seemed instinctive. It was as if there was no transition stage of changing music into explanation and back to music for him, rathei as if there existed a kinship, a simple flowing in and flowing out. He has great instrument sense, thought Skinner, listening to him try a difficult passage and make it; he feels what an instrument can do and gets a little more out of it. There's nothing he can't play, nothing he can't read, nothing he can't understand. And he's so spread out, all over music, that he could never be great unless he had the training to conduct or write. Oh, hell, said Skinner to himself, Rod is music; that's all.

Rod had progressed to the point where the old man would play a series of phrases, and Rod would repeat them, and they would go on to the next series without having to go over the first a second time. Sometimes there would be a correction in inflection or emphasis, and they would repeat the phrase in question in unison, until Rod had it right. The old man was delighted, and somewhat incredulous. He kept trying harder and harder stuff, as if he couldn't believe his ears; and Rod stayed with him.

Finally, the pipe-player held up his hand for Rod to be still. He played a short piece, all the way through. Rod nodded and started to play it. He got almost to the end, and got into difficulty. The old man played along with him and they finished together.

The crowd, standing around and watching, was delighted. Here was a soldier, an American, who seemed to love and understand their music. They applauded.

Rod smiled, and played the whole thing through alone. Skinner knew he wouldn't stop at the end. Years of improvising blues and jazz had taught Rod what came next. He had the structure, now; he understood the scale, the technique, the idiom, how the ideas ran. And he started to put Rod's stuff into it, Rod's understanding of this fine new music.

The greatest thing Skinner could say about it afterwards was that, to him, it sounded no different from what the Arabs had been playing when first they came along.

But the bystanders were excited. Several knelt to hear better. At least two ran to get friends from the nearby coffee-shop. The old pipe-player sat, smiling and nodding; there were, Skinner swore it, tears in his eyes.

But if Skinner didn't understand it perfectly, he could follow Rod's eyes, and was close enough to him to follow the thread of meaning. At first Rod played joyfully; then he changed tempo slightly, and the notes came out sad. He looked at the warm sun and played for it; he saw a dark-eyed little Arab child, and played for her, saw the sores on her bare feet, and played for them; he saw the ancient walls around him, walls that may have been standing when Christ was born and before, and they were in the music, too. And the Arabs, who stood and listened to him, smiled their approval.

After a while, Rod nodded to the singer, nodded to him as if he were another instrumentalist in a band, and the singer began to chant with Rod playing behind him. The words were those of another song, but they were made to fit the music. They were the same words Skinner had heard earlier:

"Ya salaam, ya salaam,
Salaam aleik."

(Oh blessed, oh blessed, blessed be you.)

Finally Rod nodded to the old man, and the pipe-player picked up where Rod left off, and played for twenty minutes.

When he finished, Rod patted his shoulder, and said, exultantly, to Skinner, "Did you hear that? He didn't repeat himself once." And the old man smiled at Rod, and Rod smiled at the old man.

"Salaam i-ehdik," said the old man.

And Rod, who couldn't have known what it meant but could sense that it was a high compliment, returned it to him: "Salaam i-ehdik." Later, they learned its meaning: Blessed be your hands.

The whole group moved, then, to the coffee shop, where they had thick, sweet, Turkish coffee, and Arak with ice, and slices of cucumber and tomato, and bread with Syrian spreads, to eat with the drinks. Several of the men could understand Skinner's French, and acted as interpreters, and they answered questions about America, questions about the army, exchanged political opinions, made jokes about the strength of Beirut's liquor and the passion of its girls. At sundown, the faithful were called to prayer, and Rod and Skinner sat alone in the shop, finishing their drinks quietly, while all went out, knelt in the street, and affirmed their belief that there is but one God, and he is Allah.

Skinner and Rod's friends returned, and they had more Arak, and different spreads for the bread. Without their realizing it, it grew dark outside.

"We've got to head up," said Skinner.

"Let's stay," Rod urged. "They all want us to dinner, and we could spend the night."

But Skinner had to be on duty that night, and Rod the next morning, and it seemed wisest to go. They were escorted out of the district by a cordial group of four or five, who left them at the yellow sign, begging them to return.

On their way out towards camp on the streetcar, Skinner said to Rod, "I've received a gift."

"No kidding? Let's see."

Skinner took a small, pasteboard box out of his pocket that he had gotten from a man in the cafe. He opened it and showed Rod the contents. It was filled with the greenish crumblings of small leaves.

Rod recognized them. "Maryjane."

"Not out here," said Skinner, closing the box and putting it back in his pocket. "Out here they call it hashish."

Rod whooped. "We'll get high," he shouted. "We'll fly like kites."

"Not tonight," Skinner told him. "Fred and I are on tonight. Tomorrow, when Heinz and Billy are on."

"Right," said Rod. "Tomorrow night."

As soon as they got back to the post and into the shack, Rod began to undress.

"Going to bed already?" Skinner asked him.

"You're damn right. First time I've felt like sleeping in weeks."

"Something's been bothering you," Skinner said. "You've been a pretty morose boy. But you seem better, now."

"I am better," Rod said.

"What's been wrong?"

"It's all over now. Forget it." He patted the pipes, lying

by him on the bed. "These brought me luck. It's all over now."

Skinner was unconvinced. Rod's depression had not seemed to be the simple, periodic blues business. But he said nothing.

By the next night, Rod had lost none of the elation of the afternoon with the Arabs, and it carried over into the hashish party.

They were gathered in the shack: Skinner, Freak, and Fred, who were novices. And Rod who had tried marijuana often before, as he had tried everything.

They spread a dozen cigarettes on the table, and Rod showed them how to work the tobacco out the ends, and substitute the green leaf for it. They all lighted up, and Rod showed them the Indian trick of cupping the hands over the burning end of the cigarette so that none of the smoke escapes, and it can be inhaled through a crack between the thumbs without touching the lips to the end of the cigarette.

"Makes it last longer," Rod explained. Then he established the ground rules. "If you sit around trying to analyze whether it's getting you or not, you won't get any kick out of it," he said. "Just forget what you're smoking. And, for God's sake, talk about pleasant things. If you're morbid when you begin to get high, you'll end up under the bed, thinking you've found your coffin."

"Hey," said Freak. "I know something pretty pleasant. I haven't had a chance to tell you." He had been away all day.

"Give," said Skinner.

"Blondie took a customer home last night." Blondie was the dance-hall proprietress, with whom Freak had danced.

"You're kidding."

"Nope."

"How'd it happen?"

"Well, you know, Toler and I played tennis yesterday."

"Yeah."

"Well, afterwards, we had a swim, and then some drinks and some dinner. He's a nice guy."

"Go on," said Rod. "How'd you happen to go to Blondie's?"

"Well, Toler's worried about his girl. He got a letter from her saying that some G.I. in England was teaching her to jitterburg. He didn't know what it meant, and he thought it was some form of necking. I told him it was a way of dancing, and he still didn't get it, so I said, 'Come on down town, and I'll show you'. So I took him to Blondie's."

"Then what?"

"I didn't have to show him," Freak said. "There was this big colored guy there, see, in British uniform. Blondie asked me if he was American, and could he dance like the Ethiopians in the cinema. I said I thought he was British, but she made me go over and ask him."

"So he came from Harlem?" Rod asked.

"Detroit. His name was Johnny Loyola, and he'd been born in Jamaica. He'd been back visiting the home folks when war broke out, and the British draft got him."

"Could he dance like the Ethiopians in the cinema?" Skinner asked.

"Could he dance? Listen. He was raised on Spanish stuff, rhumbas and tangos. And he learned lindy and shag in Detroit. He could even do some tap. Gee, he was good. Remember telling us Blondie was tireless?"

"Sure."

"He danced her right off her feet."

Skinner whistled. "That takes dancing."

"We went in there at nine," Freak said. "They danced without resting until after eleven. Just cleared everyone else off the floor, and danced themselves silly."

"And Blondie gave out?"

"Yeah. It got to be a contest. She was wonderful, though. After they'd been going an hour and a half, you could see that she was getting tired. The band was trying to play slow stuff to give her a rest, but she wouldn't let them. Finally she had to give up; she threw her arms around him, smiling, and hung onto his neck, and he carried her over and sat her on top of a table. She said, 'Bravo, cherie,' and pinched his cheeks, and all the customers clapped—and you know what the damn fool guy did?"

"What?"

"Took a bow, signalled to the band for more music, and cut loose in a wild tap routine that went for five minutes. It was wonderful. Blondie closed the place up and took him home."

"That's marvelous," Rod said. "Boy, I like that."

Freak, who came from the South, added, with a certain amount of self-wonder in his voice. "You know, in spite of all the kidding you guys have handed me about it, I never thought I'd enjoy seeing a colored guy and a white woman together. But I swear, I'd have been disappointed if she hadn't taken him with her."

They finished their first reefers and made enough for three more each.

Skinner told them about Rod and the Arabs, and Rod played the pipes a little for them.

They lit a third round, and Fred told them he'd been reading Heinz' new book. "It's awful," Fred said, "but it's okay, because he knows it."

At eleven o'clock, the symphony began.

It started with Skinner's saying: "Listen. All over the world. You can hear little pops." It was a still night. They all listened to the little pops.

"What are they?" Freak asked.

"People's pet theories being exploded," Skinner said.

"Pop," said Freak, softly and solemnly. "Pop. Pop."

"And," said Rod. "All over the world, ten or twelve times a minute, hearts breaking. They don't make a loud crack, because they're soft, soft. They go rish, rish, rish. Ten or twelve times a minute, all over the world."

"Orgasms," said Fred, getting into it. "Every time you snap your fingers, some guy, somewhere in the world has an orgasm. And some poor woman, lying with him, almost does but just misses." He snapped his fingers on the off-beat of Freak's rish-pop; first he would snap them loudly for the man, then softly, not quite making a snap, for the woman.

"Souls," said Skinner. "Newly departed souls, moaning, lonely in their new dwelling place." He began to moan musically, letting his voice roll up and down.

"Death rattles," Rod cried. "Death rattles to remind the souls what they have just been through." And he handed Skinner a mess gear that was lying on the table with a fork and spoon in it, which Skinner clanked softly, in rhythm.

"Latin phrases," Fred said. "All the phrases of the Roman law and the Roman church." And he began to chant Latin phrases, in counterpoint to Skinner's moaning.

"Lonely men whistling in dark, city streets," Rod said, getting up; and he began to whistle, sweetly and melodically, fitting it in with the beat, the moaning, and the chanting. He began to lead them with his hands, bringing the beat up, swelling the moan and fading it, quieting the chant and letting it come out.

None of them could have said how long the symphony

lasted. It was timeless, it was eternal, it ended in sleep.

At one point, Skinner vaguely saw Billy, the little fairy, stick his head in at the door, his face expressive of mingled curiosity and alarm. He watched them and listened for a moment. Then, apparently unsure how to take it, he asked, "What is this?"

In all probability Skinner, whose chair was nearest the door, was the only one to see or hear him, and, changing his moan to speech, he intoned, in preaching cadence, "Life is a symphony, life is a symphony, life is a symphony, squeaked out by rats. Rats we are and to ratform returning, ratforms on the platform of the self-deluding world." Billy, looking a little frightened, withdrew his head and closed the door, and Skinner, immediately forgetting that he had been there, continued his sermon. "Here we are, ratforms on the platform, trapped by our own conception of great, monitory cats; catforms on the platform, and we call them gods. Here we are, trapped in our own conception, trapped in our own pretense: that claims our music bravest, that claims our music finest, when we're squeaking our defiance, defiance by the ratforms of the catforms on the platform of the self-deluding multiform, the self-deluding world.

"What pain, then, and how bitter; what hollow, mordaunt dances, what grim destructive hornpipes, what macabre Arabesques. When we know our final folly, we find our final answer, we know, know, know, for certain that the cats do not exist. That is the great fear, that is the arch fear, that is the mad fear, that there is no fear."

Watching Rod's hands, he changed tempo slightly. "That nothing to fear exists, that nothing to fear exists. . . ."

CHAPTER

10

BUT from then on, Rod got worse.

Following the exhilaration of the hashish party, and the let-down that inevitably followed it, he swung back to the jumpiness and preoccupation that they had worried about since the first week in Beirut.

Freak and Skinner, Freak sprawled on his bed, Skinner tilting back in a straight chair with his feet on the table, talked it over.

"He got sore at Fred yesterday," Freak said.

"What about?"

"Fred was trying to kid him into cleaning up his car, and Rod blew his top. Then I said I'd help him clean it, and he hopped me and went off somewhere."

"Probably down to the Arab quarter," Skinner said. "He's okay when he goes down there."

"Playing the pipes?"

"Yeah. And drinking with the Arabs. You can tell when he's been there, because he's relatively cheerful when he gets back."

"You should be able to find out what's wrong," Freak said.

"He won't tell me. I've asked him point-blank a couple of times, and he either tells me it's nothing, or says to leave him alone."

They went over the possible reasons again, and again got nowhere. It wasn't because Rod never got mail from home; there was no one at home Rod gave a damn about. It wasn't anything to do with the war, as far as they could tell, because they were still too far away from it. The work was easy, the possibilities for recreation endless. Rod was with his friends when he wanted to be, the weather was good, the food passable, and he'd found a new kind of music to keep him interested. They came back again, as they always did, to Rod's speech in the brothel. The key to it was there, if they could only apply it.

"I just can't figure it," said Skinner.

"Yeah," said Freak.

They went over the whole thing again. They got nowhere.

Then they talked about Benny; Benny was in Raqqa; Benny was a little bored, he said, but he wasn't letting it get him.

There had been landings in Sicily. They talked about them. It was another week before Skinner found out what was wrong with Rod.

There came a hot, damp morning; the sun was offensively bright, and the sky intolerably blue. Of the seven on the post, five had gone to swim. Freak and Fred Birch had thought about it first, and had gone to ask Heinz if they could drive down in one of the ambulances. Heinz had told them to go ahead; unless an emergency came up, there was nothing for them to do; and, thinking of that, Heinz had decided to go with them. Billy, the little fairy, coming into the office and overhearing the plans, had asked if he might go, too, and, being told that it was okay, had run to get his partner, Tommy. Skinner, who had a tire to fix, offered to stay and do that, and to call the hotel at whose beach they swam if he had to leave. Nobody was quite sure where Rod was, though he had been seen on the post within the last few minutes.

Two ambulances had pulled out for the beach, and Skinner stripped down to a pair of khaki shorts and sneakers. With much sweating, he got the tire off the rim, patched the tube, and reassembled the wheel.

He went to the washhouse, and scrubbed the grease off his hands and forearms, took off his clothes and threw cold water over himself. He dried, put the shorts and sneakers back on, and started for the shack to get a shirt. The door was closed. He had left it open. Someone's there, he thought. Oh yeah, Rod.

It was Rod, all right. Rod, surrounded by his clothes, his equipment, the whole contents of a duffel bag and a musette bag strewn and stacked around him on the floor. Rod, frowning as he rolled a pair of socks and threw them into a light, denim laundry bag.

"Getting your laundry out?" Skinner asked him, coming into the room.

Rod picked up another pair of socks, rolled them, and threw them into the bag before he answered. Then he simply said, "Hi, Skinner."

"What's going on?"

"Tell me where everybody is," Rod asked.

"They've all gone swimming."

"When are they coming back?"

"Not until after lunch."

Rod nodded. "Good," he said. "I won't have to wait until tonight." He turned, sat on the bed, facing Skinner. His voice, very tired, said, "Ever hear that Teagarden record called *Jack Hits the Road?*"

"Yeah. Sure."

Rod let his body sag forward, and looked down at his feet. "Play it over for me, boy."

"You're leaving?"

"Big Rod is on his way."

"For good, huh?"

"I guess so."

"Need anything?"

"No."

There was a pause. Christ, Skinner thought, what can I say? Then he thought, If he wants to tell me, he'll tell me, and maybe I can talk to him. So he said, "How about dough?"

"I'll make out."

Skinner got out his wallet. "Better take this," he said, holding out four twenty-pound notes. It amounted to about forty dollars, and was all he had in cash.

Rod said, "Thanks. But you wouldn't get it back."

"What the hell," said Skinner. "If I needed it, I wouldn't offer it to you."

Rod shrugged, looked at him, smiled briefly, and took the money. "Thanks, Skinner, I can use it." He folded the bills and stuffed them into his pocket. "I was going to get ready now, and then go tonight. But I guess it's better to take off right now, while no one's around."

"Yeah."

"I was going to tell you before I went. You and Freak can split this crap up." He pointed with his foot to the uniforms on the floor. "Take what you want."

"Thanks."

"I don't figure on needing any clothes. I've got some Arab stuff in the bag. The socks and underwear are all colored, and I've torn the labels off. And I'm taking a few things to sell."

"How about your watch?" Skinner noticed he wasn't wearing it.

"Sold it last week. I had to get all the money I could to

buy papers. I don't want to sell my passport, yet. If I get right up against it, the guys that fixed the papers up will give me twelve hundred for it. But I don't think I'll get up against it."

"What are you going to do?"

"I won't tell you exactly—so that when they ask you, you won't know. But I'll hang around Beirut for a while, maybe a day or so. Then a friend of mine is going to take me over the mountain to his home town. It's just a little burg."

"Arab friend?"

"Yeah."

"Then what?"

"I'll stick there. Maybe work his orchard with him. Play a little music. Learn some language."

"Yeah? Is that the way it ends?"

"After I figure they aren't looking for me very hard, I might come back here. Or go to Damascus, or Aleppo. I don't know. I'm dark. I'll pass for Syrian."

"You're not very worried about it."

"No."

"What about the rap if they catch up with you?"

"They won't. Whenever anyone is looking for me, I'll know it. These people like me. If they're coming too close, my friends will hear it, and I'll be warned. So—I'll burn my passport, go into a consulate, tell them that it was stolen and that I've been held all this time. There isn't a way in the world they can prove I'm lying."

"I hope you're right."

"See, I've got a perfect way of demonstrating good faith. I tell them I want to join the army."

"Maybe so, Rod," Skinner said. "Want a smoke?" They lit cigarettes. "You may have a tough time getting back to the States after the war."

"I'm a civilian," Rod said. "I've taken no oath. The worst thing they can get me on is draft evasion. And anyway, who's going back to the States?"

"You don't want to?"

"I just don't give damn. America means about as much to me as the snot in my nose."

"You can live better, there."

"You mean you can get something called Coca-Cola for a nickel a glass?"

"Okay."

"All I've ever wanted was to be left alone," Rod said.

"You've been pretty independent."

"Sure," said Rod. "Independent of other people, maybe. But never independent of my stomach. Or my goddamn mind. Never able to take a minute and just live through it, for its own sake, the way these Arabs can."

"Yeah." There was a pause.

"No," Rod said, "that isn't why I'm leaving. That isn't it at all."

"Going to tell me?"

"Sure," Rod said, in a voice harsh with self-loathing, "I'm amazed you haven't noticed. I'm in love."

"What?"

"Beautiful thing, love. Makes the God damn world go round and round and round. Ever hear of it?"

"Talk sense," Skinner said.

"I'm in love," Rod repeated, bitterly.

"Some broad in the States?"

"No. A beautiful little someone right here. A little blond someone," his voice grew even more bitter, "a lovely, blue-eyed creature, with crispy golden curls, and a nice little pink set of male genitals."

"Jesus," said Skinner. "You and Billy?"

Rod stood up, walked over to the laundry bag, and

kicked it across the room. "That's right," he said. "Me and Billy. Just Billy and me, and Tommy makes three. Billy the beautiful fairy. Billy kissed me, when we met . . ."

"Wait a minute," Skinner said. "You've been fooling around with this kid to see what it was like. Isn't that it?"

"Oh, no," said Rod, sitting down again on the bed. "No. The fooling around to see what it was like started a long time ago. Once upon a time, Rod Manjac was not a punk. He was just a guy who liked punks now and then, for something different. It was just that every now and then, some guy would say to Rod, 'Come on. Let's go down to Weary's and get a couple of punks, for the laughs'. And Rod, being a good fellow, would say, 'Sure. For the laughs'."

Skinner could think of nothing to say.

The bitterness went out of Rod's voice. Now he only sounded tired. "You know how it is," he said. "You're fooling around. You're playing jobs. You try all sorts of things. Every now and then, maybe, you try spending an evening with a punk, just for the hell of it, but it's all right, because you're under control. You aren't doing it because you have to; you're doing it because you want to."

"And it's not that way with Billy?"

"No. Oh, Christ, no, Skinner. I'd have to go way back to tell you."

"Okay," said Skinner. "Let's go way back."

"You know how it was when I was a kid?"

"You've never talked about it much."

"The old man was a liquor-head. He wasn't a pimp, but when he needed liquor, he'd just as soon make money pimping as any other way. Know how I learned to play piano?"

"No."

"Hanging around a joint called Katz's Grill, every afternoon after school, waiting for the old man to hit it on his rounds. He never missed it, because the girls used to hang there, and he'd give them tips on what kind of money was around at the other bars, and they'd give him dough. A whore named Elsa taught me to play scales."

"Yeah?"

"They thought I was cute. They used to fool with me, comb my hair, mother me. One of them used to take me into the lady's room and lock the door. They stank of liquor and sex."

"Yeah," Skinner said. "I guess they did."

"Listen," said Rod. "That's what got me. The stink. It still gets me. I can't stand the way a woman stinks."

Neither of them spoke for a moment. Then Rod went on, speaking quietly now. "Listen, Skinner. I don't think I'm a punk. I think it's just that I've known so many women they make me sick. Maybe it's the same thing. Maybe a guy that doesn't want women is a punk. But I never felt like one before. Before, I could take a fag for an evening, or leave him alone. Or take a woman, and have just as good a time. Or say to hell with sex, and get high, and play music, which was best. But more and more, the last couple of years, I've gotten so that women kind of revolt me. I've told you before. There were plenty of times, when things were tough, when I've had to live on some woman, and that means sex whenever she feels like it, whether you're tired or not. And pretending you like it." He shook his head. "But I never thought all that was turning me into a punk."

"You mean it's really different with this kid?" Skinner asked.

"Oh, Christ, yes. Different as all hell. Listen, Skinner, this kid is like a girl in a book. Like a clever little flirt. He knows all a young girl's tricks for playing you, and he uses them better than any girl I ever saw. He flirts, he makes you jealous, he's affectionate. And he gets a hold on you. I don't know how. As soon as I get away from him, I see what a moron I'm letting him make of me, but I always go back, figuring this is going to be the last time; I'll show him who's boss, and then I'll be through with it. But I can't fight him, Skinner. He plays me against Tommy, and Tommy against me. I get disgusted with myself, and go down, and drink with the Arabs, and figure I'm all over it. Then I come back, and he's after me again, or I'm after him, and it's like being a kid in high school."

"It sounds pretty bad," said Skinner, helplessly, feeling a little sick.

"I'm probably going batty," Rod said. "I'm probably losing my God damned mind. No girl ever affected me the way he does. Why not?"

"I don't know," Skinner said. "I've read case histories of girls who get disgusted with the brutality of men when they're young, and turn Lesbian. I've never heard of it being reversed."

"You think this is the same thing reversed, huh?" asked Rod, frowning.

Skinner decided to evade. "Look, Rod. Why do you have to take off to get away from it? Why don't you just ask for a transfer, go to another post? Here's one little bitch of a guy, who's playing on a weakness he's found in you. You can't help the weakness, but you figure it's controllable if you get away from the guy. So why not take a transfer and keep it legal?"

"No," said Rod. "This outfit's full of fairies. And this things been following me for a long time. I've been afraid of it, and I've fought it, and I've lost. I'd be a pushover for any fairy, anyplace. They'd sense it in me in five minutes. This kid knew he could get me right away."

"What about out here?" Skinner asked. "What about Arab fairies?"

"The language part will keep them from knowing," said Rod. "Doing clean work will help. And there's you and Freak and Benny, you know. You guys are the best thing that ever happened to me." His voice grew bitter. "How would you like to have a nice fairy for a friend?"

"Christ," said Skinner. "You know it doesn't make a damn to us."

"Sure it does," said Rod. "Who are you trying to kid?"

Skinner thought for a moment, and sighed. "Yeah," he admitted. "I guess it does."

Rod got up, crossed the room, and got the laundry bag. "Thanks for the dough," he said. "If you come out this way for your honeymoon, I'll be the little Arab with ulcerated hands, begging on the corner."

Skinner stood up. "No other way?"

Rod shook his head and walked to the door. "Give me a day to lose myself, and then tell Heinz, so he won't get into trouble for not reporting me. And Skinner?"

"Yeah?"

"It's stupid of me to give a damn, but I'd rather you wouldn't tell the Freak why. Let him think I'm being sort of wild and adventurous. Tell Benny, if you want. And Fred."

"Okay," said Skinner. "If it gets too tight, get a message to us. We'll do what we can."

"Thanks," said Rod. He hesitated again, shifted the bag to his other shoulder, and smiled crookedly. "Take care," he said, and walked out, closing the door.

Skinner waited a day, as Rod had asked. Heinz had been very good about not reporting them AWOL when one evening in town stretched into a two day drunk, and everyone on the post made a practice of covering everyone else when such things happened. So, to keep Heinz from having to cover Rod any longer than necessary, Skinner went to him on the second day, and told him that Rod had taken off for good. He said that Rod had told him goodbye, that he had tried to dissuade him and been unable.

The members of the post took it in various ways. Heinz shrugged and filled in a report that Rod Manjac was absent without leave. He and Skinner had agreed that it was best not to say that anyone knew of a definite intention to desert.

Freak was saddened at first, but, since loyalty was the first item of Freak's code, he persuaded himself that what Rod had done was admirable, even heroic.

Fred, to whom Skinner told the whole story, thought for a little while, and finally said: "If it were anyone but Rod, I'd say he was a damn fool. Rod might just be able to get away with it."

Billy, who could probably guess the reason, seemed rather pleased; his vanity was probably gratified. And Tommy, who was much the more likable of the two, seemed, at the same time, glad to have Billy to himself again, and sorry that the solution had been so drastic.

Within a week, another driver had been sent to take Rod's place, and no one except Skinner even spoke of Rod very often, though Freak liked, occasionally, to speculate on the adventures he might be having.

Skinner became thoroughly depressed. The trouble, he thought, was the old business, of having no one to blame. You might want to kick the smug little smile of Billy's face, but that was emotionalism; you could hardly blame Billy for being true to his distorted nature. You could blame Rod, for being weak, or perhaps his father for being weak before him, if you wanted to, but it proved nothing.

So what were you going to blame? Society for being anti-social? Humanity for being anti-human? You can never blame. You can only mourn.

They neither saw nor heard from Rod again.

Skinner became so melancholy that Freak grew alarmed.

"Hey," Freak would say. "Smile. Laugh. I'm afraid you'll take off on me like Rod did."

"I haven't got the guts," Skinner would answer.

Fred, too, tried to bring him out of it: "Rod did what he had to do and wanted to do. He was a good guy who got screwed up, and was lucky enough to find a way out. You should be glad we didn't find him on the end of a rope."

Skinner's reply was, "Hell, Fred. It's not just Rod."

There was an investigation. There was questioning. Descriptions were sought and obtained. The authorities decided there were indications of possible kidnapping and murder, and Rod's name was added to a long and very secret list of disappearances which could not be definitely accounted for.

The CID sergeant who was left in charge of the case rather leaned towards the desertion theory.

"Nine-tenths of these things are desertions," he told Skinner. "But they hate to think that there are that many blokes fed up with their bloody army, so they like to pretend that the Arabs have done away with them. I wish I had a quid for every Kiwi who's living down in the Wog El Burka in Cairo."

"How do they get along?" Skinner asked.

"Find a bloody bint and move in with her. That makes 'em one of the family, so the wogs'll do everything to protect 'em. They move around after dark; sometimes their army mates bring 'em stuff to flog."

"I see," said Skinner.

The sergeant explained that he was breaking up the post. "Here's the way it is," he said. "It'd make it a lot easier for him and harder for us if he's got mates to bring 'im cigarettes and goods to sell, won't it?"

Skinner said he supposed it would.

"Well," said the sergeant, who was both smart and thorough, "the way I see it, you and this chap Lacey were his closest chums, so I'm recommending that you get posted. And this Fred Birch, now, you're pretty thick with him, so I'm asking them to post him along, too. It seems a shame to break you up like this, but it's the best way. If we don't get him in a week or so after you've gone, it'll mean he's gotten away for fair, because it'll mean he's got some Arab chums to help him out, see what I mean?"

"Sure," said Skinner, glad he would be sent away. "Any idea where we'll go?"

"That's up to your headquarters," the sergeant said. "And now, let me give you a tip to carry off with you."

"What's that?"

"Well, I won't say anything about it, it's none of my bloody business what you know, as long as you don't tell it, but I'm dead sure now the bloke deserted."

"Are you?"

"You needn't worry. It won't be in my report that you know. But if anyone questions you again, you be a little more worried about the foul play business, see. Ask him how much of it there is, and all like that. From your not asking me, see, I know you aren't worried your chum's been done in. So you must know he's all right. You probably know he's got friends, too, and that they're taking care of him. You could probably give me a pretty good guess at who they are, and how I could track 'em." He sighed, then smiled. "But you won't tell me, and I don't expect you to." He got up to go. "Cheerio."

Skinner got up. The questioning had gone on in the office-shack. "So long," he said, and shook the sergeant's hand. "I wish you all kinds of bad luck on the case."

"I'll have it," said the sergeant. "Never fear."

The transfers came through three days later, accompanied by replacements for the three who were leaving. Two of them were to be sent to Aleppo, which would be fairly good. The third would go to a one-man post at a pioneer camp in the valley.

"Which will be pretty grim," Fred said.

Skinner, Fred, and Freak had been called into the office, and Heinz explained that he had orders for transfers, but that he would leave it up to them to decide who went where.

"I've got some dice," he said. "Want to roll high-man for it?"

"No," said Skinner. "I'll take the one-man deal."

They looked at him in some surprise. "Why so noble?" Fred asked.

"It's not nobility," Skinner said. "It's just that I'd like to be alone for a while."

"Know what a pioneer camp is?"

"No."

"It'll be a bunch of black boys from Africa, recruited out of the bush to work on roads. And about four white officers, and half-a-dozen white non-coms to run 'em around. You'll get mad the day you get there, and you won't cool off 'til you leave."

"Good," said Skinner. "I'm mad anyway. It'll give me something to take it out on." But he had been closer to the truth the first time. He wanted very badly to be alone.

CHAPTER

11

SUPPOSE you are outside in the dark. You push a button. A beam of light cuts through the night, speeds through the blackness at 186,000 miles per second. For that is the speed of light.

But surrounding your beam of light all the time is darkness, waiting to rush back in when you push the button again. And the speed of darkness? 186,000 miles per second.

Perhaps you do not push the button again. Then the power grows quite gradually lower, and the darkness creeps back slowly. Until, suddenly, the power fails completely, and the darkness can come slashing back again at the height of its incredible speed.

The new post was in a town called Drun, not far from the ancient temple-town of Baalbeck. It consisted of two dozen rows of ugly Nissen huts, squatting on the flat ground of the valley floor, by the side of a black macadam road.

The pioneer regiment which occupied it was made up mostly of men from Bechuanaland, the interior of South Africa. They were big, strong, slow men, who loved to drill because it was something you did in strict time. To reward squads for excellence in work or military details, the whites who ran the camp would give them extra drill periods, and the competition between squads for the privilege was keen. After a day's work on the roads in the surrounding valley, the Bechuanas would stand or sit around outside their huts, playing rhythm games, which took the place of books and radios.

The rhythm games were a sort of sublimated pease-porridge hot, not really dancing, as one might have thought at first, since there was little change of place in them. Two Bechuanamen would stand, facing one another, about twelve feet apart. Stand, loose and still, watching one another. Then one would raise his hand and forearm in a pushing motion towards the other, and bring it back slowly to his side. The other would repeat the pushing motion. The two would stand that way, pushing back and forth, first in simple patterns, gradually in more complex ones: one pushing very slowly, say, the other tripling the time, or each pushing fast with one hand and slow with the other. Their bodies would get into it, and they would shuffle their feet, and they seemed happy, just doing that. Sometimes the game would involve four, or even six. Often, there would be four or five groups in the same area, each in a different pattern of movement, oblivious of the other groups. And if there was music being played on native instruments indoors, the conflicting tempo of it didn't seem to bother the men outside.

Sometimes, when they were sad, they would sing, chanting words, shouting and sighing in unison. Once, on a Sunday afternoon, Skinner saw one of them at the Y. M. C. A. piano in Drun, playing two of the bass notes over and over again, with varying shades of emphasis, until somebody asked him to stop.

The whites in camp were completely aloof. They understood none of the language that the Bechuanas spoke, and didn't want to. They were malcontent, mostly, having hoped for assignments to more elaborate posts, and took out their dislike of the place wherein they found themselves on the men whom they worked. Each of them, even the two corporals, had a native batman to clean quarters and run errands.

Skinner, who had been assigned to a Nissen hut with three sergeants and the two corporals, found that he had nothing to say to them, and took to sleeping in his ambulance after the first day, to avoid having to have a batman himself. He got his food in a mess tin and took it to the car to eat. He seldom saw or spoke to any of the others, except when they lined up for meals, and in the mornings when he saw them in the course of his work. In the afternoon, it was too hot to do very much, so he slept.

For the first few days, Skinner loved all the Bechuanamen, and, after that, he loved them all except one. The one he hated was the black sergeant-major, and the disgust was an outgrowth of a conversation he had one day with the Tommy who was Company Clerk.

"How do they get these guys into the army?" Skinner asked.

"Well," said the clerk, glad of a chance to take a rest from the eternal filling in of forms, "they're fighting men, do you see? And that's how it's done. They tell 'em they're to fight."

"And then make them work?"

"Right."

"But," Skinner said, "I should think after they'd tricked a few hundred that way, the rest, back in Africa, would get wise and not join up."

"Oh, well, mate," said the Tommy, who was a strong labor man. "It's this blasted Empire business. You know how they run those things. The sergeant-major bloke, back in Africa he's the chief's son. So they arrange it with the old chief. They'll make his boy sergeant-major, and give him a smashing good uniform and what-not, and they'll also make him recruiting officer. Then, for every recruit he makes, they'll give him a hundred pounds, see?"

"Yeah."

"Well, then the old chief orders his men to sign up, and, if they won't, he takes all their cattle, and punishes their families and all."

"Jesus," Skinner said.

"Then, if the man gives us trouble because he's got to work instead of fight, we get word to the old chief who he is, and it's goodbye cattle and family again."

So, after that, Skinner loved all the Bechuanas except the sergeant-major; and they liked him because he would try to talk with them, and listen when they sang.

Every morning there was a sick-parade. The men who felt badly, or who needed cuts or burns dressed, would line up outside the Medical Inspection Room, and come in, one by one. The Medical Officer sat at a desk, just inside the door, and, as a man came in, he would ask what the trouble was, getting his answer in signs, grunts, and the few English words most of them knew. He would look, if there were anything to see, or interpret as best he could if the source of trouble was not obvious, and send the man in to the orderly carrying a slip of paper on which the doctor had scrawled directions for treatment and dressing. If, as rarely happened, there was a man who seemed to need hospitalization, the orderly would call Skinner, and they would get the man into the ambulance. Then Skinner would drive to the Nissen Hut in which the man lived, the man would go inside and get his helmet and small kit, and they would drive the twenty miles to the Casualty Clearing Station at Zahle.

One morning, while the line was shuffling through, two

Bechuanamen came in, carrying a third. The one they carried was almost out. He had a couple of cuts on his head, one just above the right eye and clotted on the lid.

The men waiting in line drew back, and the three got in to where the doctor's desk was.

"He looks about done", the doctor said. "We'd better have a stretcher for him."

Skinner and the orderly got a stretcher and helped the man onto it.

The doctor came from behind his desk and knelt by the stretcher. "Clean all this away," he said, pointing to the blood, "and put a sulfa dressing on it."

"Yes, sir," the orderly said.

The doctor looked up. "You two clear out," he said, waving his hand at the men who had brought the patient in. They turned to go, and Skinner walked outside the door with them.

"How?" He asked, pointing back inside.

"Sergeant," said one, making a hitting motion with his fist.

"Bechuanaman sergeant?"

"Bechuanaman sergeant, big white sergeant, fat white sergeant. All." Again he made the hitting motion. For purpose of demonstration, the other man became the victim, illustrating how his friend had tried to protect himself by covering his face, without trying to fight back, while the man who had spoken impersonated the three sergeants, holding and hitting him.

"Why? Why sergeants hit? What friend do?"

The man who was doing the talking took breath for a long speech. "We work. There." He pointed to where they were digging a pit on the far side of camp. "Too much hot." He pointed to the sun and wiped his forehead, letting himself slump. "Fall down. Rest." He staggered, then he straightened up and assumed a fierce expression. "Fat white sergeant say, 'sonmbitch, got work.' Black sergeant say, 'sonmbitch.' " He slumped again, spread his hands. "No can work." He straightened up. "All sergeant. . . ." and again he demonstrated the hitting.

Skinner touched the man's arm. "Not good," he said. "Very bad." Then he turned and went back inside the M.I. Room.

The orderly had finished with the dressing.

"He's been beaten up," said Skinner.

The Medical Officer, who had been checking the man's pulse stood up. "I know," he said, regretfully. "It happens now and then. Only sort of treatment they understand, really. Look here, you'd better take him along to the CCS. He'll need some rest."

"I'll get someone to give me a hand with the stretcher," Skinner said.

"That won't be necessary. He's conscious. He can walk by himself." And the doctor sat down again at his desk, and beckoned to the next patient to step forward.

The orderly was helping the man to his feet, and Skinner moved to the other side so that he could help support him.

Between them, they got him to the car, and into the front seat. "Where house?" Skinner asked.

"Nineteen," the man mumbled. They were drilled to know the numbers of their houses.

Skinner drove to Hut Nineteen, and stopped the car. The working party from which the man had come was in sight, just beyond it. Skinner got out, went around the front of the car, and opened the right hand door. He motioned to the patient to get out, offering his hand to help steady him. "Find kit," he explained.

"No. No. No work," said the man, seeing that he had

apparently been brought back to the place where the trouble started.

Skinner pointed to the hut. "Kit. Kit for hospital."

The man got out, shaking his head dubiously. They walked to the house together, found his cot just inside the door on the right. Skinner got the correct things, and they went back outside again, walking towards the car.

When they were nearly to it, the man suddenly screamed. Skinner looked around. Coming towards them, grinning, were the black sergeant-major, and the two white sergeants.

"Brought him back for more, have you?" called the fat white one.

Skinner stopped and looked at them. He noticed, glancing sidewise, that his patient's lips were trembling.

"This man's in my charge," Skinner said, coldly. "Keep away."

The sergeants stopped briefly, looked at one another. Then the big white one smiled and jerked his head towards Skinner and his patient, and the three started walking towards them again.

Skinner took the step from where they were to the door of the car, jerked it open, and pushed the hurt Bechuana in. He reached under the seat, grabbed a tire iron, turned, slamming the door, and faced the non-coms again.

"I wouldn't come any closer to this car, if I were you," he said, evenly.

They stopped again.

"What's up with you, then?" asked the fat white one. Curiously, not unpleasantly.

"I'm not explaining a God damn thing. Just keep away from this car," Skinner said, smacking the tire iron against his thigh.

For a moment, nothing happened. Then the big one

looked at the fat one, the fat one shrugged and took the sergeant-major by the arm and turned him around, and the three of them walked away.

As they strolled off, Skinner heard one say, in a puzzled tone, "I thought the bloody Yanks were so set against niggers."

After that, Skinner became a very separate guy indeed from the other white men in camp. He was a little oppressed by it, not so much because of their unfriendliness to him, to which he was thoroughly indifferent, as by the depth of his unfriendliness to them. For, while the beating up had crystallized it, the unfriendliness had existed since he had first come to the camp and begun to see their attitude towards the black men under them, and towards army regulations concerning their treatment.

It is an open agreement among the petty officials of all armies, an agreement endorsed by higher command, that all regulations designed to enhance authority, enforce segregation, accord privilege, and provide for personal servitude, are to be rigidly enforced; while regulations designed to protect and shelter those under authority may safely be ignored and mocked. This was especially true, in the British army, in units whose strength consisted mostly of non-English-speaking troops. For who ever heard of a black-man, who couldn't even say, "Yes, sir," properly, reading a regulation book, let alone trying to have a white man court-martialed.

It was this situation, rather than the specific incident, which led Skinner to avoid the billet completely now. He was very much alone in camp, and that was the way he wanted it.

In the evening, he would sit quietly and watch the Bechuanamen, and listen to their singing, until they went to bed. Then he would go back to the ambulance, sit on the running board in the dark, thinking of the sadness of simple people far from home.

After awhile, as the night became chilly, he would get into the ambulance, start the engine to run the heater, turn on the big dome light, and read, or write a little, or, sometimes, try to write to Cindy.

Cindy's letters still came every day. In Beirut, he had read them all several times, with joy. Now he hardly bothered to scan through them. They all seemed to say the same thing. Or maybe they didn't. He no longer read them carefully enough to be sure.

His own letters to her, which had previously been full of everything they were seeing and doing, became short, bitter, and infrequent. He found himself doing something he had sworn not to do; he found himself taking an odd, savage pleasure in thinking of Cindy and himself and trying to discredit his memories of their time together. Slowly, night by night, and quite consciously, he was destroying, in his own mind, their entire relationship.

There existed a compulsion he did not try to understand, which made him inspect all the bright things they had had together for signs of tarnish. It almost seemed that he could not go to sleep easily at night until he had picked a favorite incident, and turned it over and over until he found a weak spot that allowed him to see it as sordid.

And the compulsion would not be self-contained. After a while of letting it work on himself, he began to try to make it work on her. He would write:

Dear Cindy:

All the bright, whimsical little things we said seem so childish in retrospect. I suppose when you're in love, nonsense about Shapes and so on seems very neat and tender, but, in the cold blue light of memory, it becomes insipid.

I showed your picture to a little Syrian girl I patronized in Beirut. She admired you. I tell you this, not to destroy your illusions, because I don't think you have any about me, but to prevent your forming any in my absence. I do so on the theory that I shall be back after a time, and that we may not be too weary to try to pick up where we left off.

If I could be sure I were not coming back, I would leave you alone to picture me as you might, for it would do no harm; but under the circumstances, I think it best for you to know that I am as faithless physically as any taxi-driver or sidewalk Romeo.

Love,
Skinner

Usually, having written such a letter, he would reread it, tell himself that it was not necessary to be cruel, and prevail upon himself to tear it up. But he would write no substitute letter to take its place, and, occasionally, when he was very low, he would mail one.

He devoted one night to composing fourteen pages of analysis of himself and her, all very straightforward, the conclusion of which was that they should face the fact that what they had had ended when they said goodbye; that what they might have was conditional on a very uncertain future; that he was changing daily, as she was, each in different ways, each influenced by totally different conditioning factors; that they would thus have grown very far apart when he got back, and perhaps she would do well to keep looking around, though he was willing to try to salvage what they could when they met again . . . though he might change in that respect, too.

He told himself that this analysis was thoroughly objective and, accordingly, mailed it. With it, he enclosed a sonnet of Gerald Gould's he had come across, which ran:

"I am frightened, sweetheart—that's the long and short
Of the bad mind I bear: the scent comes back
Of an unhappy garden gone to wrack,
The flower-beds trampled for an idiot's sport,
A mass of vermin battening there, a mort
Of weeds a-fester, all the green turned black,
And through the sodden glades of loss and lack
The dead winds blown of hate and false report.
There was a music in the early air,
When our young love was virgin as we were,
Ripe for the rose, new to the nightingale;
But now two ghosts walk showing each to each
The empty grace of ceremonious speech,
And I am frightened, and the air is stale."

Finally, one night, he worked out eight lines of his own which, it seemed to him, disposed of himself and Cindy, which put his role in the relationship in a nice little coffin, and read a properly didactic sermon:

There was too much left unsaid.
Suddenly
We had to be too close too
Quickly. You caught haste from me like a sickness.
And there has never been a chance
For us to know each other.
I have wanted too much too
Quickly; and do not realize
How young I am.

He wrote it out very carefully on a sheet of V-mail paper, and, at the bottom, he added: "You are probably a damn nice girl, Cindy; and I am certainly, at this point, a very poor fellow, but why hope?"

After that he wrote to her no more, for there was no longer any love in him: not for Cindy or for his friends or for himself; or for anything he had ever done or anything he ever would do.

He thought about what he ever would do, and he thought that he couldn't make music, though he knew the tunes, nor make books, though he knew the words and ideas.

He thought often of death.

Not specifically about his own death, but about death in general, death as a force in the world; a force for good as often as a force for evil. He thought: One must see through death and cease to respect it, as one has seen through and ceased to respect everything else. He put this into a sonnet, inscribed to Rod, which, he thought, was a very fine idea because it was quite certain that Rod would never have a chance to read it:

For Rod

What unimportant time we have is spent
For no cause. You, my friend, and I are not
Cause-people. There is no accomplishment
Mystic or practical that does not rot.
I will admit that there are negatives
We can reemphasize by written things
Or notes of music. This course always gives
Some satisfaction. So do slanderings:
To slander life is fine, to slander love,
Is best of all when things are closing in

And if authority, if those above,
Say this is sin, then, Gentlemen, we sin.
But when we think of death, let us renew
This resolution, slander dying, too.

Everything he tried to write turned into a death-song, although they were not all metrical and rhymed. Thus he wrote:

ANATOMY LESSON

Consider
The feeling of death
Inherent in the body.
My body, your body, all bodies.
Built in.
A structure of thick lead shapes,
One rooted in the brain
Connected to another, twisted through the heart,
Connected to another, pressing against the center
    of the stomach.
With blunt extensions
Thrusting into limbs and organs,
Crudely caricaturing
The calcium skeleton.

Live warmly. Warm the lead to body temperature,
And you are unaware of it.
Melancholy is an agent
For cooling lead.

Be sad:
The skeleton grows colder.
Feel your flesh throb from it,
Feel your nerves, your rose colored intestines,
Shudder, trying to draw away.

Alway some inner part will touch
The dull, remaining core
Until eventually . . .

Having written this, he went to bed. He reread it the following night. As always seemed to happen when he wrote something that he thought at the time was good, he was impelled on rereading to write something else which mocked it.

The mocker, this time, was a sonnet. Its being a sonnet mocked the form, and its content mocked the skeleton metaphor:

Here in the cabinet-drawer, lined with zinc,
  See how the doctor has laid out the soul
He's just dissected. It's a frog's, I think.
  He's left the little separate members whole.
The greenish one's the badwill, by its side,
  The undernourished goodwill, pale and blue.
(If you should hear the doctor coming, hide.
  Better look quick, he may be coming through.)
We haven't found the loveyouhateyou yet—
  Here it is, lying underneath the wit;
Here is the cone-shaped godwant, violet,
  It turns to purple if you tickle it.
(It may not be the soul; it may be brain
Or bowels. Organs look so much the same.)

It bothered him a little to rhyme brain and same, and he decided that, until he could revise the couplet to take care of it, the sonnet was unfinished. Then he thought, "What the hell? Who's going to read it? For that matter, who's going to finish it?" And he let it go, adding it to the jumble of papers in his glove compartment.

After that, he stopped trying to write poetry at all, partly because he no longer saw any reason to make the effort, and partly because he came upon some stanzas from a poem of Housman's which said most of what he wanted to say so well as to make him feel amateurish. The poem was, "Shot? So Quick, So Clean an Ending?", and the stanzas were these:

"Oh, you had foresight, you had reason,
You saw the road and where it led,
And early wise, and brave in season
Put the pistol to your head.

Oh soon, and better soon than later
After long disgrace and scorn,
You shot dead the household traitor
The soul that should not have been born.

Right you guessed the rising morrow
And scorned to tread the mire you must.
Dust's your wages, son of sorrow,
But men may come to less than dust.

Souls undone, undoing others—
Long time since the tale began.
You would not live to harm your brothers,
Oh, lad, you died as fits a man."

One's life is a pebble, Skinner thought, falling steadily through the water, towards an unknown but predictable bottom; and what does it matter if the water be shallow or deep?

In the mail one morning came a note from Benny; he had come down with jaundice, had left Raqqa, was now in the hospital above Beirut. When could Skinner get over to see him?

He had a trip to the CCS at Zahle that same afternoon, and decided that, since he was half-way there, he would drive on over the mountain and go to the hospital.

He discharged his patient at the CCS, and, instead of turning left to go back to camp, turned right and headed for Beirut. It was four o'clock. He drove fast, passed through Chtaura, and was at the top of the mountain by a quarter to five. He took it a little slower going down, figuring that if he arrived at the hospital at five-thirty, he would be able to share the evening meal with Benny. Then, as he thought of that, he realized that it would be hard to talk with Benny in his present state of mind, that for one thing, Benny would ask about Cindy, and that the explanation would be a wearisome one to make, leading to argument and debate.

He shrugged it off and continued down the mountainside.

He turned in at the hospital, and found a parking place. After he had stopped the car and set the brake, he decided he would smoke a cigarette before going in, and figure out how much to tell Benny.

He smoked. He thought, God, I just don't want to talk to Benny now. I want to talk to Rod. Rod might understand and agree. I wonder what little Arab hovel he's holed up in now? Why is it that crap things always happen to guys like Rod? I can't talk to Benny, he thought; Benny will just be impatient. Oh well, hell, I'm here; I might as well see him for a minute. He relaxed back against the seat, threw the cigarette out the window, and watched the ember hit the ground and bounce. Without stopping to analyze why, he impulsively straightened up, started the car, released the brake, turned around, and left the hospital grounds without having gotten out of the front seat.

Going back over the mountain at night was tricky enough so that it kept him from thinking.

But when he hit the level ground at Chtaura, and was headed for camp, a logical pattern of ideas began:

Suicide is supposed to be emotional–it would not be for me. For some it is escape–for me it is not. For me suicide is an intellectual position, the inevitable result of thinking things through to the end. It is the final stink, in a way, the only way of finally proving to myself that I don't actually care. The big thing is the realization that it is perfectly meaningless if I do it. That there's nothing hard about it. That it's perfectly easy. That there's a sense, maybe justified for once, of great superiority about it, because I alone realize that it has not required guts, or madness, but simply an understanding of how meaningless it is.

That was the way the pattern ran, and it seemed very clear and very simple. In the light of it, all the insolubles were ridiculously obvious.

The things to be done when he got to camp were too easy to require conscious planning. He arrived; he parked the car; he looked into the windows of the non-com's billet to make sure that no one was there. He slipped in the door and slipped out again, in a minute, with the fat sergeant's automatic. He checked it by the light from the window to make sure it was loaded.

The idea of being there, in the middle of camp, was offensive. It would be better to be away, off along the road somewhere, where he might not be found for a day or two. Putting the gun into his shirt, where the metal felt cold and final against his skin, he started to walk towards the road.

He reached the road and turned left, walking along parallel with the camp. As he came even with the corner of the camp, a sentry shouted, "Halt!"

Skinner, preoccupied, hardly heard him.

"Halt!"

Skinner continued.

There were footsteps running; he didn't connect them with himself. Suddenly a blacker shadow came rushing towards him through the darkness, swinging a gleaming blade. He had failed, he realized, to respond to the challenge. The sentry meant to bayonet him. And Skinner did an amazing thing. He kept walking, heading towards the blade.

Inches away from him the blade swerved, avoided him, the sentry threw out an arm and stopped himself against Skinner's body. He was laughing. "No hurt you," he said. "You friend." He laughed again, stroking Skinner's arm with his big hand. "Sorry. No see who," he said. "Sorry, friend."

Skinner was not sure, but it could have been the man he had protected from the sergeants the week before.

He smiled then, warmed slightly because he had been recognized, and because the man had made an effort not to hurt him when he knew who it was.

"Okay," Skinner said. They stood a minute, looking at each other.

The Bechuanaman pointed out in the direction in which Skinner had been heading. "Go there?" he asked, indicating that he would let Skinner pass.

Skinner thought a minute, and shook his head. "No," he said, and sighed. "Go back."

He turned. He started back for the place where his ambulance was parked, not quite sure why he had changed his mind, but, somehow, very much shaken.

Then, suddenly, he knew. It was because he had been wrong. Dead wrong. He had been guilty of gross self-deception, had figured something so thoroughly wrong that it was no longer permissible to act on it. He had not tried to avoid the sentry's charge with the bayonet. So suicide was not an intellectual position. It was pure emotionality, after all.

Because, if his decision had been intellectual, reflex would have stopped him. He would have tried, without reference to volition, to avoid the death that came unexpectedly. That was clear. And, since he had not tried to avoid it, reflex had not operated normally; the deep, non-intellectual core of him had willed death, and the fine logic of the evening had been so much frippery to cover it up.

"Hell," said Skinner, aloud in the night. "I haven't figured anything. I'm just awfully, God damned tired."

CHAPTER

12

THE melancholia was over now, and the hangover, which was listlessness, set in. It seemed to Skinner, looking back over the past week, thinking of similar attacks of depression that had preceded this one, that it turned life into a sort of long endurance swim. You took a lot of deep breaths and paddled along the surface, in the sunlight for as long as you could. Then you began to tire, and you lost breath and began to sink, and at first you resisted sinking, but gradually the fight went out of you. And you floated down into the dark, cold depths, where the sun could no longer reach you.

And usually, as you approached bottom, there came to you somehow strength for an involuntary, convulsive kick, which would send you drifting up towards the top, towards sunlight again. He had been as low as he would go, now, as deep as he had ever been. Now he was floating towards the surface again, indifferently, perhaps, without much struggling, but upwards, towards the surface, towards the sunlight, towards the sparkling air of normalcy. And he knew that, when he reached the top, and absorbed the sun, and breathed the air, he would strike out and swim again, with increasingly exhilarant strength until the next tiredness came.

A few mornings passed, and a kid showed up at the camp in an ambulance.

"I'm to relieve you," he said.

Skinner couldn't remember ever having seen him before. "You new?" he asked.

"Yes," the boy said. "How is it here?"

"The post is okay," Skinner said. "A little lonely, but you can be pretty comfortable if you want to stand on your Warrant Officer rank." The kid was wearing a shiny, new garrison cap, undoubtedly from the Cairo Officer's Shop; he'd stand on his rank, all right, thought Skinner, but without any particular bitterness.

He began to show the new boy around. He couldn't make himself be cordial, but civility wasn't as hard to manage as he'd thought it might be. Hell, maybe this was a reasonably nice kid. Maybe he was like Freak would be if he were coming onto a new post, and hadn't hung around with Skinner and the group, first. There was no point in being clever or unpleasant.

So he was civil, took the boy to the billet, introduced him to the clerk, and helped him arrange his things.

"Gee, it looks like a good set-up," said the kid.

"It's okay. What's going on down at H.Q.?"

"Something big. They wouldn't even let us stay around Cairo for leave. They seem to want to get you guys out in a big hurry."

"What are the rumors?"

"Well, there's going to be a big convoy from here to Egypt, and on up the desert. Everybody knows that much. Then you're supposed to be going into action."

"Sicily?"

"Maybe. A lot of guys think so."

Skinner frowned. "I don't think there'd be time

enough," he said. "That thing's about over with, isn't it?"

"Yeah. They're doing good."

"It'll take a month to get all the stuff ready and the cars in shape. It must be something new."

"Greece?"

"That would be swell," said Skinner. "Or it might be Italy; or even France."

"Around Cairo they say it's too soon for France, and Italy isn't important enough."

Skinner picked up his kit, and began to stow it in the ambulance. "I think I'll get started," he said. "There's a guy in the hospital I want to see before I go in."

He got into the driver's seat, and the kid came over and stood by the window. Skinner explained what the duties around the post were. The kid told him how the trip was, coming over. Skinner warned him that he hadn't been on too good terms with the others there, but said that he didn't think it would make much difference after the first couple of days. The kid said thanks, he'd remember it. They chatted a few minutes more, and Skinner was very careful not to say anything disillusioning, not wanting to sound like an old boy at school impressing a new boy.

After a while, they said so long, Skinner turned the car around, and drove off towards Beirut.

He planned what he would do. He would stop off, first, at the Ksara monastery, outside Chtaura, where he would buy two or three bottles of the good *Eau de Vie* they made to have for the reunion with Fred and Freak. At first he thought he might try to slip one into the hospital for Benny, too, but then he remembered that liquor and jaundice are an extremely bad combination, and decided against it. Then he would have lunch in Chtaura, drive over the mountain, see Benny, turn back, come over the mountain again, and try to make Headquarters in Damascus by nine o'clock.

Thinking of the cool cellars, full of good wine and brandy at the monastery, Skinner began to feel good. The same valley floor which had been dull and not worth noting the week before was green and fine in its midsummer fertility now, and he responded to the richness of it with a smile. Fruit trees were bearing now, and the grain was getting tall. The sun was an enemy no longer, and he pushed the windshield open so that the air could wash over his face and cool him.

He drove through Baalbeck, past the Zahle turn-off, and came to the little dirt road leading up a gentle slope to the monastery. When he parked the car at the monastery door, and turned and looked at the valley, he really felt swell. He went in, and talked to the monk who was on duty selling wines; they talked French together, and had a fine glass of red wine, and Skinner bought six bottles of *Eau de Vie* instead of three, mostly because he felt so friendly.

He drove on to Chtaura. There was a little French hotel there, in the middle of town, which the ambulance group had found served as good meals as any you could get in Syria or Lebanon.

He left the car behind the hotel, and went in. He drank sherry with some RAF guys, and they shared a table, and ate Hors d'Oevres and Omelet aux Fines Herbes and Roast Beef, and Green Salad, and pastry and Turkish coffee. The RAF guys told him how fine it was over Cape Bon, when you really knew you had won, and you hardly had to look at another plane in the sky, because you could be almost certain that, if it wasn't a Spit or a Hurry, it was a Yank.

The vin ordinaire began to hit them a little, and they joked with a woman at the next table who, one of the RAF guys said, was the mistress of an aging French officer who could only get over from Beirut once a week, leaving the other six days for the pilots who stayed at the RAF Rest Camp up the mountain.

When Skinner left the hotel and started up the mountain again, he was singing.

The drive up the mountain was tricky, and not particularly beautiful, since one couldn't very well look back down at the valley. But starting down from the top, it was one of the loveliest stretches of road anywhere. The bank fell away from the shoulder in a series of steep, fertile ravines; the surface was wide and even, the curves well-graded and gradual; traffic was seldom heavy. And, as one followed down, each curve on cleared place on the lower side brought a glimpse of the roof-tops of the city below, white and shimmering beside a blue sea.

After curving back and forth for three or four miles, the road straightened out abruptly into a down slope of a mile or so, and, at the bottom of it, the city began.

The hospital, where Benny was, was just inside the city.

Skinner stopped there, parked the car, and walked over to the admissions office. They told him what ward Benny was in, and how to find it.

The ward was long and light, with comfortable beds lining the opposing walls, only a little too close to one another. Between each pair of beds was a sort of narrow table. On its top were eating utensils, arranged in a prescribed manner, and such books and stationary as the patient wanted. Next shelf, clothes, also folded and arranged as ordained, and, on the bottom shelf, shoes, if the patient was in bed. The clothes were the fantastic Hospital Blues, issued by the British to all enlisted patients, so that they can be spotted easily if they happen to stray away from the hospital without permission. They were worn as carefully as a uniform, and were felt to be very much the proper sort of thing for a man well enough to get out of bed and help with light duties around the ward, or sit outside in the yard. The suits were cut from tawdry sky-blue cloth, roughly finished, into a loose caricature of the pants and jacket of a civilian suit. With these were worn a cheap white shirt, a bright solid red tie, and the patients regular shoes, socks, and cap.

Skinner found the nursing sister in charge of the ward, and asked which Benny's bed was, and whether he might see him. The sister was dubious. *Infectious hepatitus* patients were supposed to be isolated.

"Official business," said Skinner, trying to look like an officer.

"Very well, sir," said the nurse, and Skinner was glad he had worn a necktie. Only officers are allowed to wear them in the British army.

She led him into the second section of the ward, a smaller room where sergeants and warrant officers were bedded, then into a still smaller, semi-isolation place. And there was Benny, sitting on the bed, wearing the infamous blues.

"Stand up," said the sister sharply. "Here's one of your officers to see you."

Benny looked up. Skinner winked.

Benny leapt to his feet and saluted with the wrong hand. "Major Galt, sir," he said. "You're looking ripping."

"He's absolutely undisciplined," said the sister to Skinner, without humor. "I hope you'll report that to your organization."

"I'll see that he's punished," Skinner promised.

"They'll beat me 'til the blood runs," Benny said to the woman. "And on Judgment Day, God will say it was your fault." He sat down.

The nurse walked haughtily out.

"Benny," said Skinner, sitting down by him and stroking the sleeve of his blue jacket. "You look marvelous. Red for courage, blue for loyalty, white for truth, and yellow for jaundice."

"I am yellow, aren't I?" said Benny. He was. The skin of his face noticeably, and the whites of his eyes completely.

"How long does it last?"

"Months. I'm thinking of going back to the States and going on a bond-selling tour. I'm a dirty yellow Jap, see? Everybody who buys a bond gets to slap me. Buy a bond and slap a Jap."

"Got enough to read?"

"I'm running low. Can you get up again?"

"I'm not sure. We're supposed to be taking off right away on a big convoy. I'll come if I can. If I can't, I'll send you whatever I can get in Damascus. Anybody else come in?"

"Yeah. Freak and this guy Fred Something-or-other."

"Birch."

"Yeah. They were in yesterday on their way down from Aleppo. Fred knows a colonel on the staff here, so the bitch had to let them in."

"Did they tell you about Rod?"

"Yeah. But it sounds funny. Did Rod really just take off for the hell of it?"

"No," said Skinner. "He took off, but it wasn't for the

hell of it. He didn't want us to tell Freak, but it's okay for you to know." He told Benny the story.

"Jesus," said Benny, when Skinner had finished. "That's a very rough thing. What do you suppose will happen to him?"

"Well," said Skinner. "They haven't caught him yet, or one of us would have heard it. So he's getting away with it so far."

"Suppose he'll ever get back to the States?"

"He said he didn't care about it. But I won't be surprised to walk into a cocktail lounge in Minneapolis ten years or so from now, and find him there, playing the piano."

"Right," said Benny. "Rod is the original man who knew his way around."

"He likes the Arabs," Skinner said. "Because they know how to live for the moment."

"He's right," said Benny. "They do. But Rod will never learn it from them. None of us will."

"Why not?" Skinner asked.

"All occidentals," said Benny, "have preconceptions of satisfaction. The Arabs patiently wait for what happens, and if it makes them happy, they're grateful. But we try to figure out what's going to make us happy, and go after it. And, after we've got it, we keep trying to get more and more, even though we were probably disappointed in it the first time, simply because we think we must have been right when we were figuring."

"So what's that got to do with living for the moment?"

"Ah, you're blind," Benny said. "How can you live for today's moment in terms of yesterday's satisfaction, especially when you weren't even satisfied yesterday?"

"Benny," said Skinner. "This hospital's making you glib."

"It's not that," Benny said. "I've been writing a play." He pointed to a notebook lying on the table. "It's about a bunch of jokers who scream around trying to find moments to live for. I've just been quoting the only one of them who has a grain of sense."

"Oh," said Skinner. He picked up the notebook and opened it. On the first page was written: "The heroine of this play is named Bertha; there's nothing wrong with her. The hero is Martin; his clothes and personality are by Abercrombie and Fitch." He smiled, and opened to the middle of the book. Here he found some dialogue in blank verse: "*Bertha*: Here's the new Almanac, *Freud's Weather Book* . . . With dreams explained and many useful charms."

"Don't read it," said Benny, grabbing it from him, "It's crap. It's not worth soiling paper with."

Skinner grinned at him. "What I saw looked sort of good."

Benny snorted. "It's crap."

"You're psycho-pathic," Skinner said. "Your obsession is self-criticism."

"Nuts," said Benny, looking through his play. "It's wonderful. It scans. It's clever. It's about as original as a stink bomb in the seventh grade teacher's desk."

"What do you have to write to please yourself, *King Lear?*"

"Yeah," said Benny. "That's okay."

"Sure," said Skinner. "Somebody else wrote it, so it's okay. If you'd written it, you'd say it stank."

"Sure," Benny told him. "Bum plot. Woman characters too one-sided. Too much rhetoric." Then, abruptly, "Freak and Fred said you might be going to get in it this time."

"Yeah."

"Jesus," said Benny, impatiently, "what a time to be sick."

"How much longer will you be here?"

"Four or five weeks. Then a couple of weeks convalescent leave. I don't know whether I'll ever catch up with you guys again or not." He sounded dejected.

"Where will you take your leave? Palestine?"

"If I take it. I'll go to one of the colonies and work. Get brown and healthy and forget all about God damn wars and armies for a couple of weeks."

"You pretty fed?"

"God yes. This hospital. All the patients who are able to will stand up when the nurse enters the room. Also, mop the floors, work in the kitchen, make the beds." He began to imitate the clipped, pseudo-educated accent which British nursing sisters affect when they're pulling their rank. "Feeling badly today? Nonsense. Doctor told you to get up, didn't he? Don't speak to me that way. Remember, I'm an officer. I can get you into very serious trouble." He sighed. "It's a mess."

"You don't seem to waste much love on the Angels of Mercy."

"You should hear them. They're strictly bourgeois bitches to begin with, and they get around officer's messes and pick up these ridiculous airs and accents. Hell, it's bad enough to hear the genuine officer-class jerks pulling that crap; at least they've been brought up stupid, and don't know any better. But when these babes come around comforting the sick with a broad a . . ." he made an angry gesture by way of finishing the sentence.

"There are a few nice ones." Benny went on. "There was one little London Irish girl—she was sent home in disgrace a day or so ago. She was the best nurse I ever hope to see."

"How come they sent her home?"

"Listen," said Benny. "Are you in a puking mood? Wait until you hear this one."

"Tell me," said Skinner.

"Listen. You know these Eyeties around here?"

"The guys with grey clothes? What are they, prisoners?"

"Yeah. They work the grounds. Carry trays for guys that can't walk. That sort of stuff. Well, there was a guy in this ward. It was when I was plenty sick, and he used to bring my food. I'd say, 'Hello, comrade', to him, and he'd smile, but he never said anything. Well, one day he came in with my lunch, and I was reading *Fontamara.* It was a Penguin I'd bought in Aleppo. He put the tray down, picked up the book to move it out of the way. Then he saw what it was, and asked me in perfect English what I thought of Silone. I said I thought he was swell, and he said he thought he was too obvious. I said, a lot of good things are obvious, look at Marx. He said Silone wasn't trying to plan an economy, he was trying to create literature. So I agreed that the motivation was a little superficial in the book, but that perhaps Silone was pointing out that when you're working with simple people, you are much more likely to get them to take action against petty injustice and superficial issues than on national and international crimes. So it worked into a nice little argument. After that, I got to know him pretty well."

"What's he got to do with the little Irish nurse?"

"I'm coming to that. First I want to tell you what this guy was like."

"Okay."

"He was strictly a good guy," Benny said. "Nice. Quiet and sensitive University graduate. Anti-Mussolini, but pro-Italy. Like you might be anti-Roosevelt but pro-America.

Wrote poetry. Told me that, when he was in college, he'd translated Stephen Spender into Italian."

"Ever read any of his poetry?" Skinner asked.

"Yeah. I read Italian fine."

"I thought maybe Spender returned the compliment and translated him into English."

"Quiet, or I won't finish the story."

Skinner promised to keep still.

"Well," said Benny. "The guy was very charming. He had a lot of dignity, and a lot of fire, but he could laugh. Sometimes, though, we'd be arguing about something, and he'd get so damn sincere, he'd win on sincerity alone. I think he was more of an aristocrat than he was an intellectual—he told me once that he'd lost his peacetime commission over some sort of anti-fascist coup he and some other young officers were planning to pull, just before the Ethiopian deal. But his family was big enough to keep him out of jail. When this war came, they pulled him back into the army, only this time in the ranks. Medicals. His politics were good. See the kind of a guy I mean?"

"Sure," said Skinner. "I'll bet I can almost tell you what he looked like. Tall, slim, very straight; looked better in his prisoner's clothes than the average major does in full regimental dress."

"Yeah, yeah. You've got him. Well, we come to the pay-off. He was in love with this Irish nurse."

"My God," said Skinner.

"Don't blame him, either," said Benny. "She was something to fall for."

"Really nice?"

"Lord," said Benny. "Pretty and warm. Big eyes, big heart. A nice, instinctive sense of justice and the guts to back it up. I saw her stand up to a lieutenant-colonel one day. He wanted some poor joker to get up, and she said the guy was feeling rotten. She had too much sympathy for her own good."

"And she was all for the Eyetie?"

"I don't really know, but it seems pretty certain. She wasn't on this ward, all the time, but she used to make excuses to come down here. Of course, they had to be terrifically discreet. When she came down, they wouldn't look at one another at the same time. But there was something there. It was just coming to a head when I came into the hospital."

"They got caught?"

"Worse than that. She got pregnant. So she went to one of the young doctors she thought was a friend of hers, according to the way the story got back here, and asked him to fix it up for her. He said sure, and then ran up instead and told the commandant."

"Christ," said Skinner. "What a louse."

"The story is, he was miffed because he'd never been able to get anywhere. And then, apparently, the boys all asked one another, and had to admit that it hadn't been any of them, so they began to suspect the poor Eyetie. I don't think they ever did get her to confess it. Well, she used to cry back in the little office back there, after that. They were fixing up a nice, juicy court-martial for her, but they kept her on duty right up to the time they were ready to get her. Then they had themselves a really fine time. They'd packed the Eyetie off somewhere, of course, and the only guy who'd agree to defend her was some high-minded infant who can barely read."

Skinner nodded. "Great bunch around here," he said.

"You should see the captain who prosecuted. God, is he a fat-mouthed slob."

"What was the charge?"

"Something technical about treatment of prisoners. But they made sure to drag out as many luscious details as their masturbation-crazed minds could conceive of. One of the sergeants who was court-orderly told me about it. The whole God damn court-martial board sat there verbally raping her, all day long. The high-point came when somebody expressed the stirring sentiment that, if an Englishwoman was going to do that sort of thing, she ought to do it with Englishmen. He was roundly applauded."

Skinner stared at the floor. "You were right," he said. "That does make me want to puke."

Benny stared at the floor, too.

After a while, Benny said, "I'm pretty fed with this part of the war. This rear-area crap. All the meanness and smallness of it. It's probably the same in American rear-area, too."

"Sure," said Skinner.

"Why the hell can't people be decent to one another?"

"I don't know," Skinner said. "There's nothing we can do about it."

"I got pretty low over this deal here," Benny said. "It's made me think a lot. I think maybe I've got an answer."

"No kidding?"

"Yeah. Listen, Skinner. There's bound to be some decency around this war somewhere. Where would you think it would most likely be?"

"In the lines?"

"That's what I think. But not just the lines. In the Infantry. Where the guys with the guns are. The little, personal guns."

"You think so?"

"I hope so, Skinner. I haven't really decided, but I may try to find out."

"How do you mean?"

"We can transfer," said Benny. "Right into the American Army, if we want to. If I can get into the infantry, I'm going to do it."

"What's wrong with this thing we're in?"

"It's too much like buying a ticket. You can't lose yourself in this, Skinner."

"Yeah?"

"Why don't you come with me?"

"No," said Skinner. "No. Not for me. I promised myself that, whatever happened, whether I flew or fought or drove, I'd never take this war seriously. And I never will. It's just a big joke. If I get killed, it's the biggest joke of all. I'm not even hoping for decency in it. It would upset me to find it. I've believed all my life that life was indecent, and that war is the most grossly indecent thing of all, history's way of proving that man is born a heel. I'm not going around looking for salvation. All I want is confirmation, and what you've just told me about the nurse and the Eyetie fits fine."

"You know," said Benny, talking slowly and sorting over his words. "Our greatest fault, as individuals, is that we think of ourselves as exceptions. All the way through, when we see smallness, and stupidness, and cruelty, even when we participate in it, we figure we're exceptions. We say, 'I know what I'm doing. I'm not doing this because, as a human being, I have to as part of my human nature; I'm doing it because I observe other humans involved in it, and I want to get in and see why. I'm just an observer around here, around life. I observe, I amuse myself and the select little group of initiates I call my friends, but I don't really have to do things like this at all. And I can stop and get out whenever I want to.' We felt that way about school, and the jobs we had, and college, and now, the war. We participated and participate in all those things, and, at the same time, refuse to identify ourselves with them. But it's all rationalization, Skinner. We are identified, like it or not. The illusion of objective participation is kin to the child's illusion that he will be an exception to dying. No human being is an exception to humanity, Skinner. And this ambulance deal is an attempt to perpetuate the legend of non-participation. It lets you feel that you have chosen to try war, for the laughs, that you're at war voluntarily. I'm sick of feeling that way, Skinner. Maybe the infantry will knock it out of me."

There was a little silence before Skinner found the answer he knew he had to make. Then he said, "I don't think I want it knocked out of me, Benny. I think it's the only thing that keeps me alive."

Benny smiled sadly. "The old deathwish pretty strong these days?" he asked. It was a very gentle question for Benny.

Skinner told him about the past week.

"Same old thing, huh?" Benny asked.

"Yeah. Getting low. Way low. Same old thing."

"Life's a pain in the tail, why not try death?"

"That was it," Skinner said.

Benny thought of something. "Wait a minute," he said. "Is Cindy still writing?"

"I guess so."

"You guess so?"

"I sort of stopped reading my mail. Yeah, she still writes."

"And how many pieces did you break her into?" Benny asked, the gentleness all gone now.

"I don't know. I'm afraid I was pretty rough."

"You took it out on Cindy, because she was the best thing around."

"I wrote some stinking letters. But it's better, Benny. If I hadn't busted it now, I'd have done it later. This way she's loose already. It's better."

"You're insane. You're the only guy I ever knew who really had love, and you want to toss it. You're the only guy I know who has something to go home for, and you're kicking it away."

"It's better," said Skinner. "Things always end. And I'd rather see them go up quick, in flames, than fade slowly, and rot away."

"Listen," said Benny. "It's all over. The depression, I mean, you're okay, now, aren't you?"

"Sure. I'm fine. I'm an optimist."

"Well, then, will you stop putting yourself through the wringer, just to watch the pretty guts come out? And will you stop spilling Cindy's blood all over the pavement? Listen, Skinner, write and tell her you were nuts, will you? Tell her how wrong you were, explain about Rod and everything. There isn't another girl in the world who'd understand how you could have done it, but she will. Write her, will you?"

Skinner thought, and shook his head. "I don't think I will, Benny. Because, just about the time I got it all straightened out, I'd cross her up again. It wouldn't be any favor to her. And there's not much love left in me now."

"You're screwy," said Benny. "Screwy through and through. You're like a hungry man dissolving a great big steak in acid."

Skinner shrugged. "Let it go, Benny. You're probably right, but I can't see it."

They let it go. They kidded for a while, and then Skinner had to leave.

"Are you really going through with this American Infantry deal?" Skinner asked.

"Yeah," said Benny. "More so than ever, since I've talked with you. You're my friend, Skinner, and I like you. But you're a wrong guy. And, in a way, if I were to stay in this outfit, now that I think the way I do, I'd be a wrong guy, too." There was affection in his voice, though the words were of condemnation.

"Okay," said Skinner. "I've lost Rod. Or Rod lost himself. And you're finding yourself, so I lose you. Where does that leave me?"

"On the line," said Benny. "Ready to fall backwards as soon as something comes along to push you."

"I'm too fast," said Skinner. "I'll duck."

They shook hands. "Let's not lose touch," Skinner said. "Write me and write the Freak. Maybe we'll all be in the same part of it later."

"Maybe," Benny said. "So long."

"So long," said Skinner. They shook hands again, hating to part without first expressing some sort of approval of one another, finding some point of agreement.

Finally, Skinner shrugged. Benny answered him with a shrug, and they smiled at one another. And Skinner turned, and walked out of the smaller room, down the long white ward, and into the air.

It was twilight. It would be a cool night.

PART SEVEN

A Final Portrait

Jack the Nimble, the Quick, and the Dead

CHAPTER

13

IT WAS off again, on again, all the way up the Peninsula.

The landing, at Salerno, was rough, rougher than anything anyone had seen yet, rougher than anyone thought it could be.

But from there on, through Naples, was easier than they had any right to expect. And, instead of making a stand at Naples, as he should have done according to the figuring, Jerry had let them right into the city—mined the place, of course, and very thoroughly—but not chosen to make a stand, and so the offensive rolled on, and only the cautious said Rome for Christmas; everybody else was talking about sharing Thanksgiving turkey with the Pope.

They were not in Rome by Thanksgiving; or even by Christmas; the Pope conducted his Easter service without them. They barely made Rome by Spring.

For, first there was a stand right at the Volturno river, concentrated around Capua, which was almost as rough as Salerno, and later, after that river had been crossed, there were other rivers and other stands, and they were even rougher: The Garigliano, Minturno, Gaeta, Venafro, Casino, and the unlucky beach-head.

But after the crossing of the Volturno at Capua, and other places, it was off again for a while. Jerry was obligingly drawing back to the next natural barrier, and they started talking about Rome for Christmas again.

And, the river having been crossed, and the casualties diminishing, Headquarters could take time now to rotate the ambulances, and the drivers who had been with forward outfits were coming in to take the restful posts in the rear, and other drivers going forward to relieve; thus the posts were switched around, so that each man would have his equal share of comfort and hard work.

Skinner, having been relieved at the Regimental Aid Post he had stayed with for a month, was headed back along the road to Capua, headed for Headquarters at Naples; headed for a shave with hot water; for a bath; for a chance to see his friends, and drink, and get a woman, and eat some hot food.

He was driving back carefully, worn out, conscious of a certain pride in having done well, conscious of a certain gratitude that he had kept alive between baths.

He picked up three Tommies who were walking his way, and rode them into Capua.

"What's it like?" They asked him.

"Nice," said Skinner, "Nice and quiet. A little shelling at night, but they've got most of the mortars moved out."

"Good," said one of the Tommies. "We're going in again tomorrow. I hope it's like you say."

He let them out at Capua.

There was an American sergeant on the road between Capua and Aversa. Skinner stopped for him. The sergeant was curious about the ambulance outfit, and Skinner explained that they worked for the British. Fifth Army was widely billed as an American army, but fully a third of it consisted of British troops.

The sergeant asked some questions about the British. Skinner answered as best he could.

"I imagine the American Army is a lot better deal," said Skinner.

"The American Army stinks," the sergeant said. "A goddamn bunch of amateurs. If you put the names of all the men in a unit into a hat, and drew for who'd be colonels and who'd be privates, you'd get exactly the same percentage of good and bad officers and non-coms."

"Yeah," said Skinner. "But you get treated well. Good pay, good equipment, good food—comparatively, I mean."

They came into Aversa.

"I'll tell you how I feel about the American Army," said the sergeant. "How I feel, and every guy feels, who isn't an officer or some other kind of moron. If I had it to do over again, I'd rather spend the time in a clean jail. It's a great career, the army. For pigs. If I ever have a son, and he wants to join the U.S. Army, I'll do him a big favor. I'll say, 'Turn your back, my boy', and when he does, I'll kick him in the spine and cripple him so he won't be able to make the physical."

They came to where the sergeant's unit was, and Skinner said so long and let him out.

There was no one else to pick up between Aversa and Naples, though the road was jammed with civilians loaded with household goods, who were making their way towards town or away from it.

At headquarters, Skinner went to see the man in charge of the Fifth Army company, and was told that he had a rest coming to him.

"We're sending you to Aversa," he was informed. "It's a CCS. Not much work. Lacey and Birch are up there, and some others. They're friends of yours, right?" Lacey was Freak and Birch was Fred.

"You bet," said Skinner.

"They've set up their own little mess at Aversa; we've

got eight cars, and there isn't really enough work for four, though we have to keep them on hand, just in case. We can't really spare anyone for leave, but you'll be able to catch your breath up there."

"Thanks," said Skinner.

"And Galt?"

"Yeah?"

"Your M.O. at the Aid Post sent word about you. You must have done a hell of a fine job."

"Everybody up there broke their backs," Skinner said. "It wouldn't have been human to do a bad job."

He drew some money, then, collected his mail, and drove downtown. He found a parking place where his vehicle would be guarded, and left the car. He went to a barber shop and had a shave, and let the man massage his face for half an hour. There was a public bath nearby, and he went in and stayed for an hour. Then he inquired directions to the Red Cross club, and found it, and drank four or five cups of coffee, which tasted wonderfully well after a steady month of tea. He went upstairs in the club to the music room, and played all the Debussy and Ravel they had.

Going out of the Red Cross Club, he ran into a guy named Kildress whom he knew slightly and liked, and they went to a shop on the waterfront that Kildress knew of, and bought two big bottles of alleged champagne.

They took the wine and walked along back alleys, paralleling the Via Roma, where little girls of fourteen had joined their older sisters in soliciting. They found two pleasant girls, and shared the wine with them in a room rented for a quarter. Skinner began to feel alive again.

It was still afternoon when he arrived at Aversa.

Freak was there, at the mess, to greet him. Fred would be back soon.

"It's wonderful here," Freak said. Both he and Fred had been relieved earlier than Skinner, and had been off the line for over a week. He showed Skinner over the mess.

It consisted of three small rooms, in the front of one of the unused buildings. The CCS had taken over the grounds of an Italian school, and there was a great deal more room than was really needed.

The first room they saw had a table, scrounged from the Aversa courthouse, and a dozen odd chairs picked up here and there.

"This is the dining room," Freak said. "Fred and I got the table cloth last night."

"It's beautiful. Where'd it come from?"

"Off an altar," Freak said.

There were candlesticks, too, with candles, also from the church, in them. "It must look pretty civilized at night," Skinner said.

"You'd never know there was a war on," Freak confirmed. "Except that you can hear the barrage when there's an air-raid at Naples."

In the second room there were a divan and a radio, a rug, and more chairs.

"Someone's taken a lot of trouble with this place," Skinner said. "How long has it been going?"

"About two weeks. They sent us out a cook from headquarters, and we draw rations down there and scrounge more from the Americans. A couple of moonlight nights was all it took for most of the furniture."

In addition to the other luxuries, there was an Italian named Naproni who had attached himself to the mess as a sort of handyman, black market bargainer, assistant cook, entertainer, personal servant and host. A genial, ingratiating man who had been released from political prison where he had been placed probably because of an incurable mischievousness. He had had an incredible background: soldier in Ethiopia where he had shot off his trigger finger to get out of the infantry, renegade to France, from there, much to his surprise, a victim of drunkenness and his own good-nature, to Spain where he had driven munitions for the Mateotti Battalion of the International Brigade. At the end of the Spanish war, he had destroyed his identification, placed himself in a prisoner of war camp, and waited to be liberated.

In the evenings, Naproni would, as waiter, serve dinner; as servant, clean up; then come to the living room and drink with them, pouring wine with the air of master of the house. And sing fine songs in a true, if slightly maudlin tenor. The songs he sang were the popular airs from Italian opera, mostly, and a handful of others for which there was no explanation.

He was teaching Freak *O Sole Mio,* and they had perfected a florid duet which Skinner heard them sing that night.

Fred was with them, then, and so were half a dozen others. It was a very pleasant place to be.

The candles were lit; the supper had been good; they were all drinking wine. Naproni went into *Torno al Sorrento,* and thence into *The Red Flag,* the fine old socialist marching song, which the Abraham Lincoln group learned from their European comrades:

Avanti popula
Alla riscosa
Bandiera rossa, Bandiera rossa

"This is swell," Skinner said, luxuriating.

"You think this is good," Fred said. "Wait until night after tomorrow."

"What's going on?"

"We're having a party. Freak is getting some American nurses from the new hospital. They've just gotten overseas, and they think we're wonderful."

Things were quiet on the post the next night, and Skinner was able to go in with Freak who had a date with one of the nurses, and was to make the final arrangements for the party.

The girls Freak knew worked in a big general hospital which had just moved in and was situated just inside the outskirts of Naples, high on one of the surrounding hills.

They went to the Nurses' Quarters, and Freak asked if Lieutenant Marilyn Ormsbee was there, and was told that she was. After a moment, the lieutenant came downstairs and proved to be a nice-looking girl with long legs and brown hair.

Freak introduced Skinner, and asked Marilyn if she could get someone else, and Marilyn ran upstairs, and came back with a little blonde named Johnny. Johnny, in her own little blond way, was a nice-looking girl, too.

The girls said they couldn't stay out very late that night, because they wanted to be out real late the next night, which would be the party, and Skinner and Freak said that was okay, and they went out to dinner.

They had a fair dinner, at a place the girls knew, behind closed shutters. It was a big room on the second floor of a once-fashionable restaurant. The main dining room was boarded up now, and some of the tables had been moved upstairs into what had been a private ball-room. It was full of nurses from the hospital and their dates. There was smoke to breathe instead of air, because of the blackout precautions, and a piano to sing to, and plenty to drink.

They ate. They drank. They sang.

Skinner was delighted with Johnny. She had a way of

saying things that were just far enough removed from being dumb to be cute, and a trick, when she delivered them, of leaning towards him and taking his hand, like a little girl telling a secret.

Across the table, Freak and Marilyn went into a clinch.

"It looks like they're trying to eat each other," said Johnny.

Someone played *Stardust* on the piano, and they got up and danced in a little circle, between their own table and the one next to it.

"Some people get dreamy when they hear that piece," Johnny said. "But I just get sad."

"Why, Johnny?"

"They were playing it on the radio one night, when I was about fourteen, and Mama caught me kissing a boy goodnight on the front porch. The boy was afraid to ask me for another date."

About nine-thirty, the sirens began, and the lights were put out. People crowded around the stairs, getting in one another's ways and laughing about it. No one was very frightened.

Skinner and Johnny worked their way outside. They could hear planes, and the barrage was starting. They were still quite near the hospital, and, because of the hill, they felt quite safe and remote, the raid being directed against the ships in the harbor far below.

Most of the couples were going towards the air-raid shelter at the hospital, but Skinner led Johnny over to where the ambulance was parked.

"It's too pretty to miss," he said. The car faced up the hill, so they let the back doors swing open, and sat on the floor in back, with their feet out over the end, resting on the rear step. There was a bottle of Scotch under one of the seats that Skinner had drawn that afternoon—as warrant officers, they got a whiskey ration each month.

They sipped the Scotch and watched the tracer patterns, the bomb flashes, the spectacular explosions of the heavies in the sky. It was a pretty thing to see, until you thought about it. And then it was still pretty.

"This is the way to fight a war," Skinner said, putting his arm around her, and taking a light pull at the Scotch bottle. "If it were only as harmless as it is lovely."

"A lot of people will be hurt," Johnny said. He handed her the bottle and she tasted it. "Oooh," she said, giggling, "that's strong." She took a little drink and gave the bottle back.

"I think that's a plane going down," Skinner said, pointing to a streak of fire way out over the bay.

"Oh," said Johnny, and snuggled up close to him, hiding her eyes.

"It's gone," he said, and, as she looked up, he kissed her. She responded briefly, and drew her lips away.

She cocked her head and looked at him. "What a way to spend an air-raid," she said. They each had another drink.

Down in the town, the sirens were sounding the all-clear. "I'd better go in," Johnny said.

Skinner thought it well to leave the car where it was, in case Freak should be trying to find it, so they walked back to the nurses' quarters, hand in hand.

On the way, she asked, innocently: "Have you been up to the front?"

"A little."

They walked alone in silence. "I wish I could see the front," Johnny said.

"I might run you up sometime," he offered, idly.

She picked him up on it. "When?"

He stopped, startled and amused, and looked at her. "You foolish little blonde," he said. "What on earth do you want to go up forward for?"

"I want to see it."

"But, honey, there's nothing to see."

"I don't care."

"It's just fields, and burned out tanks," he said, minimizing.

"I want to see it." Little girl stubbornness.

They resumed walking. "Okay," he said, lightly. "Sometime when you're off, I'll take you on a tour. Like a congressman."

"Will you take me tomorrow?" She challenged, stopping and cocking her head in the odd way she had.

"Can you get out tomorrow?"

"I'm not on duty, but I'm supposed to stay in. But I can slip out. Listen." There was no one around, but she lowered her voice. "You come to the main entrance at ten o'clock, and I'll meet you by the stairs. Will you?"

"Sure," said Skinner. "And we'll go up and kill four Germans each."

"Be serious," she said. "I really want to go."

It was screwy, he thought, but why not? He could drive past Capua, around the artillery position he had passed two days before, and they could hear the guns go off in comparative safety.

And, he thought, maybe on the way back, we can find a little side-road.

"Okay," he said. "I'll be there at ten."

CHAPTER

14

IT WAS a fine, sunny morning.

Fred woke Skinner for breakfast at eight o'clock. They went over to Freak's car, and woke him, and Fred made them toss for who would take a short run at nine.

"We'll toss," said Skinner. "But Freak will have to go, anyway."

"Why?" asked Freak, rubbing his eyes, and trying to wake up.

"I've got a date," Skinner said. "Remember?"

Freak sat up. "Right," he said, and hummed a fanfare. "The charge of the blond brigade."

They went over to the mess, and Naproni fried their eggs in olive oil—he had been up early making deals with canned rations.

"What's it all about?" Fred asked.

Skinner told him while they ate.

Fred thought it was funny. "I used to know a girl who always made me stop when we passed a wrecked car," he said. "It must be the same instinct."

"Wait till you see the one we've got for you tonight," Freak promised.

"You'll think you're the one who's been in a car wreck," Skinner said.

They finished eating, and went out into the sun. Skinner shaved, and put on a clean shirt. Freak took off on his run.

Fred came over.

"What does this little sight-seer of yours look like?" he asked.

"She's small," Skinner said. "About half-puppy, half-kitten. Comes up to here." He held his hand level with his breast, and did a dance step. "Boy, she's really fine. A touch of Mediterranean romance for this kid; maybe a leave on Capri together when we get to know each other . . ."

"Just the ticket." Fred smiled.

Skinner dance-stepped again. "I'm happy about her," he said. "And I have great ideas. You, me, Johnny and friend, the Freak and his girl: a touch of Italian moonlight, a little vino. Fine evenings in villas. . . ."

"Apartments . . ."

"Cornfields . . ."

"Ambulances . . ."

"The hospital will follow us right up Italy," Skinner said. "If we play it right, there'll be something waiting for us whenever we come off the line."

They were quite happy about it. Then Skinner said, "It's okay, isn't it, Fred? To take her up there? How was it where you were yesterday?" Fred had made a trip to one of the aid posts.

"Quiet as a whisper," Fred said. "Didn't hear two shells all day long. What the hell, you don't have to go in range."

"Right," said Skinner. "I was figuring on getting around the artillery and turning back. There's no counter-battery is there?"

"No," Fred said. "The batteries are all in the orchards, pretty well hidden. And Jerrold isn't wasting shells trying to find them."

In a way, the front wasn't a front at all. The front was pockets of resistance scattered along the line of German retreat to slow down pursuit: a self-propelled gun, covering a road; a pill-box set to fire grazing-fire along the side of a ravine; some eighty-eights behind a hill. Behind them, the main body of the German army carried out a systematic and highly planned evacuation. At some point, perhaps the next river, they would stop, move into prepared positions, and wait. Things would be messy again. The ambulances would carry wounded instead of V.D. cases. But now it was a war of patient men. Patient sappers clearing mines, patient flyers and artillerymen levelling eighty-eight positions, patient foot-patrols and armored cars, cleaning up pill-boxes and probing out information. And patient drivers of a hundred sorts of truck, bringing up supplies, moving whole outfits forward a mile or so each day.

"It's not really the danger that worries me," said Skinner. "It's the way the thing sounds."

Fred waited for him to go on.

"It's sheer playboyism," Skinner said. "Dashing young ambulance driver takes pretty girl into line for excitement." He sighed. "Oh, well, I'm obviously going to do it. And I'll enjoy it, and think it's amusing, and feel like a very good fellow. I'd really bitch, though, if it were told to me as something someone else had done."

"Sure," said Fred. "What kind of stinker would do a thing like that? Can you imagine an ambulance driver, a fine young humanitarian volunteer, taking a girl he's trying to make, up to see the dear boys die?"

"Never," said Skinner. "Such things just don't happen. Human beings aren't made that callous."

"Right," said Fred. "Know what we ought to do?"

"Is it horrible?"

"Makes me shudder." He shuddered.

"Frighten me," Skinner said.

"Well, we pick a quiet field. You drive her out there, and you say, 'My God, Johnny, put on your helmet. This is it'. We've got guys planted around in the bushes, and we open up."

"I leap out of the car, and you shoot a neat hole in my hat."

"You hit the ground, pulling her down with you, but shouting defiance."

"And you guys start lobbing grenades in the other direction, while I recite the Declaration of Independence."

"You pick her up, throw her in the car, and make a brave dash for it."

"And you get your junior marksman's badge for missing us."

"Oh well," said Fred. "So you each lose an arm and a leg."

"Sorry,' Skinner said. "I want Johnny with both her legs."

And he drove off towards Naples, humming the song he had heard Naproni sing the night before. You and me in a gondola, Johnny.

Johnny looked good. She looked so good, coming down the stairs, that he had to run up and meet her, so that he could touch her. He wanted his hand to be against her arm or her cheek, because she looked so alive. But actually, he couldn't touch her right away, because then he would have to explain, and the explanation might alarm her. True, they had kissed, but as strangers, not as friends.

So he stopped, part way up the stairs, and smiled, and waited for her. And all he said was, "Hello, Johnny," being careful to make it sound as if hello were all he meant.

You and me at Pompeii, Johnny.

"Let's hurry," she said, smiling back. "I don't want to be caught going out."

"Chief nurse around?"

"Yes." She took his hand, and gave him a breathless little smile. They ran down the few remaining steps together, laughing softly, like pleased children.

Laughing as an expression of pleasure, not because there was anything funny; like pleased children.

They ran along the bright marble floor, towards the door, and a stray sergeant, who was hurrying along the corridor, stopped to watch, and shook his head at them, comically.

They went out into the sunlight, and down the outside steps to where the ambulance was parked. They got in, and he started the engine, shifted into second, and drove towards the gate.

"Johnny," he said. "Are you sure you want to go?"

"How far are we going?"

"Until you tell me to stop," he promised. They were silent for a little while, but he felt perfectly at ease. With this girl, there was no compulsion to hunt around for things to say. After awhile she started talking about Naples.

"It's dirtier than Africa, I think. I mean, the streets aren't, really, but somehow it looks dirtier." She looked at him expectantly.

"Do you know why, Johnny?"

"No. Tell me."

"You probably never went into an Arab house. No matter how dirty the street may be right up to her front door, an Arab woman keeps the little hole she lives in spotless."

"Really?" asked Johnny, admiring.

"The Arabs are terrific people," said Skinner. "But I'm not going to spend the whole morning telling you about them."

"Aren't you?"

"No," he said.

"Tell me what it's going to be like."

"Well, it won't be the kind of front you're thinking of, honey. It's just an artillery bunch here," he mapped with finger smudges on the windshield. "And another here, and more here and here. Then up here are some infantry, sitting around, hoping no one will tell them to move up any further, and maybe doing some patrolling when they have to. And maybe every few days there'll be a little local barrage, and these infantry boys," still more smudges, "will have to put on a small push. Then Jerrold will get wherever he's going pretty soon, and there'll be a nice, noisy front for a while. That's the way it is, this war."

Johnny was impressed. It was too easy.

"Look, Johnny," he said. "I'm telling you what I've heard, not what I've seen."

She laid a hand on his arm, and she didn't say, "Oh, you're so modest, and so wonderful," but the way she smiled and squeezed his arm was a good enough equivalent.

You and me on the tower of Pisa, Johnny.

They were going through the outskirts of the city. Skinner slowed down. "That's the airfield," he told her, pointing.

"British or American?"

"British. The Americans are out that way."

"Did you know, the first time I saw you, I thought you were a pilot. From your jacket."

"No such luck, honey."

"Would you like to be?"

"Not in the army, though that's a terrible thing for a red-blooded American boy to say."

"Oh, I don't think so. I don't like pilots."

He laughed at her. She wrinkled her nose back.

"Johnny," he said. "I declare today Thanksgiving. I give thanks that you're a foolish little blonde, and not a tall, educated brunette. I give thanks that you react like a woman, instead of figuring things like a man."

"What a thing to say."

"Johnny, Johnny, I give thanks." He stopped the car and kissed her.

They were outside Naples now, where there is a mile or two of road that runs beside green fields. There was sun, and the sky was blue.

She smiled, and she was sweet as sugar candy, remember the old song? And everything is fine and dandy all life through. He brushed her lips with his again, because it pleased him that she should look so pleased.

"What was that for?" She dimpled, she glowed.

"Johnny, Johnny," said Skinner. "We are blocking important military traffic on a highway leading to the front lines, and I don't care; I just don't care." He sang the last phrase.

"I think we ought to go, then," she said, with composure.

He started up again. They passed through Mileto, and he pointed to the ammunition boxes, stacked and camouflaged along the side of the road, the stacks going back a mile or so into the field.

"I should think the people would move away," she said. There were children playing among the boxes, older people using them to sit on. At one farm, a woman was doing her wash, with her tub set on a box of small arms ammunition.

"Wouldn't you like to live in an ammo dump, Johnny?"

"Live in an ammo dump!"

"Sure. Brush your teeth in nitro-glycerine; sweetens the breath and gets those hard-to-reach crevices. Cook your breakfast on incendiaries . . ."

"Oh stop," she laughed. Then her face puckered. "Really, aren't they afraid?"

"They've been through a lot of wars, Johnny. It's an old story, a part of normal life. Most of them have lost sons or husbands—six, seven years, now. Ethiopia, Spain, France . . ."

"They get," she reached for a word and found it. "Fatalistic."

"I'm proud of you, Johnny," he said, rather soberly. "Yes. They get fatalistic. If Jerry finds the dump, that's all. But this was their home before it was an ammo dump, and it will be their home afterwards. If it wasn't this, it'd be some searchlights, or there'd be a tank company to be bombed. What the hell, Johnny, the triumph of spaghetti over Stukas."

They drove through the big old arch, by which you know you are in Aversa. They passed the C.C.S., where the mess was, and he pointed it out to her.

"That's where the party will be tonight," he said.

"Swell."

"How many girls are coming out?"

"Six. And I make seven."

"You make six and a half."

She hit his shoulder lightly. "Hush," she said.

"We have a little Scotch, and a lot of brandy, and a whole ocean of wine," he said.

"Going to get me drunk?" she asked placidly.

"Ply you with liquor, Johnny. Very evil designs."

"Bad man?"

"You talk like that, and I'll stop the car and really kiss you."

She stuck out her tongue at him. "Don't tie up traffic, Skinner."

You and me in the Alps, Johnny.

"Look, the ravages of war," he said. There was a burned out truck by the side of the road.

"Can we stop?"

"Sorry. We've passed it now, honey. But we'll see plenty more."

"It's funny," she said. "It never looks as bad as you think it will. They told us in Oran that Naples was practically levelled by bombs, but it doesn't seem so bad. And Bizerte —there's lots left of Bizerte."

"We're coming into Capua," he said. "I think you'll see what you're looking for." They had to turn off the road onto a dirt track, which detoured them around the ruins of a bomb-twisted railroad overpass. When they pulled up the bank on the other side, they were in Capua.

Capua was like the newsreels, like the cover on *Life*, like an atrocity picture. Capua was a city of dust.

Johnny said: "This is like what I imagined."

"Are you glad you're seeing it?"

"Well," she said, carefully. "It's very interesting."

"You pretty little ghoul," he said. "You know you love it."

"Don't say that." She smiled. "I have wanted to see it— and it isn't as if there were any dead people lying around."

They crossed the Volturno on a pontoon bridge, which was even more like the newsreels, and Johnny was delighted. From Capua, they drove on more slowly. There were shell-holes, wrecked equipment, occasional crosses to see.

Around three o'clock, they stopped by a wrecked Italian half-track, lying on its back. Skinner opened the rear of the ambulance.

"For lunch we have Spam and Lima beans."

"Not Spam," she pleaded.

"What about some nice bully beef, Ma'am?"

"Is it fresh?"

"Canned it myself, yesterday."

"Oh, all right. Let's have bully."

He got out his primus stove, and a couple of mess tins.

"We'll splurge," he said. "I've got margarine to fry the bully in." Bully beef and lima beans tasted fine. They ate quickly and happily.

"Do we have to go right away?" Johnny stretched back lazily on the grass.

"Lie still," he said. "I'll wash the dishes." He rinsed out the messtins with water from his water bottle, and gave her some to drink. He sat beside her and looked at her, and they smiled at each other, for no reason. They smiled at each other for every reason in the world.

He remembered, for the first time in many days, that there was a girl in the world named Cindy. Who had understood his jokes. With whom he could talk ideas without being unintelligible. In many ways, he thought, being with Johnny was better; but he could not be sure he wasn't kidding himself, so he abandoned the train of thought, and got to his feet.

"Let's go up and get shot at," he said.

"I'm lazy."

"Not scared?"

She jumped up. "Don't be mean," she said, and pushed him. He picked her up, trapping her arms, and, laughing at the way she struggled, carried her around to the door of the car.

"Get in, little target," he said.

They drove on.

The road was not very crowded. Once a British M.P. stopped them, thinking, apparently, that Johnny must be a civilian girl. She had no hat on, and looked about as military as a ball of pink yarn.

"You can't carry that girl," said the M.P.

Johnny grinned at him. "Why not?" she demanded.

"Talks English, does she?" said the M.P. to Skinner.

"I'm an American nurse," said Johnny, sweetly, holding out the wing of her collar so that the sun caught the little gold bar pinned to it.

They went on, and Skinner said, "He was so surprised, he forgot to ask what you were doing up so far."

"Am I the first American woman to get this close?" She was as pleased as she could be.

You and me and the fountains of Rome, Johnny.

They were getting into the artillery positions, now, and Skinner stopped the car to check his map. They heard a gun go off, somewhere, but otherwise it was quiet.

"Johnny," he told her. "There are quite a few young German fellows, a mile or two over that way." Actually, it would be a good bit farther, he thought.

Johnny was thrilled.

An affable American corporal from a nearby emplacement strolled over and talked to them.

"You're not real, are you, baby?" He asked Johnny pleasantly.

"I don't know. Pinch yourself and see."

"Anything happening?" Skinner asked him.

"Not a thing."

There was a machine-gun talking very quietly, quite far away.

"Have we come far anough, Johnny?"

She hesitated a moment, then she said, decisively, "We have." She gave him a sidewise glance, trying to look sly, and he was so happy about her that he said, just to make it easy:

"I'm every bit as scared as you are. Let's turn around and drive back, just as fast as we can." The corporal laughed, and turned away, walking back towards his gun.

Skinner turned the car, and they started back. It was almost evening. There were no other cars on the road.

About two miles from where they had stopped, the road turned right, and ran parallel with the line for a way. It was just after they made the turn that it happened. A stray German plane, probably returning from a dull observation mission, saw them going alone, and dropped down, suddenly to strafe them. Skinner double-clutched, went down into third, and swung off the road. There was a quick, snapping sound, and a pattern of little holes, which would otherwise have appeared on the left-hand side, appeared on the right. Johnny gave a little squeal and was dead.

There was a sort of hole in her forehead.

Very slowly, he drove the car back onto the road, and stopped, and touched her—she was warm. And lifted her hand—it was lifeless.

For nearly half an hour he sat where he was, very still, staring ahead. Gradually, he hypnotized himself until they had never made the trip at all. Instead, it was morning again, and he was at the Aversa mess, talking with Fred. He was telling Fred that Johnny had sent word that she couldn't go, that she was on duty.

You and me in Vesuvio, Johnny. You and me in Venice, you and me drinking wine. But all warm things grow cold: ashes, sand at night in the desert. Tears.

Finally he got out, without looking at her, went around

and opened the back doors. He pulled a stretcher out of the rack and opened it on the floor. He walked around to the right side, opened the front door and lifted her out of the seat. Carried her to the rear, up into the back, put her on a stretcher. Put a folded blanket under her head, for no reason. Got out, closed the doors, and got into the driver's seat.

When he got home, to the C.C.S., he could think about it. He could find Fred who would help him think about it. When he found Fred, he could let himself realize what had happened.

And so, driving fifty back to Aversa, it hadn't happened at all. He kept his mind blank, was conscious only of the necessity for following the road. The thoughts of court-martial and consequence, and the dead feeling which is real sorrow, would come tomorrow. Now he had to get to his friends, and they would do something about Johnny, who had a sort of hole in her forehead.

To turn in at the gate of the C.C.S. was so automatic that he would never remember how the guard flashed a light in his face, and said,

"Hello, Skinner."

He drove to the car-park, left the car, and walked a few yards to the mess, where his friends would be.

It was only just outside the mess, when he heard the laughter of girls, and the voice of Fred, drunk, and Naproni, singing the Loyalist marching song from Spain, that he remembered there was a party on.

CHAPTER

15

IN JAIL, mail came once a week.

It was in the twelfth delivery that Skinner learned the extraordinary thing: Cindy was in Italy.

The note had been addressed direct to him, so she knew where he was. It was, for the most part, cheerful. She had seen Freak and Fred. She was puzzled about not finding Benny. She realized that they had drifted pretty far apart, but she blamed herself as much as she did him, and, if he wanted, she would like to come and see him.

It was the U.S.O. that had brought her over. She was one of the girls in a small show built around a magician; she handled props, and helped with the patter. It wasn't much of a show, but there was a chance of getting into a play, now that she was on this side. They would probably cast several things, as soon as the situation permitted. Was he comfortable? Was there anything she could bring him?

Being in Italy was just plain luck. Most of the shows had gone to England or Africa, or out to the Pacific. Well, it was all a gamble. But as soon as she realized that his unit was in this area, she had tried to look him up. At first they had been reluctant to say where he was; then she had learned. He should have written her about it, even if they had drifted apart. He should have let her know.

Skinner, so that his back would be turned on the stupid face of his cell-mate who sat on the other bunk, watching him read, got up and walked to the window. He felt a spark of interest in something outside the terms of daily existence for the first time in a good many days. She hadn't really come to Italy to find him, he reasoned; that she was in Italy, was, by her own statement, all very accidental. And why should she want to visit now? It was curiosity, perhaps, or, at best, misplaced loyalty—not to him, but to her idea of how to act in such a situation.

It was a bad thing, really, to have had this letter. Jail was all right, once you had taught your mind that jail was the world, that nothing beyond the buildings, the guards, and the other prisoners, existed.

At first his resentment of prison had been very strong, strong enough to kill the sorrow he had felt for Johnny's death and the manner of her dying. Strong enough, too, to drive out the gratitude he had felt to the court-martial board, which had treated his gross misuse of military vehicle and warrant officer privileges, very leniently. The officer who had conducted his defense—which was a simple plea of guilty—had explained to him, even before the trial, how the verdict and sentence must go.

"You see, they'll want to go easy with you, since you're a volunteer, serving without pay, and a gentleman, and so on. Any of us might be in the same boat, might have been out sparking an A.T.S. girl, or something, without benefit of trip ticket, and had some sort of accident; might easily have been me, for that matter. On the other hand, they can't let you off scot-free, because of the girl involved having been American, because your Americans are likely to make a frightful row about it."

At the trial, there had been a few questions to establish the facts, a few more to determine whether anyone else was implicated. Then, as predicted, the verdict had been guilty, and the sentence lenient: one year imprisonment, subject to review by higher court; and separation from the service upon release.

Gradually, sorrow and gratitude had been absorbed, first by resentment, then by curiosity. He had felt, after the first week and for perhaps a week thereafter, a quite genuine interest in the way in which the attitudes of prison life were a distorted reflection of the life outside. This was not a punishment camp. The men here were criminals. They had raped, black-marketed, stolen, or murdered their way in, and the army was through with them. They would serve their time, do their labor, and be discharged without honor back into civilian life. So there was no attempt to mold, here; no attempt to punish. The purpose of this place was confinement. And, within the confinement, there was a distinct social order, standards of approval and disapproval: here the good citizen was the man who stood up to the guards, sneered at the prison officers, was sullen with priests and social workers.

As he had always reacted against approval patterns, so Skinner had reacted against this one. He was obedient, polite, reserved, and snarled back at his fellow-prisoners when they cursed him for it. So that, although it was no part of his original intention, he was comparatively well-treated, in that he was left alone and not much bullied.

But having analyzed what the patterns here were, and determined his attitude towards them, his interest in prison life was over, and the strain of having no one to talk to began to affect him.

When solitude is imposed from without upon an active mind, the effect, at first, is an immense increase in the flow of ideas and phrases through it. Alone, and in silence wherein social intercourse has been reduced to an occasional exchange of bestial monosyllables, the mind is freed for extraordinary flights. But, as communication continues to be denied it, the mind grows weary of its own brilliance, having no way to evaluate its effect upon other minds, and there grows a protective listlessness.

Now had come a letter proposing that the listlessness be endangered by a visit from a world twice-removed.

Visits from the world once-removed were not too bad. Neither Fred nor Freak, who had come every week at first, less often as the fighting moved them farther away, had tried to probe his attitudes and emotions. Freak, apparently, continued to believe in the unquestionable rightness of Skinner Galt, and Fred, who did not think in terms of making right and wrong judgments, had never, except in the odd times when moods coincided, been close enough to Skinner for either of them to want to expose emotional bottom to the other. So the visits had been pleasant, and the visitors had concerned themselves with the bringing of news, gossip, and assurance of affection, making no attempt to disturb the listlessness, in which, apparently, they recognized a kind of equilibrium.

Cindy, if she came, would recognize the equilibrium, but it was doubtful that she would accept it. And that would be bad. It would be better if she did not come.

And so, Skinner rejected the offered visit. He did not even answer Cindy's letter.

The following Sunday, when the guards appeared to tell him to come and receive his visitors, intuition knew that she must have disregarded his failure to reply.

Cindy was looking well—a little strained, probably because of the circumstances, a little thin, probably because of the nature of her occupation. Uniform neither became her particularly, nor failed to; it was simply what she wore. Freak had come with her; probably had driven her here. Freak looked well, too. A guard stayed in the room.

Skinner sat down at the table, opposite them.

Freak smiled, then, when he saw that neither Skinner nor Cindy was smiling, looked first boyishly embarrassed, then earnestly solicitous.

She said, "Hello, Skinner."

He said, "Thanks for coming," in such a way that she would understand he didn't mean it, yet not ironically.

Freak, who hated tension, said, "Maybe I shouldn't have come, Skinner, but I thought. . . ."

He smiled at Freak. "It's okay. Nice to see you. How's the show, Cindy?"

"All right."

"It's a darn good show," Freak said.

"It's not much," said Cindy. "But we try to make it as good as we can."

"I've never seen you on the stage," Skinner remembered.

There was a silence, as he thought, And won't; she's not likely to play the prisons, and she probably thought the same thing, and Freak said, "She's fine on the stage, Skinner," to try to cover up.

"How do you feel?" she asked him.

"All right. The food's all right. We get plenty of rest. We work hard."

"You're pale."

"Prisoners are." He thought she winced slightly at the word. "Let's not be coy about where I am," he said. "This is a prison."

"Yeah," she said. Freak looked unhappy.

"Hell," said Skinner. "Let's not be phony. We can be friends, or we can have a prisoner-social worker relationship, or any way you want it, but let's not be phony."

"We'll be friends," she said. It was a plea.

Suddenly he wanted to be nice, not because he felt a return of personal warmth for her especially, but because he began to sympathize with her position. "Look, Cindy, I am a guy who was responsible for a girl's death under rather unsavory circumstances. That makes me quite a wrong guy, and society has places for wrong guys called prisons. If we get it all said like that, we can go on from there." The last phrase suggested a continuation of some relationship between them, and since he was unsure of himself in the remembrance of emotions, the sympathy evaporated, and he added, "If there's anything to go on to."

Her next question took him by surprise. "Skinner, did you love this girl?"

"Of course not."

"Excuse me for asking, Skinner. But I wanted to know."

"It's okay."

"I don't really understand that part of it."

"Okay. I won't expect you to."

"Can't you tell me?"

"It would take a long time. It's not important. Maybe Freak can tell you, on the way back, how it is about girls."

"Sure," said Freak, sounding a little puzzled but willing to help out if he could. "Maybe I can tell you about it." She looked at Freak and smiled at him.

"Skinner, you have nice friends."

"Thanks."

"Oh, darling," she said, probably unaware that she had used the word. "We're being awful. Can't we open up with one another?"

The appeal was strong. He hesitated, momentarily, and resisted it. "No."

"Please, Skinner. Talk to me."

"What do you want me to say?"

"I want to know about you. What this is doing to you, what all these things have done to you. What you think of yourself. What you're becoming."

"That's very easy, Cindy." He paused for an instant, while it came clear in his own mind. "I'm becoming dead."

It startled her into silence. She looked at him apprehensively, and Freak, too, seemed uneasy.

Skinner said: "Identity is a funny thing, and I'm losing it. Skinner Galt is on the way out. He had his day, now he's going. When I get out of here, I'll be someone else. Poor Mad Galt, perhaps, or Sailor Galt, or Virgil Galt, or even Galt the Ripper. But I'll be Tom Galt. I'm sure of that. I won't be Skinner. I'm sick of Skinner. He's too God damn clever, and he hurt a lot of people."

Cindy made a great and wonderful effort, and conquered pride. "I'll wait, if you say so, Skinner. I'll be Mrs. Tom Galt."

Again he felt the strength of the appeal, and this time it took more than will to resist it. "I'm sorry, Cindy. It's a chance I can't let you take: for your sake and mine, too. No one knows who Tom Galt will be. No one knows whether it was he or Skinner who loved you."

There was a pause. Then she said, slowly: "Skinner is still hurting people."

It angered him. "It's because they've disturbed his metamorphosis. Death and birth are not the spectator sports that you Twentieth Century humanitarians have tried to make of them. Dying is a private affair."

She stared at the table in silence, and he knew that she was fighting to control tears. But he had to make it final.

"Cindy," he said, flatly. "You shouldn't have come."

There was only one answer, and she made it, though he

could have made it for her. "I came because I loved you."

It was, he told himself later, sentimental; a banality he would have regretted giving in to. But, without consulting will or conscience, he started to reach a hand across the table towards her hand, and the word darling was close to his lips, when he noticed that Freak was standing.

Indignation and sorrow replaced the boyishness in Freak's voice: "That's not true, Skinner. She didn't want to come. She came because I asked her to."

That was it then. Even as he had lost Rod, and Benny, he had lost Freak. Even as he had lost Cindy, he had lost his friends. And that was it.

Identity is a two-way business; it exists in one's own recognition of it, but it exists also in its recognition by others.

But dying, now that it was all but done, came hard, and Skinner made a last effort to defend himself from Cindy's grief and Freak's accusation. And, in so doing, put into words what Benny had known, what Rod had felt, what Freak had learned, and what Cindy could not admit.

"We were war-born," he said. "Listen, the war made us. Let the bad joke of the past die decently, along with the clowns who tried to make it funny."

As he said it, he realized that it was not a defense he was making, but an appeal for pity, and he rejected his own appeal, saying: "Go away. Please go away now."

They got up.

"Goodbye, Skinner," said Freak.

"Goodbye, Tom," said Cindy.

He stood. He watched them go without feeling. Then, his mind tensed with the crowd of realizations catalyzed by the visit, he turned to join the guard, wanting very much to be back in his cell. There he could get this all in order: how Freak would not understand, but must cease to admire, and how Cindy would understand but must cease to love, and how Benny would have understood, did understand, and how, once the war arrived, it was already over, because people realized that it could not be endless.

And how Rod would have understood and wanted them to die together.

They made a right turn, and another. Somewhere, in the middle of this long corridor, was his cell, where, once these things were in order, listlessness awaited him, and he walked towards it impatiently.